About the Author

Kathleen Harryman lives in York, with her husband and two daughters, and family dog and cat.

After attending writing groups, Kathleen was inspired to write her own book based around the city where she lives. Stories run through Kathleen's head whilst out walking the family dog. The miles disappear and are replaced with stories that are then brought to life in print. Writing is a natural part of Kathleen, and she enjoys watching the characters come to life

Dedication

For Dad – for the things you have done, and all the thing you
continue to do. But especially for being you.

Kathleen Harryman

When Darkness Falls

AUSTIN MACAULEY PUBLISHERS™

LONDON · CAMBRIDGE · NEW YORK · SHARJAH

A CIP catalogue record for this title is available from the British Library.

ISBN 9781786299635 (Paperback)
ISBN 9781786299642 (Hardback)
ISBN 9781786299659 (E-Book)

www.austinmacauley.com

First Published (2017)
Austin Macauley Publishers Ltd.
25 Canada Square
Canary Wharf
London
E14 5LQ

Acknowledgments

I would like to say a special thank you to Annette Longman – Chief Editor, Hayley Knight – Senior Editor, Walter Stephenson – Editor, Jessica Norman – and everyone in the Production Team, where would us writers be without you. I would also like to say a huge thank you to Ellie Johnson – Marketing Coordinator, you are a very special lady. And everyone at Austin Macauley Publishers, that makes all this possible.

This thank you is for my wonderful family; I am truly blessed. Your support and encouragement keeps me going:

For my husband, Stephen and our girls Victoria and Maddison, I love you so much.

June and Neville Chappell – mum and dad, I can't tell you enough how much you mean to me.

Maureen Kildin – my twin sister, we have certainly enjoyed a lot of coffees and wine together. May it continue.

Julie Chappell – my big sister, I don't think you will ever grow up. Good for you.

To Emma H. Jaqueline S. Tara K. Denise L. and Sarah E. thank you for your support.

And finally, as always and forever, the biggest thank you must go to *you* the reader, I could never do this without you.

Chapter One

What's wrong with being a psychopath?

No, really, stop and think about it; psychologists give you this fancy little title, because they have this need to categorise you. I think it gives them a sense of satisfaction to nod their heads and say *'psychopath'*, just so that they can slap themselves on the back and congratulate themselves on assigning a label to explain your behaviour. Psychologists first used the term 'psychopath' in the 1900s, you would have thought that by now they would have evolved somewhat, but no. Hervey Cleckley (1941) was the first psychologist to develop a list of criteria, just to allow the medical world to label you as a psychopath, and why? To fulfil their need to place a tick in a box, that's why. They define a psychopath as having Antisocial Personality Disorder; and because of this you are viewed to have no thought or feelings for anyone. No remorse or shame for your actions. People view you as being egotistical, manipulative, and capable of lying to achieve your goals. Well, put like that, it could be anyone of us, *right.*

Some of you may disagree with me, fine, then answer this.

Have you ever lied to get what you want? Manipulated people to make sure you got your own way? And tell me, were you sorry? Felt any shame about it when you accomplished your goal? Bet you didn't.

So why should I be any different from you?

OK, well yes, apparently, we psychopaths are dangerous; couldn't argue with that. We also have a tendency to be violent and cruel; again, I can't really argue with that. However, don't we all have these tendencies? Take the alcoholic that blames the alcohol for their behaviour and the violence that they unleash whilst under the influence. The drug addict that needs their next fix, and isn't about to worry what they have to do to get the money to pay for the drugs, they so desperately crave.

I apportion blame to nothing, or no-one for the way I am. I own every action I undertake. And yes, I enjoy the violence and the manipulation that it takes to get what I want. In short, I like being me.

According to scientists, my behaviour is a result of a lesion, on a part of my brain responsible for fear and judgement, known as the amygdala. As I like to do my research and, for those that don't know, the amygdala is apparently the centre for emotions, emotional behaviour and motivation, and so forth. It is also responsible for detecting fear, and preparing for emergency events, you know the fight or flight scenario. It explains to scientists, (and we all know the need scientists have for rationalising everything!), why psychopaths don't really experience the effects of fear or softer emotions, like love. See I can't help being the way I am. I really was born to kill.

When it comes down to it, we all have a little bit of a psychopath in us.

Well, the chap strapped to the chair in his apartment kitchen was probably going to disagree with me because when he woke up, I was going to kill him. And I wasn't going to feel a damn bit of remorse about it.

9

I'd dropped him the pill hours ago and was now getting a bit fed up of waiting for him to wake up. I'd wandered round his apartment twice and found no value to be had. Of course, I wore gloves and was careful not to leave any trace evidence behind that would lead the police in my direction. I'd read this book once in which Dr Edmond Locard said *'every contact leaves a trace.'*

I'd given this little statement some consideration, and came to the conclusion; what if trace evidence could be manipulated? If at every crime scene the perpetrator (that would be me) left something behind, and carried something away with them. Could I then not choose what I left behind and destroy what I took with me. It seemed so simple to me.

It was also one of the reasons why I had decided long before I set out killing people that I didn't want to participate in trophy collecting. That kind of thing got you caught.

I couldn't really see myself collecting my victim's eyeballs, or cutting off their fingers or hair, storing them in a jar, and getting them out every now and then to have a peak, to make me feel good. No, my trophies were the memories of the kill. The way my victims fought before they died. Or how they whimpered and cried. But most of all, it was the blood. I loved seeing their blood leave their bodies.

I got the feeling that psychologists liked to define a serial killer by their trophies. It was as though trophy collecting and being a serial killer went together. A serial killer is thought to collect their victim's body parts, like someone may collect stamps. I prided myself on being different. I didn't need to be the next Edward Gein, taking my victims skin to make a lampshade, or using breasts and skin to make a vest.

No, I knew why I killed, and didn't need anything to remind me. I killed because of Tracy Bennett. Because I hated Tracy so much that I wanted to make her life an absolute misery. I wanted her to feel that her life had become unbearable. I wanted her to disappear for good. Her demise would make me complete. I knew this with such certainty that it occupied most of my time.

When I wasn't killing people, that is.

Unfortunately for Tracy, I'd seen the way that she had looked at the man that was slumped in the chair in front of me. I'd caught her deep intake of breath as she breathed in his aftershave. Noticed how her eyes dilated as she looked at him, and liked what she saw.

That was enough for me to become very interested in Patrick Barnes.

I'd once heard that the police didn't like random, and Patrick Barnes' death would appear random because sitting on a bus next to Tracy Bennett would not lead the police to a pattern. My last victim had been drinking coffee at Starbucks when he had smiled at Tracy from the window as she had walked past. Tracy had smiled back. Big mistake buddy.

Tracy was your modern-day leper, the bringer of death. The unfortunate thing was, was that she didn't know it. *Yet.*

The worst of it was that Tracy Bennett didn't even know I existed. She didn't want to know that I existed. She was so wrapped up in her own life that she never stopped to notice me staring back at her. I wouldn't mind but it wasn't as if she had amounted to much in the last fifteen years since the *'incident'*.

OK, when she'd been kidnapped, beaten and raped, at the tender age of eight by Uncle Kevin, who wasn't even really an uncle but a so-called family friend, it wasn't a good thing to have happened to her. Still, she could have accomplished more than she had. Tracy had a very high IQ, not that you would know this if you met her. Tracy hid her intelligence, believing that it set her apart from others. She was always so desperate to be accepted, to fit in. See that's the problem with Tracy, she's so needy. She never thought to get even, to right the wrong done to her. She should have cut off Uncle Kevin's balls when she'd had the chance. I know I would have.

Take Peter Kůrten, who became known as the Vampire of Dűsseldorf. What made Peter kill? Well you could blame it on the terrible beatings that his father freely gave him when he was a child. Of course, he could have just been born that way. A little like me. Still the main point here is, Peter didn't waste his life away like Tracy. No, he got even. Well, technically, I guess you couldn't say that because he didn't kill his dad, but he did kill a hell of a lot of other people.

Some may say that the most frightening thing about Peter Kůrten is that when they came to execute him by guillotine, he asked the prison psychiatrist if, after his head had been severed from his body, would he still be able to hear the blood gushing from his neck? Weird right! Well get this, when the psychiatrist told him that was possible, Peter turned around and said *"that would be the pleasure to end all pleasures."* And they say I've got problems.

Tracy was the driver. The one everyone saw and felt sorry for. Me, I was the one nobody wanted to know about. I couldn't really blame them. I wasn't what you would call easy to get along with. Psychopaths aren't known for their easy-going nature.

I've known Tracy Bennett for a long time, most of her life in fact. I've watched Tracy Bennett as she's grown up, from a gawky uncomfortable eight-year-old, into a beautiful woman. Her dark chocolate wavy hair hung down her back, like a wave rippling across the ocean. Stormy blue grey eyes stared back from long thick eyelashes. She might be average in height, but that was about the only average thing about Tracy Bennett. Her body was muscular, without being unfeminine. She kept herself in shape, spending hours at the gym or pounding the pavement. She made me keep myself in shape too.

Well, I couldn't go around killing people now could I, and not look after myself. I maybe slender in stature, but I was muscular. It helped with moving my victims' bodies around, and positioning them where I wanted them.

Patrick Barnes was soon going to understand what kind of girl he had picked up in The Parish up on North Street in York. So much for the good-time girl he'd been expecting. I smiled to myself.

Wait till he found out that he was not only tied to a chair, but was very naked as well.

This was not a sexual thing. No, I liked to see where I cut. To see the blood.

When a knife goes through clothing, it hides the damage it does. A blood stain on a piece of fabric really didn't move me. Just where was the fun in that?

Another consideration was the depth of the cut. A knife can do a lot of damage and kill a person long before you want them to die. And that situation isn't good. I often wondered if anyone truly appreciated my skill. My victims never seemed to, and I didn't know what the police thought because they never published what they found in any detail. They just gave me a title 'The Yorkshire Slasher'. Not very original and really, I didn't slash. I took great care *not* to slash! It had taken quite a few bodies to perfect my technique.

I looked round the very expensive apartment again. The apartment was situated next to the river Ouse in the old Bonding Warehouse Building. Very luxurious, and would set you back more money than I could earn in a lifetime. It didn't help that I was very bad at holding down a job. There were traces of femininity everywhere. That would be the ex-wife. She had obviously had a passion for country twee, not that I thought it suited this type of building. The old pine table and carver chairs, the overhanging rack above the range, twee.

The apartment was cosy, the walls were warmly painted in soft caramel, while the curtains that hung by the windows added a touch of density, with their sweeping blood red background and pale cream lilies painted across the fabric. The flat only had one bedroom and the living area was open plan.

I looked across at Fred who I had placed by the kitchen cabinets near Patrick, in his size twelve army boots. Fred was six feet and a few inches, and depending on how much air I blew into him, he was either broad or came up a trifle on the thin side. Fred was another one of my trace evidence markers. He was the best, because of his portability.

Fred was all about blood spatter, or rather the void in the pattern. By planting Fred, I was leading the police to think that two people had been involved in the crime. I did hope that they appreciated the lengths that I went to, to give them something to work with.

Patrick gave a moan. His thick black mop of hair moved as his head came up. I saw him blink and then watched as his brain started to take in his surroundings, and me, stood in his kitchen, knife in hand.

I was ambidextrous, which was handy when you were literally getting away with murder. I always made sure that I used my left hand to do the stabbing and used my right hand for everything else because, well most of us must have seen at least one episode of CSI, to know that the police take these things into account.

Take for example the case of Joan Wolfe who was murdered by her boyfriend, August Sangret. Her body was discovered on the 7th October 1942 – Godalming in Surrey. Her skull had been smashed into forty pieces with a heavy wooden stake. She had also been attacked with a knife, my weapon of choice. I had no respect for someone who didn't take the time to learn some finesse. A killing should be carefully planned and executed, as an artist would cover a canvas with paint, with care and attention.

Dr. Keith Simpson reconstructed Joan's skull and found three stab wounds at the front of the skull, along with other wounds in the palm and right forearm below the elbow, an aggressive and somewhat feral attack in my opinion. No finesse. I felt I was something of an expert in this, which Patrick Barnes was soon going to discover.

In this case, Dr. Simpson was lacking in his description of the actual knife, and in this I felt more of an expert than he was. After all, he made everyone wait some considerable time before concluding that the wounds had been done by, and I love this description, *"the point of the weapon must have been something like a parrot's beak."* What, seriously? A parrot's beak? OK, we are talking 1942 here, and resources weren't what they are today. No Google. Still...a parrot's beak? I felt annoyed at his lack of research. Dr. Simpson could have undertaken further investigations, looked at the curve of the blade and compared it to a hawkbill blade to see if it matched, or maybe a clip point blade or a trailing point blade, all of which have curved blades which could have resembled a parrot's beak to those less trained in such things. You get the picture. Dr. Simpson also (and this brings me back to my comment about using my left hand to kill with) concluded that, as the stab wounds had been made close together and high on the left-hand side of the skull, that in his opinion it indicated that the wounds had been made by a right-handed person. And now you can see what I mean about CSI taking these things into account.

We may have moved into a more technical world than in the 1940's, however the basics were still the same. Angle, depth, position, it all stacked up against your average killer.

"What's going on?" Patrick's voice was heavy from the drug I had slipped him once we'd got to his apartment. He'd been too busy thinking about getting my knickers off to notice. Bet he wished he'd paid more attention now.

"Well Patrick, just so you know, I think you have a lovely....*no*... great body. I can tell by just looking at those abs that you've been looking after yourself. I know Tracy Bennett would have liked them." Patrick looked down at his chest, taking in the thick bands of muscle that lined his abdomen, before his eyes took light of the silk ties that bound his arms to the chair. I could almost taste the confusion that was so heavily written across his face.

"Who's Tracy Bennett?"

I gave Patrick a considered look. "Tracy Bennett is the girl you sat next to on the bus, and when I say she liked what she saw, *well*, I mean that. It's just too bad she's never going to get a chance to sample the goods." I could see the cogs firing in his brain as Patrick tried to recall the event that was going to lead to his death.

The carver chair had come in handy. It meant I could tie Patrick's arms to each side of the chair, palms facing the ceiling.

It gave me more flesh to carve at.

The irony of 'more flesh to carve' and Patrick strapped to a 'carver chair' wasn't lost on me. In fact, it brought a smile to my lips. It's always the little things, isn't it?

"Great body or not Patrick, you're going to die tonight." His eyes widened as my words sunk in. "On the plus side, you'll die knowing you look gorgeous, and I'm not just saying that. I mean it."

Patrick licked his lips. I reckon he was trying to decide if shouting outright that I was a crazy bitch was going to get him anywhere, or if he should try the *hey- come-on-I-know-you-don't-mean-it*, let's pretend I get you, scenario.

It didn't much matter; either scenario was going to get him dead.

I laughed and bent down so that he could see the rather voluptuous outline of my breasts. Pulling guys was so easy. Tits on show, long legs poking out from a skirt my father would have said I'd forgotten to put on, and long red hair that moved around my waist tantalising and soft to the touch.

If Tracy Bennett was a beauty then I was exquisite, and unlike Tracy, I knew what men liked, even if they never got exactly what they came for.

My grip tightened on the Robert Welch Signature 20cm carving knife, with its long-curved edge that hung down by my side. It was the only one I could find in Patrick's kitchen that looked like it could do some real damage. Before Patrick could focus, I sliced across his right cheek, whipping the blade against the soft tissue.

I felt the knife lick at his cheek, gently digging into his flesh. Blood came to the surface quickly, trickling down his cheek and onto his chin where it dripped onto his chest. I liked what I saw. That was the thing about cutting the face, blood came quickly, and things looked a lot worse than they really were. If I had wanted to really scare Patrick, then I'd have cut him along his forehead first. That was always a winner for blood flow, although it never caused any real harm.

Patrick cried out as the cold metal bit into his flesh. "You crazy *bitch!*" So, he was going for that approach.

"Why Patrick, what's wrong baby, don't you want me anymore?" I smiled nastily at him. He could scream all he wanted to, his neighbours were away for the weekend.

That had been Patrick's opening line to me, as we had walked out of The Parish to his apartment. *"The neighbours are away for the weekend, so we don't have to be quiet. I want to hear you scream."* Ha, like I would ever fall for a line like that. Though the neighbours being away made things more interesting; I liked to hear them scream.

Patrick tugged at the ties, they weren't going anywhere.

I enjoyed watching him try.

I drew the knife back around and sliced it across his other cheek. The panic that seized him told me that he knew I'd meant it, when I'd told him I was going to kill him. This was going to be it for Patrick Barnes. He started to shake and his breath came in deep gulps, as though he couldn't get enough oxygen into his lungs – a panic attack.

I walked behind him, hips swaying, and bent down, my lips inches from Patrick's ear, I took a deep breath. I felt him shiver and watched the beads of sweat that appeared on his skin. "You smell of fear Patrick." He whimpered like a puppy that had had its toy taken away from it. I smiled and drew the blunt edge of the knife along his neck. His skin tensed under the cold steel. Patrick swallowed, but didn't cry out. His body ridged with fear.

Slowly I came around to face him, the cold steel of the knife never leaving contact with Patrick's body. I straddled him, sliding the knife against his chest. He froze holding his breath. I smiled ever so sweetly, flipped the knife around and ran it lightly along his collar bone, down his chest to his navel, almost like a woman would run her fingers across their lover's body. I ran the knife back up and along the opposite collar bone forming a deep v. Patrick started to scream as I drew the knife upwards, his blood drip, drip, dripping from his body. He couldn't kick me off as I'd nailed his feet to the wooden floor while he was out cold, a fact he hadn't noticed. I guess a woman welding a knife at you can make you forget all types of things. The wooden floor in the kitchen had been a real plus; tiles had become way too popular nowadays. I didn't really like strapping legs to chairs, they tended to bounce a bit too much. Nails – they stopped a body from moving.

I stood back and appraised my artwork.

Hmm, it needed a bit more work. Like an artist moving paint across a canvas, I began to work the knife across Patrick's body. My body danced around him. The knife slicing at differing depths, never too deep to cause harm but enough to rip apart the skin and allow the blood to flow. When I stopped, there wasn't a patch left on Patrick's body that wasn't bleeding, apart from where the back of his body was covered by the chair. Blood splattered around the kitchen area, a creation of its own. I took a second to appreciate the deep arches in the blood patterns, as it had hit the kitchen units and trailed across the floor.

Patrick was weeping uncontrollably, shame all the emotion he was sending out was lost on me. I did feel somewhat let down by Patrick Barnes; such a big man, and yet here he was crying like a little baby. I leant over, my face close to his, his eyes widened in fear. "Poor baby, almost over." I'd tied Patrick's arms to the chair so that his palms were facing up for a reason.

I never did anything without a reason.

I applied more pressure and drew the knife along his forearm to his wrist, doing this meant that I would hit one of the two main arteries that ran along the forearm. It didn't bother me if I hit the ulnar or radial artery or both, the end result was the same – death.

I repeated this on the other arm and moved to the wall opposite where Patrick sat slumped in the chair. I slid down the wall, and licked my dry lips as I watched the blood drip, drip, drip to the floor. The pleasure I felt was immense, as the blood hit the floor and coated it red, in a red veil.

It's amazing how quickly blood leaves the body. A nice sized pool of blood had formed on the wooden floor, and Patrick had stopped screaming a few minutes ago, wouldn't be long now and he'd be dead.

I liked this part the best.

I liked to watch the blood form in a puddle on the floor.

Watch life leave the body.

Did you know that every puddle is different?

There are so many variables. It can depend on the surface it drips to, how the body is sat, the way the floor tilts slightly, like I said all sorts of things. Bet that never occurred to you. But then you're not me. You couldn't possibly find the wonder in such things, because your emotions would tell you it was wrong; that you shouldn't find pleasure in such things. You don't know what you're missing.

It was all over so quickly. Too quickly.

I could feel myself coming down from the high I'd been on. I pushed away from the wall walking round the puddle, careful not to step in it. I washed my gloves in the sink, never taking them off, before I walked round to Fred.

A nice puddle had formed around Fred's size twelve boots. I pulled out the plug and squeezed out the air. Fred deflated, and I lifted him easily out of the boots. He was a bit slimy. Patrick's blood had made him quite the slippery little thing. Still, he'd served his purpose and I lifted him away. I appraised the void that he left behind as I rolled Fred up against my body and put him in a plastic bag before putting him in my handbag. I cleaned off my gloves again as I didn't want to get blood on the inside of my bag. That kind of evidence is very bad.

Slipping off my heels and adding a few extra pairs of socks to get the pressure in the shoes right, I slipped my feet into Fred's boots which I'd packed at the toes with a few wrist weights, and walked to the door and down the hall to the outside door leaving a trail of bloody footprints behind me. As I reached the threshold, I slipped them off and walked back to Patrick's flat. I'd left his door open and as I turned into the flat, I caught sight of Patrick's body. I took a breath. He truly was beautiful. Turning I put the boots in a plastic bag and then into my handbag.

Manipulation, of the evidence, that's what it's all about.

Gives the police something to work on; *busy, busy, busy.* They were always busy, busy looking in the wrong direction.

It was a good job oversized bags were in fashion.

I pulled off the extra socks and put my feet back into my shoes, pulled my coat off the sofa slipping my arms in and walked towards the door exiting the apartment. I didn't look back at Patrick Barnes; I'd already appraised my artwork and found it satisfactory. There was nothing left to see.

My heels clicked on the hard surface of the floor, leaving behind a broken set of bloody footprints. I was careful not to walk too close to Fred's. I'd gone to a lot of effort to make them, I didn't want them fusing with my own. I wanted the police to believe that two people had killed Patrick. Keep them busy looking in the wrong direction.

I wasn't worried about what evidence I would be leaving behind. The shoes I wore were a size too big. The inner soles I'd put in the shoes stopped my feet from sliding forward, evening out the pressure of my feet and the footprints I left behind.

According to Patrick's calendar that had been pinned to the wall in his kitchen, his cleaner was due the following day. His neighbours would be back early the same day that the cleaner came. The neighbour's cat wouldn't get fed tonight, as Patrick was no longer around to feed it. Still on the plus side, I'd let it into Patrick's flat, so it could have a play with the evidence.

I calculated that by the time the forensic crew came, that too many things would have interfered with what little I'd left behind to become worrisome. Still, and this is the main point, the blood splatter would still be in place for them to chat about.

My clothes were black and blood didn't really stand out on black like it did on other colours. See, I liked to think of everything.

The wind gripped at my hair and I pulled down on my leather gloves as I walked down Skeldergate, back towards The Parish. There was a bus stop right outside the pub. I looked at my watch;

it should be here in about ten minutes. I began to search the contents of my bag and started to sort out some change as I walked to the bus stop.

It had started to rain, which was a plus because my footprints were already being washed away from the pavement, cleaning the soles of my shoes. I'd still clean them with bleach when I got back home, just like I'd treat Fred to a good-old-let's-get-rid-of-the-evidence deep clean. My bag I'd throw. I had lots of them at home. And I'd made sure that there was no trace evidence to link the bag back to Patrick's death.

I looked at my watch, it was just approaching eleven.

I'd be getting an early night tonight.

I pulled on a hat as I got to the bus stop. The hat covered most of my face.

A few minutes later and the bus hissed to a stop. I climbed on. The driver didn't even bother to look at me as I asked for my ticket. I made my way to the middle of the bus, sliding across the seat to the window. There were four other people on the bus, huddled into their coats, or too busy on their smart phones to notice me.

It really is amazing how technology causes people to become blind to things.

Chapter Two

Abigail Hill came waddling between cosmetic counters, to Tracy's make-up counter, smart phone in hand. If Mrs H saw it, she'd have a fit. Mrs H was the cosmetic department manager at Hopstocks Department Store. The name rolls off the tongue, doesn't it? I refer to it as Hopscotch's Department Store. The workers all behave like kids.

Hopscotch's sat on the corner of St Helens Square and Blake Street in York's city centre. It was made up of lots of separate buildings, which had been knocked through to make one large building. Lots of larger shops in York were like this. Hopscotch's had five entrances the larger of which took the customer straight to the cosmetics department where Tracy worked. Her counter was small, when you compared it to the major cosmetic houses such as Estée Lauder, YSL and Lancôme.

It suited Tracy.

Small and insignificant.

The grey suit did nothing for Abigail; she was a little too wide across the hips to be wearing a pencil skirt. The skirt length was unflattering, dropping just past her knees, accentuating her heavy-set legs. The jacket fitted a little too snugly across her mid-section and fell to the top of her thighs in a box cut, making her legs look shorter than they already were. At 5'3", Abigail really couldn't afford to look any shorter than she was.

Abigail was one of those people that were constantly dieting. She knew every diet that had graced our planet, not that they ever seemed to be effective for her. Knowledge was not always about practise. Her blue eyes were wide with excitement. Her mouth curved up in a way that a mouth does, when the person thinks they've got ground-breaking news to pass on. Abigail was a gossip, who never let the truth get in the way. In fact, by the time Abigail got through embellishing the story, there often wasn't a scrap of truth left. But hey, the story sounded *so* much more interesting.

I watched from a distance, waiting for Abigail to relay her message to Tracy, who had finely stopped dusting the glass counter of her make-up stand. She was such a goody, goody, bordering on being boring.

"Did you see the news this morning?" Abigail asked, plonking her bum on the cream faux leather chair by the counter, and putting her greasy hands onto the newly cleaned glass surface.

Tracy looked at Abigail's hands as they smeared prints all over the glass, and sighed. Abigail didn't wait for an answer. "Some guy got killed last night in one of those posh apartments down by the River Ouse. You know the old Bonding Warehouse place. They say that The Yorkshire Slasher has struck again." I bristled, *I did not slash!*

Tracy looked at Abigail, shock painted across her perfectly made up face. She smoothed down her navy dress which clung to every curve and accentuated her small waist. You either have or you don't. Tracy did, Abigail didn't.

"Wow! It's not been that long since they found that other guy. How many is it now?"

"Five, but I reckon there's been more, and the police don't want to tell us. You know in case it puts the tourists off." For once Abigail was right; there had been a hell of a lot more than five. Still, I didn't think that the police were holding back information regarding the numbers; they just hadn't found the other bodies. I had hidden them well. The killing had been sloppy, and I didn't want to put the police off. Practicing had had its uses, but no artist really wanted to be known for their less than perfect work.

Tracy pushed her high chocolate brown ponytail behind her back. "I can't believe that this is happening, in York too."

"Ha, you have got to be kidding me. You live in a very bloody city, Tracy. The Romans cut off people's heads and stuck them on the gates of the city, just to teach everyone a lesson. Reminding them what would happen if they broke the law. It was only a matter of time until we got our very own serial killer."

I hadn't chosen York to do my killings for any reason other than it was where Tracy lived. I admit to wondering what the profilers made of me. Was I the usual abused kid, who had suffered at the hands of their so-called parents, or the loner that didn't have any friends? Ha, what a load of bull. I had never let anyone abuse me, and had anyone tried, they would have found their life span shortened significantly. As for friends, well, who needs them? Friends just tie you down.

"Really, Abigail!" Susie Johnson walked over, her high heels clicking on the tiled floor. She picked up a tube of mascara, and started applying it. "You wouldn't be saying that if The Yorkshire Slasher kidnapped you. *'Hey, it was only a matter of time before you killed me'.*" Susie mimicked, as she shook out her waist length blonde hair, sending it tumbling down her back. Susie was like a Barbie Doll. Her boobs were too big for her tiny, tiny waist. Her thirty-four-inch lean legs were constantly on display. Today was no exception, her skirt was bordering on becoming a belt.

I only hoped she was wearing clean knickers.

25

The only reason Susie got away with it was because the Store Manager – Mr Humphreys liked looking at her legs, and if he wasn't looking at her legs, then they never made it past her boobs. I don't even think he knew what she looked like, facially that is. He was a bit of a dinosaur. Looking was about the only thing he was probably capable of these days. Susie's comeback to the critics that dared to voice an opinion on the lack of skirt length, was that she worked in hosiery, and was only 'demo-ing' the product. Nice comeback.

I looked at Susie's tight fitting shirt; the boobs were on their way to popping the buttons and becoming today's exhibit. I wondered if this was the second set or third set. If they got any bigger, she'd need a forklift to keep them in place, never mind a bra. I didn't see the attraction myself. It did get me wondering, as to how much silicone I would need to cut through, before I reached the blood.

Abigail picked up her phone and flipped the screen on. "Have you seen what's going on out there?" Her face suddenly lost colour. "You know you're right Susie, it could have been me. I live really close to the Bonding Warehouse." I wanted to tell her she was safe, she wasn't even close to being on my list. *Yet.*

Susie sent Tracy a look, before she raised her eyes to the ceiling. "Abigail, you live on Butcher Terrace, that's like a million miles away from this place." Susie picked up Abigail's, phone. Displayed on the screen was a picture of the Bonding Warehouse with a lot of police tape around it.

Abigail reached for the phone. "If I lived a million miles away I wouldn't be here. I'd be in Spain or New Zealand, or something. Anyway, you're only being bitchy because you live on the wrong side of the river."

"Fulford is *not* on the wrong side of the river." Susie made a threatening gesture with Abigail's brand new iPhone.

"It is so. You're only jealous because I'm closer." Abigail tried to reach for her phone. Susie held it above her head. Shorty didn't stand a chance.

Tracy reached for the phone and gave it back to Abigail. Susie stuck out her tongue at Tracy, she sighed.

Tracy looked at her friends. "I think we're off track here. Someone died last night."

Abigail's eyes lit up. "I know; it's *so* exciting! Do you think that The Yorkshire Slasher is a looker? Hey, if they caught him, I could become one of those prison brides. I saw a programme about it the other week."

I stared at Abigail, she really wasn't my type.

The police hadn't released much information, which is probably why Abigail thought I was a chap.

I'll be honest; I did find it rather irritating. Just because I was female, it didn't mean I wasn't a killer. Fred was good, but he had his limitations. He was the right type of chap for Abigail though. Being a blow-up doll, Fred would never have to suffer through one of Abigail's conversations that began with me, and ended with me. And my victims thought I was egotistical and self-absorbed.

Abigail's phone sounded out an alert tone. "Oh, they've named the dead guy. Wow, he was a real looker." I couldn't argue with that, he'd looked even better once I'd finished with him. There was something about a knife's work that left me breathless.

Tracy and Susie leant forward. "A looker! He's gorgeous Abigail." Susie added as she tapped the screen making Patrick Barnes' picture bigger. "I'm betting there's a six-pack hiding beneath that T-shirt."

Abigail stared at the picture. "I think you're right. What a waste." I disagreed with that statement. Patrick Barnes' death hadn't been a waste at all. I had enjoyed every second, and every cut I had made. In fact, Patrick was now famous, something he would never have achieved had he lived.

"It's awful, look he was married." Tracy pointed to a picture of his wife. Ex-wife let me just add.

"It says ex-wife, they weren't together anymore." Abigail sighed. "He was available, now that's a waste."

"They could have got back together, and now they won't ever get the chance."

Susie and Abigail looked at Tracy.

"You're such a romantic Tracy. They probably wouldn't have got back together."

"How can you be so sure about that Susie? It says that they had only been separated for a few weeks." Tracy really was lame, she looked at the world through Disney covered glasses. She never saw the bad things; even after Uncle Kevin, she trusted people too easily. She should have been born a dog. That's why she needed me, not that she recognised this. It made me mad, so mad, that all I could obsess about was making Tracy pay for her oversight. Using a knife on her would be too easy; no, I had other things planned for Tracy Bennett. Utter destruction of the person, was more like it.

"Because he would have met me and forgotten all about his ex," Susie said smugly.

"Why you? You might not have been his type."

"You're fooling yourself Abs, if you think he'd have picked you over me. You'd have given him a stoop. The guy looks to be about six feet to me." Six-foot-four-inches and two hundred and ninety pounds of pure muscle, actually. I would know, I'd had to move him off the sofa onto the chair in the kitchen. Nailing his feet to the floor had been pure frustrated pleasure; the unhelpful sack of human flesh hadn't made moving easy, and it had taken more time than planned. Given that I was quick to anger, you can imagine how hammering nails into his flesh had made me feel.

"Who you calling short?"

"Oh, not you, obviously!" Abigail jabbed Susie in the ribs.

The three of them laughed. It grated on me.

Made me really mad.

I hated to see Tracy happy.

Patience, patience, patience, I reminded myself, and took a breath.

"Hey, where were you last night?" Karen Stillman came stomping over, her obvious displeasure apparent not only in the way she beat her feet against the tiled floor, but also on her chiselled features. For a girl she was very masculine looking.

Karen was one of those people you either liked at first sight or hated. I hated her, Tracy liked her. Figured really, she'd take any stray in and call it friend.

"I'm off," Susie muttered as Karen approached.

Susie had as much liking for Karen as I did.

Karen was in her late thirties and was known to be bad tempered, with more mood swings than a two-year-old. Her shoes were solid flat loafers and her skirt (unlike Susie's), fell to her calves in a loose fashion. The jumper she wore did little to present any curves to the world. There was no make-up on her face, and her ginger hair frizzed around her head like a set of snakes bidding for escape.

Karen worked in accounts and spent most of her time hidden away there, which was probably as well because she wasn't known for her sensitivity.

Abigail ignored Karen's approach and began fiddling with her phone.

"Well?" Karen rounded on Tracy. "We were supposed to meet at Harkers last night after work, remember. It's not like you could get lost, it's on the opposite corner." Karen pointed a finger to where Harkers was, one door down from Hopscotch's. Tracy looked at Karen in closed mouthed silence. "Well, I looked like a right prize sized, you know, sat there waiting for you."

"Don't worry, no one will have chatted you up." Abigail just couldn't help herself.

"I'm sorry Karen, I must have forgotten." Tracy quickly covered over Abigail's comment.

"Forgotten? Well I guess that's OK then. And there I'd been thinking you'd had some type of emergency. Knocked down by a car, got trapped under a bus or something. But no, you forgot. What were you doing last night that was so engrossing that you forgot?" Karen didn't take any prisoners, when she was mad, she was mad and you got it all, nothing held back.

Tracy's forehead wrinkled in a frown. "I don't remember." I smiled to myself, that's right Tracy, you lost a lot of time last night didn't you.

"Oh, well, that's just great. I thought we were supposed to be friends. If I wanted a friend like you I'd have got a cat."

"Look I'm really sorry Karen." Tracy fidgeted with the duster and bottle of glass cleaner in her hands.

"Not good enough." Karen stormed off, leaving Tracy opened mouthed with another sorry that had yet to come out and be formed into a word.

Tracy's gaze caught the other girls on the cosmetic floor looking at her. I could almost feel the guilt that rose up in Tracy. Personally, I didn't really get the emotion; all it did was make a person sad. Why do people want to feel sad?

"Well that went well." Abigail's eyes didn't leave the screen on her phone. "You're going to have to go to Betty's and get her a bun or something. She's going to be like a rabid dog all day if you don't." Abigail injected as she got off the chair, trailing more fingerprints over the glass. "It's OK for you; you don't have to work with her."

Tracy sighed, "I'll get her something at dinner time."

"I don't know why you want to be friends with her?"

"I feel sorry for her. She's always on her own."

Abigail sent Tracy a meaningful look. "There's a reason for that."

"People shouldn't be on their own."

"Tracy, she's a person, not a dog. Dogs don't like to be on their own. People quite often do."

"You don't."

Abigail grinned. "I can't help it if I'm a people person. Someone needs to spread a little cheer around the place."

Mrs H rounded the corner. Her bleached blonde hair was stuck up like the spikes on a hedgehog. The hairstyle suited her prickly nature.

Hidden away as I was, I shook my head at her as I watched her approach Tracy and Abigail who had yet to notice her. She was like a tiger sensing her prey. Unlike a tiger, Mrs H was as cute as a bear woken too early during hibernation.

In her late fifties, Mrs H had a tendency to forget about what was appropriate for someone of her age to dress like. She was like Madonna without the cash. Today she wore a faux leather black skirt that came two inches above her knees, her bright red shirt was almost transparent and while her bra was pretty, I didn't think people needed to see it. A black suit jacket was thrown over her arm. In her right hand she carried a black briefcase, like she was some lawyer, or something rather than the cosmetics manager at Hopscotch's Department Store. Her acrylic nails were painted red and were about as practical as a family of four having a two-seater sports car.

In a waft of perfume, she stopped at Tracy's counter. "Abigail, if I'm not mistaken accounts is on the second floor."

Abigail jumped, and quickly slipped her phone into her pocket. "Was just going," she muttered as she slid off the chair, moving it closer to the glass counter. Abigail looked at Tracy who was looking a little pinched. "See you at break time."

Mrs H rounded on Tracy, while her nails remained unsheathed, her claws were definitely out. "Tracy, I can't say that I'm happy." No change there. "Your figures are down and your counter is a mess, this is not a good start to the day." For dramatic effect, Mrs H moved her black jacket away from her wrist, taking a look at her watch like there wasn't a clock on the wall above Tracy's head. "I'll be back in five minutes, please make sure that the counter is spotless and then we will look at how you are going to make your weekly target; your shortfall so far is four hundred, and considering that it is Saturday tomorrow, you are going have to do something quite spectacular, to make it up." I could feel Tracy withdrawing into herself. She had a tendency to do this when she became agitated.

I watched Mrs H strut over to her office, red six inch heels tip tapping and felt an idea form.

I had just found my next creation. Victim was so weak, and really, I did create some outstanding artwork.

A bit like when Lady Gaga wore that meat dress, and what a fine creation that had been. Had I been a cannibal, I would have followed her anywhere. It's not often a person dresses for the occasion, and really that dress would have produced the perfect stock.

Mrs H had it in for Tracy. I didn't know why and I didn't care.

Tracy was mine, and I wouldn't have the fifty-year-old something sinking her manicured claws into her.

No one picked on Tracy but me, and especially not Mrs H.

I needed a focus, and Mrs H was it. She'd be a screamer that was for sure, so I needed to take this into account. Hmm, my mind spun as ideas formed.

One thing was for sure, for any murder to be successful there was a lot of planning and surveillance to be done. I couldn't afford to be sloppy.

Not if I was going to execute my rather well thought out plan for Tracy Bennett.

Chapter Three

I sat in the black Ford Fiesta that had seen better days five years ago, looking out the driver's side window. I kept the car for two reasons, one – it still worked and didn't cost me that much to run, and two – I couldn't afford to replace it. The paintwork was a mix of rust and black metallic, and the front seat had a few coffee stains on it. I wasn't a particularly tidy person unless I was killing, then I was meticulous in every way.

I was parked outside Mrs H's house nestled nicely between a dark blue SUV and a white hire van. I'd been watching the house for thirty minutes now, and was just finishing the dregs of my coffee. I looked at the clock on the dashboard, it was five thirty. Mrs H wouldn't be back for a while yet. I had spent the last four weeks trailing her, observing her routine. The times in which the cleaner came and went, the hours in which Mr H went to work and came home. I'd learnt quite a bit, and found some rather interesting surprises, which I was going to ensure worked to my advantage.

I looked at myself in the mirror. Today I was a blonde. The cold ash tones suited me; they added extra steel to my eyes which were violet today. Wigs and contacts, it really was amazing how they could change a person's look.

I was dressed in thick black leggings and a fine knit black jumper; my black coat was slung across the neighbouring seat at the front. On the back seat was my oversized black bag, all packed and ready for the kill. A happy thrill shot through my blood, I couldn't stop the smile that spread across my lips. Sweet anticipation, it was such a lovely feeling.

Mr H wasn't expecting Mrs H back for another hour or so. Unlike Mr H, I knew his wife had left work early saying she had a headache and after calling into the supermarket for a few things, would be home in – I looked at the clock again – about forty minutes.

This should be fun.

I sometimes felt like an Oracle when it came to my victim's lives. I knew them so well, predictions came easy; their routines, the little things that they never saw coming. It always surprised me how much people missed, while living their daily lives. Take Mrs H, she had no idea what she was about to walk into. Me I'd known for some time. I admit it did give me a sense of superiority. Knowledge truly is a very powerful thing. Besides I really was better than them. I wasn't the one that would be dead soon because of my own blindness. I was still free to kill. Not even the police could stop me. Yep, I was better than them too.

A blue fifteen plate Nissan Micra came rolling down the road. It signalled and turned into the H's drive. I watched the low autumnal sun as it hit the immaculate flashy blue paintwork. I could see the damage that would soon be done to it, once the wife (that being Mrs H) came home.

Mr H, the dirty bastard, was entertaining his bit on the side, in the family home – *really*. Not only that, but the dumb bitch had parked her car on the drive, nose first. She'd have to back the car off the drive before she could leave. That would give Mrs H all the time she would need to inflict a lot of damage onto the paintwork of the car. It constantly amazed me how people never seemed to be prepared for the unexpected.

Being the thoughtful person that I was, I had borrowed the shovel from the neighbour's front yard and rested it against the H's house before Mr H had got home. Now, that could do some damage to a car. Foresight was one of my specialities. Funny how people never seemed to stop and think things through properly, well not me. I liked to take the extra time required to make sure that I had taken account of everything. And I do mean everything.

The side piece of trash looked to be in her early thirties. That alone would probably have been enough to send Mrs H over the edge. Mrs H was obsessed about her age, and had had two facelifts that I knew of. I didn't get it. It could be because at twenty-two I was considered young. But still, couldn't you enjoy life no matter your age? The world seemed to be obsessed with age. The young wanted to be older and the older wanted to be younger. Me, I was perfectly happy being me, no matter my age. So long as I was killing, I was perfectly happy.

How did Mrs H think dressing like a lamb, when really, she was more mutton and well past her prime, and past the age of slaughter, would make her feel young? I didn't get it. She just looked ridiculous and gave bad advertisement to women in her age group. Take Helen Mirren. Now that was class, make no mistake. Mrs H would have done better to copy her rather than try and copy Madonna. At least Madonna looked after herself, undertook regular exercise and really did have a very fit body, unlike Mrs H. Well it was all too late now.

I'd watched Trash carefully get out of the car. Long lean legs covered in a pair of thigh high spiked boots poking out from the open car door. Her long black coat momentarily caught the wind as she'd stepped out, showing to the world that red lacy underwear alone was not substantial clothing for the autumnal weather. She quickly gripped the coat to her, as Goosebumps formed.

Trash had a pretty oval face, long lashes framed brown eyes, and her caramel hair fell about her shoulders in a cloud of soft playful curls.

As the door to the house opened, Trash opened the coat. It was as well that Mr H wore glasses because I think his eyes would have popped out and fallen to the floor without the glass to act as a barrier.

Mr H hungrily licked his lips and quickly pulled the woman to him, closing the door. Judging by the banging coming from against the door, they hadn't made it upstairs.

Really, people were beyond my understanding sometimes. Excitement and pleasure could be found in many ways but why risk losing everything, just because you couldn't keep the two separate.

A hotel bill was a lot less costly than a divorce and Mrs H would take him for everything he had, including Mr H's very nice and very expensive fifteen plate Mercedes-AMG GT Coupe in canary yellow, or whatever posh name Mercedes called yellow, as well as his pension.

From the wing mirror I saw Mrs H approaching in her flashy red BMW John Cooper Works Convertible Mini. I sat a bit straighter, and waited for the fallout.

This should be good.

The opportunity Mr H and Trash had presented me with, was just too much to pass up, and really it would be rude of me to walk away. So, I watched and waited.

This was going to go better than I had planned.

I patted Mrs H's mobile that sat on my coat. I had taken it from her office that morning. She wasn't that popular that she had noticed. And no one had rung or texted since the phone had been in my procession. Sometimes things were just too easy.

The front door opened and Mrs H walked into the house. The screaming began almost immediately. Within seconds the front door opened and Trash ran out, Mrs H snapping at her like a rabid Rottweiler. Mrs H was shouting in such a high pitch that the words became incoherent. What a total waste of energy. If you had something to say, you should ensure that your audience heard each spoken word. And Mrs H was gathering quite an audience.

Some neighbours had stopped their activities and stared open mouthed. Others twitched their curtains, sticky beaking from behind the fabric, thinking they couldn't be seen. It was a shame that this performance would soon be forgotten, overridden by my own outstanding artwork. Death and murder overtook sex and betrayal by quite a bit.

Mr H fell out of the front door after his wife, stumbling to the ground as he lost his footing. His trousers were round his ankles, and he was still pulling up his red silk boxers. I laughed. I felt like I was watching an old slapstick movie.

In the space, it took him to peel himself off the concrete path, Mrs H had whipped off one of her six inch stilettos and was now scraping the metal heel against the Micra's beautiful blue paintwork. Trash had dropped her car keys, the stupid bitch, and was grovelling on the floor her coat billowing around her.

She hadn't had time to put her knickers back on, and well, nice cheeks or not, they were turning red as the cold air hit them. Given everything that was happening here, nobody was going to remember the black beaten up Ford Fiesta that was for sure. Mrs H took advantage of the time it was taking Trash to retrieve her car keys, and reached for the shovel which, may I remind you, was there only because of my foresightedness, and began beating it against the windows and bonnet of the car. Glass cracked, and metal buckled under the pressure of the shovel, and the paintwork became less immaculate and more like a car ready for the scrap heap.

A shoe can only do so much damage, but a shovel, now a shovel could do a hell of a lot more, especially when the person wielding it has a lot of aggression to blow off. See I can do thoughtful.

In ten minutes Trash had the car reversed off the drive and down the street at a speed of over twenty miles an hour. The Micra flew over the speed-humps in the road, and I could hear metal crunch and the scraping of the exhaust as it hit the hard surface of the road as Trash drove the car over the speed-humps at a speed they were never meant to be taken at. It was a shame that there wasn't a police speed van in the vicinity. Well, I couldn't plan and implement everything. Sometimes a girl had to rely on the police to police. Oh wait, they were probably all looking for me. *HA!*

Mr H had pulled up his pants, as his wife walked over to him. Lucky for him she'd thrown the shovel onto the drive. I laughed as she gave him a big shove. He lost his footing. The house was set on a slight hill, and Mr H went roly-polying down the bank, and only stopped when he reached the lamppost. Thump! That had got to hurt. He hadn't had time to zip or button his pants and the trousers now twisted around his ankles again, tripping him up as he tried to stand. Oh, this was better than one of those reality TV programmes. I had tears in my eyes as I laughed at him.

The front door flew open again, and Mrs H threw an armful of clothes at him before slamming the door closed. I heard the locks slide into place. He wasn't getting back in tonight.

Mr H looked bewildered, as though he just couldn't work out quite where it had all gone wrong. Really? Well, fortunately for him I was around, and by the time I'd finished with Mrs H, there would be no need for a divorce lawyer. He'd get to keep the car, house and his pension, all to himself. He might not know it, but he would owe me, and maybe one day I would come back round to collect.

Isn't it quite extraordinary how murder can benefit people? You hear so much from relatives about how their life will never be the same again and oh, the pain, and oh, they really miss their loved one. Then there was the blame, the why, the unfairness of it all. Well, Mr H wouldn't be missing his wife, or looking for someone to ask why; in fact, he had a lot to gain from her murder. Hmm, maybe the police might start to suspect him? Maybe they might see him as a copycat? I had to have my following.

Followers were people that couldn't think for themselves, that's why they chose people like me to lead them. I don't mean to dis my followers. It was nice to think that someone appreciated me, liked my artwork. Some people, like me, were born to lead and some born to follow. It was just the way it was. I liked the thought of having followers. My work was too good to go unnoticed.

Mr H fumbled with the car keys that had been thrown at him along with his clothes, and wallet. He walked over to his car. His shoulders were slumped, and his hands shook as they held the key fob. A broken man, or just shaken at being found out? The neighbours quickly started getting on with their chores, the curtain twitchers left for better entertainment.

The slamming of the car door signalled the end, and as the car roared to life and began making its slow journey off the drive, I couldn't help but feel things had played out really well – for me.

I sat in the car for a couple of hours, waiting for my moment. I had to get this right. I didn't mind waiting, it added to the excitement of killing Mrs H.

I looked at the clock, by now Mrs H should be onto her second bottle of red. Well on her way to becoming paralytic. That's how I wanted her; unable to react quickly, her brain a little too groggy to work out what was happening, until it was too late.

The sky outside had darkened and the clock on the dashboard tripped to eight. I grabbed my coat.

It was time.

Putting Mrs H's mobile into the right pocket of my coat, I did up the buttons and reached into the back for my bag. Given what I had in it, it was more than just a bit heavy, and not easy to pull through the gap between the front seats. Three door cars, they were totally impractical for all kinds of reasons.

Mrs H opened the door at my hesitant knock. I didn't want to appear too eager. Mascara ran down her face, and she looked haggard. No wonder Mr H had found Trash so attractive.

It took her a while to recognise me, but once my face came into focus, she all but glared at me. "What do you want?" It was as well I wasn't expecting any polite chit chat.

I took out her mobile phone from my coat pocket. "You left this, and I thought you might need it." I wiggled it around, and watched her head start to spin. Oh yes, she was well and truly drunk.

Mrs H went to take the phone and missed. I tried not to smile. "You don't look so good, has something happened?" I found doing caring quite difficult, but I think I might have pulled it off because Mrs H became a blubbering mess.

Oh good.

I pushed passed her. "Come on let's go inside, the neighbours don't need to see you like this." Let's face it, the neighbours had seen the best bit, no need for the outtakes.

I led Mrs H into the kitchen and surveyed the layout. Open plan seemed to be the way to go these days.

The kitchen was made up of white glossy units and cupboards. A Centre Island ran down the length of the kitchen on which sat a slab of black granite. I looked down at the floor. My nose wrinkled in distaste, cold white sparkly tiles.

I hated tiles.

Mrs H, as drunk as she was, was going to be a kicker.

I led her over to the cream leather sofa that wrapped itself around the two far walls, defining the sitting area. Mrs H fell back onto the sofa, and I passed her a glass of red wine. It sloshed over the leather and onto her red leather pants, leaving a dark stain behind. She began drinking, muttering something about men, and can't be trusted. I tuned her out. Listening to her whinging was only going to set my nerves on edge.

I hated talkers.

Life was shitty. It's just the way it was. Why whinge about it. Get even. Take what you wanted. A much better solution, if you ask me.

I went back towards the kitchen area, and pulled a chair from under the glass table. Mrs H was slurring into her wine glass, and a few well planted *hmms* and *ahhhs*, from me seemed to pacify her by way of conversation. My timing had been off a few times, not that Mrs H noticed. I set the chair in front of the sofa, setting my bag onto its black shiny plastic seat. I pulled out Fred and began blowing him up.

Fred seemed to have an effect on Mrs H. She stopped whinging, glass midway to her lips. "Who's he?"

I looked at Fred and gave him a considering look. "This is Fred. You could say that he's my silent partner." I smiled. Ha, ha, ha, that tickled me.

I took off my coat and laid it on the granite of the middle island so that it wouldn't get covered in blood. I left my leather gloves on.

"Why do you have a blow-up doll?" Red wine fell onto her white blouse.

"You're spilling your wine." Mrs H looked down at her blouse. I took the wine glass and placed it onto the floor.

"Come on, we'd better get you out of that before it stains." It was a reasonable request and Mrs H obliged without question. I took the blouse. "Better take the bra off as well, it's only going to get messed up."

She blinked, but did what I said. That was the nice thing about alcohol sometimes. It made a person more pliable, and stopped them asking too many questions, or even thinking. Mrs H was a somewhat pathetic drunk. Her anger had dissipated and sadness had set it. She fell back onto the sofa crying. I took advantage of this and began pulling off her trousers and knickers.

"What are you doing?" What did it look like I was doing?

"I want you naked." Before she could respond, I took hold of her arms and pulled her off the sofa, and had her on the chair. She swayed unsteadily and I had to press her back against the chair, to stop her from falling to the floor.

I plucked out some zip strips from my bag which I had moved onto the vacated sofa and tied her wrists together, palms showing. She kicked out. "What-you- doing?" her words came out as one big slur.

Ignoring her, I grabbed her left leg and zip tied it against the leg of the chair. Grabbing the other leg before she could kick out again, I zipped it, pulling the strip tight. It bit into her skin. I smiled as she began to wiggle. There was no point really; she was very securely fastened to the chair although the chair did wobble when she swayed too much. That was another reason I liked wooden floors, apart from when the nail sunk into the flesh and hit the wooden floor, blood instantly rising to the surface. It didn't matter how much swaying a person did, they just never moved away from the spot they had been nailed to. The chair didn't bounce forward or topple from side to side. It just stayed put.

"What are you doing? Get off me! I want you to leave. I want to be on my own." She had to be a talker.

At least fear was making her words come out more clearly.

I sighed and bent forward. Her eyes swarm in front of my face as she tried to focus. "You're sobering up. Not good." Damn.

Mrs H began thrashing around and screaming. Really! I backhanded her across her left cheek. Her head snapped to the side. Stunned, she slumped in the chair. That stopped her.

Turning, I picked up Fred and began placing him against the sofa to Mrs H's right side. I took out his weighted boots from my handbag and slipped his plastic feet inside. Fred swayed but stayed where I wanted him. I stood back and checked the angle from the chair. I inched Fred a little closer. It was important that I get a nice void in the blood splatter along the edge of the sofa.

I liked to imagine the forensic team going over the scene, making comments, as they dabbed for fingerprints. Looking at the blood and the story it told them as it had sailed across the air, before making its mark on the walls and ceiling, and so on. They were busy little bees in my head, making comment about lack of DNA and fingerprints. How the victim must have known her attacker, as there was no forced entry.

The fibres from the wig I wore would send them in all sorts of directions. I liked the thought of them scuttling off to identify the manufacturer of the wig, and who they had sold them to. Narrowing down their search area, and always questioning. That was the thing about trace evidence, one question opened up another, always fighting for an answer, for clarity.

Mrs H was blubbering incoherently.

I walked back into the kitchen, and selected a carving knife from where it sat on the counter top. Metal grated against it as I slid it out of the wooden enclosure. Oh good, one of those self-sharpening ones. I looked at the blade and smiled.

There was something to be said for the cold beauty of a knife. With just one quick slice the blade could cut through flesh, either killing or releasing a nice flow of blood, aiming to terrorise its victim into submission

It all depended on me, and what I wanted.

The knife was nicely balanced considering it was just a plain ordinary kitchen knife. But then the H's never settled for cheap. The expensive cars they drove and the high quality handmade kitchen, said that they dealt in quality, luxury items. Lucky for them, they could afford it. I flipped the knife around, watching the light play along the sharpness of the blade. This would do very nicely.

I walked over to Mrs H who was dribbling, snot falling down her face. What a truly horrible creature she was. I bent over and lifted her chin.

"I'm not really a patient person. You can understand that I'm sure, the way you've been going at Tracy. I wonder what she did to you; too young maybe, or too pretty?" I smiled at the woman before me. It wasn't a nice smile. "Well, you don't have to worry, when I've finished with you, you will look far prettier than Tracy Bennett."

Mrs H saw the knife and screamed. She'd not been listening to a word I said. Her lungs filled with air and came out in one long agonised scream. I sliced the knife across her chest bone. The light pressure of the blade smoothly opened the skin and blood trickled down her chest. Mrs H promptly threw up and slumped in her chair unconscious. Nice.

My nose wrinkled and I breathed through my mouth. She was covered in vomit and the blood had become lost in it. I tried to control the anger that rolled under my skin. Why couldn't the woman do anything right.

This wouldn't do, it wouldn't do at all. I felt the pleasure of the cut leave my system, disappearing with the blood. Anger boiled through my blood and I rocked my head back and screamed out my frustration, clenching my fists at my sides. Unlike Mrs H, there was no fear in my scream. It was the scream of a feral animal. My cheeks puffed out as I tried to gain control. I would not let this piece of shit spoil my artwork. I had to come back down. I had to concentrate. I took a number of long breathes, taking in air as though it were more than a lifeline. My anger cooled, and I started to see the kitchen again.

I looked round the room. On the sideboard sat a large glass vase filled with flowers. You'd be surprised to learn that I wasn't a flower kind of girl. What was the point in them? They lasted, what a week then what? You went out and bought yourself some more. Dead money if you ask me.

I threw the flowers on the table. The vase was heavy with water. I emptied the contents over Mrs H. The water hit her square in the chest and washed away the vomit. I went to the kitchen and refilled the vase. This time Mrs H sputtered as the ice-cold water hit her face, and fell down her body. Oh good, she was awake.

Her eyes opened and she looked directly at me. Fear shadowed her face. Her nightmare hadn't gone away. "Help! Help! Help!" she screamed.

I rolled my eyes. "Oh please, like someone is going to come to the aid of a pathetic person like you. You threw the only person that could have saved you out the door." Her eyes widened at my words.

I picked up the knife off the sofa. "You ready Fred?" Not that I expected him to do anything, or answer.

I raised my left arm, and pushed forward with the knife. The blade cut across Mrs H's forehead, blood streamed down her face, she began to cry, sobbing uncontrollably.
Such a small cut. So much blood!
My heart beat quickened in pleasure.

"Just in case you've not worked it out, you're going to die tonight." Mrs H sobbed, and whimpered, and screamed. "Not so much fun is it when someone picks on you? Think how Tracy felt. Not that I care about Tracy, but she is mine. Mine to destroy

46

and you were interfering in my business. You can understand how irritating that kind of interference can be, I'm sure."

I danced around Mrs H's body, my knife lightly pressing against her skin, laying open the epidermis and dermis layers of the skin, releasing blood, but never going too deep. My feet spun on the floor, my left arm swung, the wig flowed around my shoulders and back. I was a dancer, an artist, always creating, always poised, and always, always in full control.

Mrs H had stopped blubbering some time ago. She'd reached that point where the brain had started to shut down, to protect what was left of the person inside. Fear had taken over, and her heart beat out a rapid beat, the blood ran faster down her body. The mind and the body made to protect, to endure, each reacting to the basic need for survival.

I lightly trailed the knife down her forearms to her wrists, leaving a small trail of blood behind, but not enough for her to bleed out too much. Mrs H whimpered, tears rolling down her face, merging as one with the blood. I looked at her face, so fearful, so lost, and changed my mind. No, this was a little too personal for that type of kill today. I grasped hold of the short length of Mrs H's hair, and tipped her head back exposing her neck. I liked to vary the way that people died. It gave the CSI unit another angle to consider. Did I share the killing with my partner? Like I would ever let anyone share and take the credit for my creations.

I didn't want all my artwork to be the same. Same was boring. It also meant that unlike others before me, a copycat couldn't really copy, because sometimes I opened up my creations' wrists, other times I might slit their throats, or take out their heart. My different styles of killing kept things fresh, kept it beautiful. The only thing that was the same was the blood that trickled from the body, drop by gorgeous drop.

I deepened the pressure of the blade as it rested against Mrs H's neck, and slid the knife quickly across her neck. I felt the knife tug at the skin, could almost hear the skin tearing apart in my mind. Blood flew over Fred and the sofa, coating the floor, ceiling and walls. I took a breath and savoured the deep pleasure that cascaded over my body like a net of emotions.

I looked round the room, so much blood, everywhere. Wave after wave of pleasure took me. It wasn't enough, Mrs H wasn't quite dead yet. Life still flowed; fresh blood came running out of the cut I had made. I watched in wonder.

I stood back as Mrs H gurgled, and the blood ran down her chest onto the floor. I watched the puddle form, and tilted my head as it took shape. The heart would give out soon and the blood would stop its journey; life gone.

I sat on the floor and let the pleasure of this kill wash over me. Time slowed down and I breathed deep. I felt euphoric.

It was all over with too soon. Why did it never last?

With a sigh, I pushed myself off the floor, leaving the knife resting on the tiles. No point in taking it with me, I'd only have to get rid of it. I'd once taken pleasure in hiding the knife; it gave the police something else to focus on. It gave them another angle to the killings. I soon tired of finding different places to hide the knife. And really, they weren't that much closer to finding me.

Fred was covered in blood. I had probably got carried away a little bit too much. Still, as I looked at Mrs H, I thought she might be one of my best creations. I had done a simply stunning job. I smiled as I congratulated myself.

Her face was now made up of thin blood lines, and her breasts were hanging at odd angles, which allowed the blood to flow in different directions as it travelled down her body. Cuts lined her arms and legs. Even her feet were covered in welts of blood made by the glittering silver blade of the knife. There wasn't much flesh left to look upon. She was gorgeous.

Now it was clean up time.

I also needed to see about tampering with the evidence, make things a little bit more interesting for the police. I didn't know who would find her, or how long it would take. The cleaner wasn't due for another three days and who knew when Mr H would find the nerve to make his way back here.

I looked out at the patio windows. Outside the sky had gone a deep fathomless black. No stars to light it up tonight. Even the moon was in hiding. And that gave me an idea. I opened up the patio doors sliding them back all the way. The nights quiet was broken by two cats fighting in the distance. Next door a dog barked, and I remembered Mrs H complaining about her neighbour's new puppy that seemed to prefer her garden to her neighbours. Walking back into the kitchen, I opened the fridge. It was crammed with also sorts of interesting foods, at the back of the fridge was what I was looking for. I reached inside and took out some cooked chicken. Pulling it apart I began leaving a trail of meat around the kitchen floor, scattering the meat over Mrs H's body as I walked past. Opening the glass doors, I stepped outside allowing the chicken to fall from my hands as I walked over to the connecting fence to next door. Someone had thoughtfully covered up a puppy sized hole, and I ever so thoughtfully pushed back the wire and bricks, careful not to allow the wire to scrap or tear at my gloves. Despite the time, I heard the puppy running over paws thundering on the ground and a wet nose appeared. I gave it gentle tickle behind its ears as its head poked through. I was rewarded with a swift sniff and lick of my black gloves.

My work was done.

Half an hour later I made my way to my car, threw my bag onto the front seat and started the engine. Mrs H's house was bathed in a soft light. I'd left the puppy happily eating its way to Mrs H's body, its feet sliding in the blood. The puppy was a blonde Labrador, a nice colour. Soon its coat would be painted red. *Red* – a far nicer colour than blonde; red would match its cherry brown eyes.

Again, I wondered how long it would take them to find Mrs H. I was impatient to see how the police would react to my latest artwork. It didn't matter how hard they worked, they weren't going to catch me. Not unless I wanted them to. I was becoming somewhat of a celebrity, and I was riding high on my fame. Even as I had the thought, my lips were already twitching into a smile.

I was betting it would be the husband, come to make his apologies, and do an immense amount of grovelling. He might be upset when he found her, and yet in the back of his mind, I reckon he'd be glad.

I had eliminated a problem for him. He should be grateful.

Of course, it could be the owners of the puppy. It would be quite a shock for them to see their once blonde Labrador red. But would they think that it had killed a rabbit or some other small creature, rather than make the connection to Mrs H's lifeless body.

I pulled the car away and made my way home.

Chapter Four

"Tracy! Tracy!" Abigail banged against the front door, sending the wooden door rattling against the frame.

I watched Tracy as she emerged from the bedroom, and made her way sleepily down the stairs to the front door. Her hair hung down her back and fell over her face. She wore a pale blue vest top, and checked blue pyjama shorts. Her feet lazily slithered across the carpeted floor. She yawned as she tugged on her dressing gown, covering up her legs.

Tracy opened the door and Abigail flew in to the house and into the living room. Not quite sure what she expected to find. Susie shot Tracy a worried look over her shoulder as she followed Abigail. Tracy locked the door behind them, and followed her friends into the living room. She stood looking at her friends scratching lazily at her head, and yawned again.

Both Abigail and Susie were dressed for the gym. Abigail was under the misconception that Lycra made her tummy flatter and her hips non-existent. It didn't work. Pink neon Lycra especially, did nothing for her complexion, or shape. But hey, it was very girlie so she had accomplished something. Her blue eyes were wide with concern, and her short-bobbed hair flew wildly around her face as she came rushing towards Tracy.

Susie flipped back her long blonde mane and thrust out her chest. Typical Susie, she never took a day off from being a sex kitten. The Lycra bra wasn't coping too well under the pressure of her false boobs. I wasn't so sure if her attire was saying sexy chick or porn star. She definitely wasn't saying class. The Lycra shorts were short, very short. Short enough that her bum cheeks made an appearance. There was certainly a lot of flesh on display. Though her stomach was flat, it wasn't firm, not that I think any male ever got that far up, or down to notice.

"What's going on?" Tracy looked confused as she hugged Abigail back. Ha! She was missing three days of her life and had no clue.

Susie pulled Abigail off Tracy. "Tracy, we need to talk." She threw her arm around Tracy's shoulders, guiding her towards the sofas. "We've not seen you for three days. We've tried calling you, but you haven't picked up. You haven't contacted work, to let them know you wouldn't be in. In fact, it was as if you'd fallen off the edge of this earth. This is the second time Abs and I have been round." Susie came to a stop at the pale blue, once over stuffed sofa.

"And the Yorkshire Slasher has killed Mrs H!" Abigail injected. I bristled at the name.

Tracy's face paled further. "What?" It was unclear if the 'what' was related to what Susie had said, or Abigail.

I watched her as her eyes flew round the room in alarm, taking in the worn Persian rug and equally worn out coffee table, littered with scuff marks. A small flat screen TV stood to the far right near the fireplace. The fire had yet to be cleared out and lit. A bookcase stood at the opposite side to the fire, lined with romance novels. That was as far as Tracy ever got to a date these days.

I could almost hear her thinking, as she stared at the duck egg painted walls. Three days was an awful lot of time to lose. I smiled. She'd never lost that amount of time before.

Susie looked at Tracy's ashen face. "I'll make us a cuppa; you do have milk, don't you?" Susie asked as she walked towards the kitchen, which fed off the living room.

Tracy woke from her stupor. "Yes... I think." She didn't sound so certain. Not surprising really.

Abigail flopped down on the sofa next to Tracy. "You're lucky that Slasher killed Mrs H." She placed a hand on Tracy's arm. "Not that I'm saying that you would want to benefit from Mrs H's death. However, it has sent Hopstocks into a mad flurry of activity. The police have been in asking loads of questions and everything, so they haven't had time to think about you, and with Mrs H being dead and all, nobody's really noticed. Well Susie and I have, but no one else." That was Abigail, ever the pragmatist.

"Here drink this." Susie stuck a mug of steaming liquid under Tracy's nose.

"It's coffee. I don't drink coffee."

Susie looked at Tracy. "On this occasion, I think you need it, especially if you're going to maintain any type of sanity through Abs constant stream of chatter." Susie had a valid point.

"But the coffee isn't mine, it's my lodgers, Lauren's."

Susie rolled her eyes. "Seriously, I don't think she's going to notice a few missing grains. It's not like she counted them or something." I wouldn't bet on that. I had noticed.

Nobody ever saw me unless I wanted them to.

I'd been with Tracy now for nearly fourteen years. I'd been with her when she still lived at home with her parents. I'd even been there when she went to school. And she didn't even know I existed. Never felt me watching her. She'd never met me, and here I was living with her in the same house. Some might think that that was rather odd. Didn't people ask for references or something? After all, with a serial killer on the loose, you can't be too careful, now can you?

No, not Tracy, she accepted the fact that I lived here. Never asked any questions, and never really thought about it, odd, right? You could say that we had an odd type of relationship.
I liked it that way.

Fourteen years and I had waited, oh so patiently, waiting, and watching for the right time to destroy Tracy. Over the fourteen years my anger at Tracy Bennett had festered into hate.

Have you ever felt controlled by someone, unable to act as you wanted because of that person? Then you might understand a little about how I feel. Tracy was driving me mad, I wanted utter control. I wouldn't get it, not until Tracy was no more.

Tracy Bennett was my one obsession.

Tracy took the coffee from Susie. I'd make her pay for that.

"So, Mrs H is dead. Gosh that's dreadful." Tracy blew into the hot liquid.
"I know. But why Mrs H! It doesn't make any sense." Abigail sounded very affronted about the whole thing.
Susie looked at Abigail. "Really, would you have preferred it to have been you?"

"No, but then who was to say that when Slasher saw me, he wouldn't become a changed man; I'm all woman and know how to please." Abigail winked, wiggling her boobs sending her whole chest wobbling.

I'd kill her just to shut her up. One swift stab into the heart and sweet silence, hmmm wouldn't that be nice. Actually, thinking about it, the throat would be better, she wouldn't be able to talk then, just gargle.
"Abs, you're amazing, and we love you. But I don't think that Slasher is taking any extra baggage on right now. What do you think Tracy?"

54

"What? Oh, yes." She wasn't really listening to either of her friends. I knew how they felt; she never listened to me either. If she had, maybe, just maybe, I wouldn't have wanted to destroy her like I did. Who was I kidding! Of course, I would.

"I can't get over it. Mrs H is dead. Are they sure it was Slasher?" Tracy asked.

Abigail nodded her head. "Definite."

Susie sat on Tracy's other side. There was a whole empty sofa opposite them at the other side of the coffee table, however they all sat on the one sofa like sardines in a tin.

Abigail lent forward. "Rumour has it that Slasher killed her at her home. Does that mean that Mrs H knew who Slasher was? Do you think that's why he killed her?" Abigail shook her head. "Well, anyway, apparently, Mr H had been having it off with some young thing. No surprise there really, is there. At first, they thought it had been Mr H, you know copycatting Slasher and all that." I told you didn't I! I just knew the police would try and take the easy route. Hey, don't let proper policing get in the way will you. All that time the police had wasted with Mr H, could've have been spent looking for me.

Abigail smiled. "Well, apparently, he was holed up in a hotel room after being thrown out by Mrs H when she learnt about the affair. Rumour has it that she walked in on them, you know…"

"Really!"

"Oh, come on Tracy, it can't be that much of a surprise, the woman was a right bitch. Look how she picked on you," Abigail said.

Susie slurped at her tea. "I hate to agree with Abs, I really do, but she does have a point. The woman was a cow." I'd say more of a pig, she had definitely squealed like one. Ha, ha, ha.

Abigail gave the mug in Tracy's hand a hard look. "Why didn't I get a drink?"

"Do I look like a waiter?"

"Tracy got a coffee." Abigail pointed out.

Susie shrugged. "I was being nice, and before you say anything, that one act of kindness exhausted me." These two should have been sisters, they certainly bickered in that unique way that siblings do.

"I'll make you one." Tracy started to rise from the sofa.

Susie pushed her back down. "No, you won't. God gave Abigail two legs for a reason."

"You're getting more like Karen on a daily basis." Abigail moaned.

"Ooo, hark at you." A smile spread across Susie's face. "Go on get your drink, and give us a break from your beautiful voice."

"I might as well it doesn't look like we're going to get to gym." That was a shame I liked going to the gym.

Tracy looked at Susie and Abigail, as though noticing their gym clothes for the first time. "Don't worry, it's not like Abs does any real gym work when she goes. All she ever does is sit on the bike and ogle the guys, pumping iron." I couldn't argue with that. That's why Abigail never lost weight or even toned up. She was as flabby and unfit as she had been on the first day that she had joined the gym.

"I can still hear you!" Abigail shouted from the kitchen.

Susie ignored her. "What's happening Tracy?" There was no missing the look of worry on Susie's face.

For one awful second, I thought Tracy was going to start crying. She'd only lost three days. Oh, for God's sake, the woman needed to pull herself together.

"Nothing, I just haven't been feeling so good lately that's all. I must have taken some sleeping pills." Like sleeping pills would make her loose three days.

I could tell from the look on Susie's face that she wasn't buying it, but didn't press. It was the only nice thing about Susie. She never pressed for an answer, when none was on offer.

"OK, well, I take it that you're feeling better now." Tracy nodded her head up and down. "Good because it's Monday and it's our day off, so if we're not going to the gym, which obviously, we aren't, why don't we go into Leeds."

"Leeds, that sounds fun, we can do lunch over a bottle of wine," Abigail said munching on biscuits, and carrying a cup of tea.

"What?" Abigail cocked an eyebrow at Susie. "I found them in the cupboard. It seemed rude to leave them there."

"It's OK, Abs, you enjoy them. I don't even remember why I bought them. I'm not a biscuit person." You didn't buy them, I did, and by the looks of things, Abigail was going to consume the lot. I hadn't even had one!

I watched the friends as they chatted. Tracy was starting to feel better, and I could feel myself fading more and more into the background.

Anger rose inside me, hot and sharp. Maybe I should step up my plan.

My eyes narrowed on Tracy. She was laughing now. I needed to kill someone.

That cold anger that burned inside of me took over. Killing made me happy. I had to think about my next creation. That would get me through this. Stop me feeling so confined, so trapped. I looked at Abigail. As pleasing as the thought was, killing Abigail would be a step too close to Tracy at the moment. Mrs H's death already had the police crawling all over Hopscotch's. I wondered if they had found the wig department yet.

That's where I'd gotten my stash of wigs from. The police wouldn't be able to trace payment to me because I'd stolen them. Security wasn't so hot at Hopscotch's. It had been over four years now, and the missing wigs had been written off as part of a break in. Hopscotch's had lost an awful lot of stuff that night. Adding to the list by taking the wigs was nothing, compared to the thousands of pounds' worth of stock the thieves had made away with. I had stood and watched them. They hadn't noticed me there. Too intent on what they were stealing, to notice me. It had been easy to slip in and fill my big bag with wigs. That was the thing about planning, patience always won in the end. Now, as I felt my anger rising, I took a breath, I should remember that, patience always won out in the end. I took another breath, and with it I tried to disperse my anger.

Susie and Abigail were peeling themselves off the sofa.
"See you in an hour." Tracy nodded at Susie.

"What you going to wear?" Abigail asked Tracy. Oh please, for once do some thinking on your own.

"I think my black jeans, and a jumper. It's cold out there." Not that you would have noticed the way that Susie and Abigail were dressed.

I smiled because I knew for a fact that Tracy wouldn't be wearing the jeans. They were in the washing machine. I'd washed them twice now to get rid of Mrs H's blood, and then left them in the washer for Tracy to discover. I felt my smile widen as I thought about the look of confusion that would cross Tracy's face as she tried to work out why they were there.

"You sure you don't mind driving?" Susie asked Tracy.
"It's fine Susie, I don't mind, I've only just filled the car up with petrol and it would be cheaper than if we all got the train. I don't really fancy drinking at the moment, so it's no heartache."
Susie and Abigail left. We were alone again, just the two of us. How cosy.

I watched Tracy as she picked up the cups and walked into the kitchen. I could almost hear the song she sang in her head. Yep, she was starting to feel better.

An hour later, with make-up on her face and a pair of blue skinny jeans and a pink silk fitted jumper on, Tracy collected her baby blue down Puffa jacket from the hook by the door. She had been unperturbed about the black jeans, which had made me cross. Her good mood was driving me insane!

Her silky chocolate hair hung down her back in soft waves. Her make-up lightly applied. She looked stunning, even if she was wearing EMU boots. Not that I had anything against them. It's just that Tracy never wore heels. I couldn't call the two-inch things she wore for work heels. With her long legs and narrow waist, heels would really get her noticed. She might even get a date. Well, if I didn't kill them first, she might get a date.

Excitement ran through me, as I considered the possibility of killing yet another admirer of Tracy's. It could be why she only ever indulged in romance novels these days. No male ever survived long enough to date her. Ha!

Tracy started singing to herself. Abigail and Susie's visit had lifted her spirits and she was back in her happy place. It irritated the shit out of me. I was finding it incredibly hard keeping a lid on my anger. It was taking up a lot of my time right now.

Tracy locked the front door and walked over to her car. The black Fiesta was nestled between a Honda and a Peugeot. Both cars were newer and nicer than Tracy's. With a lot of manoeuvring, Tracy finally got the car out of the parking space. That was the problem with terrace houses, parking was premium, and sometimes people parked way too close. No consideration on how others were going to get out. Had it been me, I'd have smashed into the front and backend of the Honda and Peugeot which had parked so close to me. That would teach them a valuable lesson, one they wouldn't repeat, and if they did, I would have found their owners and killed them. Problem solved. Simple really.

The red petrol light came on as Tracy parked outside Abigail's. Her eyebrows pinched together as she looked down at it. I smiled triumphantly at her confusion, which was quickly melting into concern and fear.

Abigail flew out of her front door, slamming it shut and locking it behind her. Her red coat was thrown over her arm. She wore a pair of deep red trousers and a plum sweater that pulled across her chest. I noticed the six inch black boots she wore, which did actually help to slim down her legs and give her some much-needed height.

For once, I had to admit Abigail looked nice. Nice.

That was one hell of a compliment coming from me.

Abigail swung the front door open and got in. "Bloody hell Tracy, turn the heat up its freezing in here." She didn't wait for Tracy and started twiddling with the heating dials.

"I need to call and get some petrol."

Abigail sent her a look. "I thought you said you'd already filled up. *Really,* Tracy what's wrong with you?" Abigail didn't have any of Susie's diplomacy.

Tracy paled. "Nothing's wrong. I don't use the car that much it must have been longer than I thought since I filled it up."

Abigail lent over Tracy giving the fuel dial a once over. "Let's get to Susie's first then you can fill up, before we hit the A64. You know how much Susie will bitch if she's kept waiting, and she'll more than likely blame it on me." That's because it was more often than not Abigail's fault. The only thing that Abigail did at super speed was talk.

"So, who do you think will replace Mrs H?"

Tracy's eyebrows shot into her hairline. "I don't know. Surely they won't replace her straightaway?"

"Of course, they will, Hopstocks is a business, they can't afford to leave you reprobates in cosmetics alone for too long."

"We're not reprobates."

"Sure you are; you just don't want to admit it. Hey, don't you remember that time that you all had that competition to see who could get the men to spend the most on Christmas Eve."

"I'd had a lot to drink."

"So had they. Still that's no excuse."

Tracy smiled. "I did hit my target and got that extra four percent in my wage."

"I don't think I'd ever seen you work it like that before, the men were eating out of the palm of your hands. One of them was positively drooling."

Tracy laughed. "You're being daft. I don't think I have that kind of pulling power."

Abigail looked at Tracy. "I don't get you. You're very pretty Tracy, why you're on your own? I don't understand. I'm beginning to think that you've sworn an oath or something, like nuns do. You're definitely living a nun's life."

Tracy laughed off Abigail's comment as she approached Susie's house.

Susie was stood outside tapping her foot as Tracy pulled the car to a stop. Not a good sign.

"Out!" Susie stood with the front passenger door open.

"I'm comfy," Abigail protested.

"I don't care! You know I can't get into the back with my long legs. These babies weren't meant to clamber between seats. Three door cars don't suit them."

"It's not the legs you want to worry about." Abigail pointed at Susie's chest, which surprise, surprise was on display.

Susie smoothed down her very low cut snug green sweater. "I didn't pay a fortune for these buggers to hide them away."
Abigail snorted in response.

Tracy lent forward looking at Susie's navy blue almost skirt, and no tights. "You do know that it's late October Susie?"

"I've got a coat." Susie raised the so-called scrap of fabric in the air, which was supposed to be a coat.

"Do you possess a skirt that's longer than two inches?" Abigail asked staring at Susie's skirt.

"Nope, I have nice legs, why would I want to hide them?" Susie grabbed Abigail's arm. "Come on, I'll help you out, I'm getting cold."

Abigail huffed but got out the car, and flung the front seat forward, scrabbling in the back. "You do know that if you actually wore clothes appropriate for the weather, you wouldn't be cold."

"I hadn't considered that. Thanks, I'll take it on board when I hit eighty, like you two."

"Hang on." The urgency in Abigail's voice stopped Susie from pushing the car seat back. "Hot damn, Tracy, I've left my Zimmer Frame at home, we'll have to go back for it. Don't speed like last time, when you hit thirty, a slow torturous twenty all the way will do." Tracy laughed.

Susie huffed, and flung the car seat back. "You're just too funny."

Abigail threw Susie a smile. "I know."

Susie settled herself in the front seat closing the door, and finally shutting out the cold air. "Come on let's get going." Tracy accelerated.

Abigail's head appeared between the seats. "We need petrol."

Susie looked at Tracy. "I thought you'd just filled up. You know what, never mind, let's get a move on. Unlike Abigail I haven't chewed on a pack of biscuits."

"I offered you one."

"No, as I recall, you spat a load of biscuit crumbs over me and Tracy."

"That was me offering you a biscuit."

"Well next time, finish your mouth full first, and place the biscuits where others can reach them."

Abigail shook her head. "Why would I do that? You might actually take one."

Tracy laughed, which earned her a sharp look from Susie. "Don't encourage her."

Chapter Five

Bored, bored, bored.

Tracy had been back at work for four days now and nothing of any consequence had happened. I don't know what I had expected; perhaps the police to do their job?

The gossips were out though. If I had to hear about Mr H's affair with Trash one more time, I swear someone was going to get dead. The only good thing about the whole thing was that I had finally been given recognition from the police for Mrs H's murder. It had taken the police nearly a week disclose this information to the media. And I think they only did that due to the pressure that had been forced upon them by the media. The papers were my friend, their reach was wide and their thirst for my story infinite. I had even caught a TV show about my killings. Psychologists were out in force, trying to convince the world that they knew me. Understood why I killed. Their hypotheses on what motivated me were a load of crap. They had absolutely no idea. All they were doing was piggy backing on my fame; leeches the lot of them.

The police had spoken to Tracy about Mrs H, as they had done with everyone else. Building a picture of the woman's last moments, I guess. From the look on their faces, they hadn't been able to learn a great deal. Ha! Did they really think that I was that sloppy?

I'd been considering leaving a few clues behind for them. Give them something to work on. I had soon ended that little thought. I wasn't about to do their job for them. I'd quickly filed that thought away.

Hopscotch's had finally finished interviewing for a replacement for Mrs H. I'd seen a few of them going up to the main offices on the top floor, and had to say that they were a dreadful lot. One woman looked like she should be in an OAP home and had struggled making it to the top of the stairs. Her white hair had been shot through with purple stripes. Her hairdresser needed shooting. She reminded me of Mrs H. Age denial was an awful thing. The look Karen had shot her when she'd passed her on the stairs was a classic. Karen could make stone crumble with one of her looks. It seemed that we were both of the same opinion about this latest candidate.

I was pleased to note that the woman hadn't been successful. However, the man strolling down the elevator from soft furnishings, sandwiched between Mr Humphreys and Mr Hopstock Junior, looked very orange and hawk like. I took an instant dislike to him.

Mr Humphreys was dressed in his normal grey pinstripe suit. The trousers had started to shine a bit, and were beginning to pull across the hips and waist. What was left of his hair had been combed over. There were about ten hairs. At least the hair was white. The harsh lighting in the store caused the hair to become transparent. It would be better if he just ridded himself of his desperate need for hair, and cut the limp strands off. His skin was ruddy, not because he spent too much time outdoors, but because of the drink. Mr Humphreys liked his whisky. Not that he ever drank on the job, but he certainly liked a good tipple after work.

In contrast Mr Hopstock Junior was a slight man. At five four he was on the short side, however his presence got everyone moving. Self-confidence rolled off him in waves, he commanded respect, and everyone gave it to him. In his late forties, he was rather old to be labelled 'junior'. If anyone could carry off such a title, this chap could.

Junior wore a dark coal suit; the label that went with the cut of his suit probably cost more than what I earned in a month. Still I liked Junior. He was a handsome man with dark skin and black hair which had started greying slightly at the temple. It gave him more of a distinctive look. Some men, like Junior, got better with age. This was a man that was secure in his own skin. Didn't need to impress or project his fears onto others. He just was. That's what I liked about him.

I thought about Patrick Barnes; despite his great body and good looks, his wife leaving him had raised some very insecure emotions. It was one of the reasons he had been so easy to pull. While outwardly he put two fingers up to his ex-wife, his apartment had told a different story. He clung to his ex-wife like a baby clings to a comforter.

Mrs H hadn't been much better, with her need to look twenty years younger than she was. Age, I admit, has the fastest trainers known to man. One minute you're in your early twenties and life is great, the next you're in your fifties and things are starting to droop.

I looked at the orange chap that stood next to Junior and wrote him off. He had no idea what he was in for. These girls on cosmetics were more temperamental than a room full of rabid dogs. Mrs H may have been welcomed into the pack simply because she was a woman, but she had never been accepted and there was a big difference.

Tracy stood by her make-up counter giving it the once over. Her chocolate hair had been plaited at the nape of her neck and coiled around her shoulders, falling down her front. She never wore a lot of make-up, unlike the rest of them. But then she didn't really need it. The blue company logo'd dress fitted her body like a second skin. I'd taken it in and shaped it for her. Not that she seemed to recognise the change, or even appreciate it. That was ungrateful Tracy for you.

Mr Humphreys stopped at Tracy's counter. Out of all the girls in this section of the department store, Tracy was by far the nicest, and the most compliant.

"Tracy, this is Mr Andrews our new Cosmetics Manager. I want you to introduce him to everyone. I am sure that he will want to spend some time going through everyone's sales figures and targets. Please make sure that they are made available to him."

"Yes, Mr Humphreys." I don't know why she bothered answering him. Mr Humphreys had spotted Susie strutting her long legs across the shop floor with an arm full of tights. When she dropped a pack, I watched him lean forward to get a better look.

You would think that wearing short skirts, as Susie does, that she would bend her knees to pick up the dropped tights; nope, not our Susie. Shy and retiring she was not. And with very little cellulite to mar her pert butt, she was all for showing it off. And so, she bent her body, legs straight, and picked up the tights. Flexibility was another one of Susie's very many feline talents. You can understand why the men liked her so much. Nice pink knickers winked at everyone. She straightened up, threw back her long blonde hair and continued on her way.

Mr Humphreys gave a wishful sigh, and without a word, and forgetting about Junior, raced over to where Susie juggled the tights. Given the extra weight he carried, I reckon he'd have a bit of a sweat on when he got there. His awful aftershave would only blend with the sweat, giving him a decidedly spicy sweat laced aroma. Not for the faint of heart. I'd been on the wrong end of that smell before. He was like a bee sensing the jar lid being taken off the honey pot. His only problem was that this honey pot wouldn't take any flak from him. Susie knew how to work the system, and she also knew just how to keep Mr Humphrey's at the right distance, without him realising what she was doing.

"Thank you, Tracy." Junior glanced over at Mr Humphreys with a disapproving look. All I could think was, I could take care of that problem for you. The way I saw it, I'd be doing Mr Humphreys a favour, he was a worthless piece of flesh. I had too much on at the moment, with Tracy. Once I got rid of her, well I'd be free to help Junior out.

I watched as Junior walked back to the escalator heading for his office.

"Tracy, was it?"

"Yes. Mr Andrews, would you like me to show you round and introduce you to everyone?" Tracy beamed up at him, her best 'welcome' smile on her lips. I could have told her not to waste her time. Mr Orange was not going to play nice. I prided myself on reading people. Let's face it, I couldn't go around killing people without being able to read them well. Take Patrick Barnes, I knew he had a weakness for red heads; you only had to see the ex-wife to know this. Patrick was also a breast man. I'd handed him his dream when I'd hooked him. Long red wig, tits almost popping out of my top. The length of leg I'd had on display had sealed the deal. It was the last dream that Patrick had had.

Mr Andrews looked down at Tracy, his hawk like face wrinkled up in displeasure. "No, show me my office and when I'm ready, I will call you in and you can bring everyone to me one by one with your sales figures." I saw Helen look up from her make-up counter across from Tracy. Her short black hair had been sleeked back away from her face, making her square jaw line look even more masculine. Her sharp blue eyes narrowed, and I could tell just from that one look, that Mr Orange was not going to survive long.

Helen was hormonal, most of the time. In her early twenties, she seemed to go from one crisis to another. Today she had just dumped her latest boyfriend, of one week, because apparently, he didn't care about her. He'd wanted to go watch Leeds play with his mates, as in the 'lads'. I wasn't into football myself and neither was Helen, so I could understand why he didn't want to take her. Not that she would have gone. Six inch stilettos weren't football wear, and Helen had yet to realise that they made heels any lower. Helen was needy. I hated needy.

I rolled my eyes. The man had no idea what he was taking on. His attitude wasn't helping things either. I wasn't quite sure who this man thought he was. He had no class, and nothing within the deep recess of his personality that could redeem him. I shrugged, this one wasn't worth killing. The girls in the cosmetics department would soon see to him. They may look like little immaculate beauties, but don't let this fool you. Their painted claws were sharp, and their tongues sharper. Not as sharp as my knife, but sharp enough to see Mr Orange on his way out.

Tracy quickly led Mr Orange to his office. I was smiling quite happily to myself about this, waiting for his reaction. No one had thought to clear out Mrs H's office since her demise. Her top draw contained a box of tampons, next to which was her HRT pills. There were also a couple of pair of shoes, a spare pair of knickers? I didn't even want to know why she kept them in her draw at work, and a few pair of tights, some of which had been worn and never cleaned. Mrs H might have dressed expensive, but she had not been tidy. That's what happens when you employ a cleaner at home, you forget you're capable of picking up a duster or emptying a bin yourself.

Tracy opened the door to reveal a rather cramped office which had once been a store cupboard. The beige carpet, beech veneered desk with shelving above it, did little to enhance the cramped space.

"This is not what I was expecting." What a shocker. "Mrs H wasn't impressed by the lack of space either.

But Mr Humphreys says, that a cosmetics manager needs to be out on the shop floor, not stowing away in a cosy office." From the look Mr Orange shot her, he was as impressed by her comment as he had been about his office.

"Sorry, I didn't mean to imply... I should go. Would you like me to bring one of the other cosmetics girls?" Mr Orange opened up the top draw. How I managed not to laugh when he saw the tampons, I don't know. His top lip curled in displeasure, and when he saw the dirty tights and spare knickers, his tan turned a degree brighter, with two red spots forming on his cheeks. I could warm my hands against those cheeks.

"No, you can get a bin bag. I want all this gone when I get back."

"Where are you going?" Tracy's eyes were wide with shock.

"Not that it is any business of yours, but I'm going for a coffee."

The rebuff slipped off Tracy without notice. She had other concerns. "But morning break doesn't start until ten and we aren't allowed to use the cafe." Another cold look was shot Tracy's way, as Mr Orange pushed past her. He obviously thought himself to be too important to abide by the rules, or to get to know his staff. He was creating shockwaves, rippling through the cosmetics department like a storm. A wave of displeasure and anger was building, as big and destructive as a tsunami wave. And if Mr Orange wasn't careful, it would hit him in less than a week. I began to question how he'd got through the interview process. What did he have that was so special? I wondered, if I opened him up, and picked at his insides, that I would find that special quality. Or would he, like most, just fail to impress.

Helen came sidling up. "Well he's a joy, isn't he?" She looked round the office space. "Don't bin the print shoes, I'll take them. Mrs H only bought them because she knew I wanted them, and there was only one pair in my size left in stock. She thought she was being clever because we were the same size. Well, look who's laughing now."

Tracy looked pale. "I'll get them for you."

Before Tracy could hand over the box, Helen snatched them out of her grasp and held the shoes up to the light. "See she hasn't even worn them; lucky me."

"I don't think I really want to do this," Tracy said under her breath as she looked about the office, not that it would have made a difference. "It's just really sad."

"What's sad?" Helen shot over her shoulder. "I'll get lots of wear out of them, and I've just got the perfect outfit to go with them. Hey, do you think Mike will regret going to that football match once he gets a load of me in these."

"I think it's going to take more than a pair of shoes, to make him want to give up football," Abigail said as she walked towards Tracy.

"You're just jealous because you're single." Helen injected, still looking at the shoes.

"Nah, can't say I am. You can't keep a man to save your life. Besides aren't you single – *again!*" Helen stomped off without further comment. Abigail had a way of closing down conversation.

"What's happening?" Abigail looked at Tracy who still stood on the threshold of the office.

"Mr Andrews wants me to clear out Mrs H's stuff. I don't think he was impressed with the tampons."

"I bet he wasn't. So, where's Mr Jaffa now?"

Tracy placed a finger on her lips. "*Shh*, don't call him that, he might hear you."

71

"Why where is he?" Abigail looked around her. "He's gone for a coffee, while I clean out the office."

Abigail shrugged her shoulders. "Then he'd need really big ears to hear me from the canteen."

Tracy shook her head. "I don't think he went to the canteen. He's more of a café type of person."

"You mean he thinks he's too good for you lot."

"You drink coffee in the canteen," Tracy pointed out.

"Yeah, but he hasn't met me, so he wouldn't know if I was worth drinking coffee with or not." Abigail's ego was bigger than Mike Tyson's.

Tracy reached for the roll of bin bags that sat in the corner of the office. "Fancy helping me? I really don't fancy doing this on my own. Don't you think it's a bit spooky?"

"The only spooky thing in here is all the dregs in the perfume bottles on the shelves. It's like a cosmetic graveyard in here." Abigail picked up a perfume bottle. "Seriously, there's more dust on these nearly empty bottles of perfume than on your bed frame."

Tracy's eyebrows shot up to her hairline. "My bed isn't dusty."

"Might as well be for all the action it gets."

Abigail ignored the long look that Tracy gave her. "Come on then, if you want a hand, I haven't got all day. Besides Karen is going to come out of her meeting soon; and if I'm not sat at my desk when she's back." Abigail drew a finger across her throat.

"I don't think Karen's going to slit your throat for not being at your desk."

"You're right. I'll be the one slitting my throat, just so I can't hear her going on and on."

"She's not that bad. Besides wouldn't ear plugs be a little less permanent"

"Easy for you to say, you don't work with her. And speaking of Karen, have you two made up yet."

Tracy shook her head as she emptied the contents of the top draw into the dustbin bag that Abigail held open. "I get the feeling it's going to take more than a cream bun from Betty's."

"Look, if you want, and only because I'm nice, why don't you see if she wants to come for a drink with us after work."

Tracy hesitated as she reached over for the rest of the empty perfume bottles. "Really! That's really nice of you."

Abigail beamed. "I know, but you're the one that's going to have to tell Susie." That I had to see.

Tracy lost some of her smile. "Well, I think we're done here. I'll just wipe down the desk and shelves."

"So, you going to break the news to Susie?"

"No, I think I might try and get Karen to pull round another way."

Abigail laughed. "You're such a coward." Susie didn't like Karen. In fact, it would be fair to say that Susie hated Karen. I wasn't sure why. Yes, Karen was a total drag at times, and very cutting. Fashion wasn't something that Karen thought about, and it showed. Thinking about it, yes, I think I could totally understand, why Susie didn't like Karen. They were polar opposites.

"That's easy for you to say." Tracy sighed.

Footsteps sounded behind Abigail, and I saw Mr Orange appear. "And who might you be."

Abigail jumped at the sound of his voice. "Me, I was just leaving. Here Tracy, let me take that bin bag for you." She shot Mr Orange a big grin. "Always happy to help, that's us lot in accounts." Abigail's shoes beat a hasty retreat towards the escalator. And just because it was Abigail, she started to do the Jaffa commercial, full moon, half-moon with her hands. Tracy blinked trying not to laugh.

Coughing to hide her smile, Tracy picked up the wipes. "Sorry Mr Andrews, I just need to wipe things down, and then it's all done."

Mr Orange looked less than impressed. "Had you spent more time cleaning, and less time talking, then it would be done by now." Who did this guy think he was? If he didn't look out, he'd be my next creation, just so I could teach him a lesson, he'd need to be *deadly* serious to listen to me and well, that would give Hopscotch's a bit of a reputation they could do without.

From where I stood, I gave him a look that told him exactly what I wanted to do to him. For the first-time Mr Orange noticed me. Yep, been here all along! He took a step back, as the coldness in my eyes settled over him. That's it Mr Orange, you just be careful, you have no idea who you're dealing with. I thought about that, you know I've heard people say that before. *"You have no idea who you're dealing with"*, some people who say it are pretty lame. Not everything is about money and position. So, what if Junior fired him, he'd still be alive, and able to find another job. Once I'd finished with him, not even the angels would want to look upon him.

That thought alone made me smile.

"The office is fine. Go. I'll be out in a minute to see everyone." Tracy looked a bit surprised by the fear that was so evident on his face. She didn't understand that he'd just seen the face of death.

Poor Tracy, she was always the last to know. Like the fact that Uncle Kevin had been released from prison. Apparently, he'd been a good boy. Wait until she found out. It would send her into orbit. Her little world was starting to break, and she didn't even know it.

I was counting the days until her mum and dad got the nerve up, to drive across to York from Harrogate, and tell her. You'd think that Harrogate was a hell of a drive away, say, like driving from the Brecon Beacons to Inverness which were over five hundred miles apart, and would take the best part of a day to get there. Nope, Harrogate was quite literally a forty-minute drive down the A59, even at the slow speed in which Tracy's dad drove his new Škoda Fabia. You would be forgiven for thinking that the car had only three gears, slow, very slow and reverse; that was the three main settings at which Tracy's dad drove.

A letter had arrived at Tracy's a few weeks back. Lucky for her, I was the one that found it. I liked to go through Tracy's mail, as boring as it usually was. However, persistence often pays off. The contents of the letter I had decided, would be enough to send Tracy over the edge and disappear for some considerable time. That was fine; I'd have time to play and live a little, while Tracy slunk off and wept in a quiet corner somewhere. The problem with that is that just like last time, Tracy would get over it and be back. I didn't want Tracy back. I wanted her gone for good. So, I burnt the letter that her brother Danny had sent. Tracy would take the news better from her mum and dad. Besides, I'm a big believer in parent responsibility.

The office door closed in front of Tracy's face. I watched her walk back to her counter and start prepping her figures. They didn't look good. She was down ten percent on last year's and twenty percent down on her overall monthly target. No way was she going to get that back, especially when she found out about Uncle Kevin.

Chapter Six

I'd been watching Mr Bennett try and park his car for fifteen minutes now. The street was a little less busy than normal, plenty of parking spaces for a change. For the average driver, there was enough room to reverse in nicely.

Mr Bennett however was under the misconception that he drove the number four double decker bus, that ran a service from Acomb into York city centre rather than a Skoda Fabia. Mrs Bennett had got out of the car to see him back, and had been waving her hand in the air enthusiastically for some time, trying to get him to back a little closer to the car behind. It had started to rain and I could see that Mr Bennett wasn't going to rush this.

Tracy being Tracy had leapt to her mums' rescue, and was now hot footing over to her, brolly in hand. Mrs Bennett took the offered brolly and moved to the house, leaving Tracy brolly-less in the rain to see her dad safely into the parking spot, that would have easily housed two decent sized cars. The rain began to beat down faster, quickly drenching Tracy. Her jeans were sticking to her, her pale pink jumper was starting to take in the water and stretch towards her knees. Tracy's trainers squelched as she moved, and her hair clung to her face and back. Mr Bennett stalled the car for the sixth time. The engine groaned back to life and began kangaroo jumping forward. Tracy flapped her arms. Mr Bennett ignored her and started backing the car into the space again. The car stalled and Tracy sank her head into her hands, shaking her head.

It took another twenty minutes for Mr Bennett to park the car, and become satisfied that it was parked right. Mrs Bennett was looking a bit worse for wear, her irritation growing, while she remained dry under the brolly. Mr Bennett refused to become aware of his wife's black mood. Tracy ran back to the house and they stepped inside. Mr Bennett looked at Tracy and seemed genuinely shocked, as she did a grand job of portraying a major water leak, dripping water all over the hall floor.

"You're very wet Tracy." Tracy blinked at her dad. The Bennett's were a treat, and I really enjoyed spending time with them. That may surprise you.

The Bennett's were so oblivious to the things that went on around them, that it was hard to feel any resentment towards them. The fact that they, like others, never noticed me didn't bother me, which was a rarity for me. The difference with the Bennett's was that they treated everyone in a similar way, so it was hard to feel alienated. I reckon if ET landed his space ship and came for super, they wouldn't flinch, and just ask him to pass the sugar.

"I'll just go change. Dad, why don't you both go in the living room, I've started the fire and I'll make you a cuppa when I get down." Tracy kicked off her sodden trainers, and ran up the stairs as her dad pushed open the living room door and shook out of his coat. Hardly a drop of rain on him! Mrs Bennett was still shaking the brolly out, not that it would stop the puddle of water from forming on the tiled floor. I didn't know why she had to manhandle the thing; it really wasn't the brolly's fault.

I watched Tracy as she striped off her clothes, and threw on some pink jogging bottoms, a long sleeved white sweat-shirt, and some white socks. She'd lost a bit of weight recently. If it wasn't for me, I didn't think she would eat at all. Nobody took that much notice of Tracy's eating habits, but let me tell you, they're sparse. I knew the body image that she saw when she looked in the mirror. It was of a person four times her size. This had developed, like everything else had, after Uncle Kevin had kidnapped and raped her. I was a little sketchy about the details, as I didn't know Tracy when it all happened. But, from what I had learnt over the years, her time with Uncle Kevin had left her quite depressed, with a hell of a lot of self-loathing.

I didn't understand the self-blame thing. Had it been me, I'd have killed him. Believe me, there is always a way, a gap in time, an opportunity that someone would have overlooked. Somehow I'd have found it, long before the police could take action. I'd also have made sure that Uncle Kevin suffered for what he had done, and believe me, I have the imagination and the desire, to inflict a lot of pain. His time in prison was no recompense for what he had done, nor would it turn Tracy back into the carefree girl she had once been.

I had never known the girl that Tracy had been before, but I had seen pictures. Families, they always like to get the photo albums out, and show everyone what a regular, normal family they were. Personally, I didn't think that normal existed. Normal was a projection of how we are expected to behave. Anyone exhibiting behaviours outside of the 'normal' equation, are termed as 'abnormal', or given some fancy name that a psychologist has thought up, to group a particular behaviour together. I should know, look at the fancy title they gave someone like me – psychopath. I mean really! I wonder how long it had taken them to come up with that one. Bet they all patted themselves on the back when they'd thought of it. But really, what was normal? Just suppose that I was normal, and everyone else was abnormal. Then really, it was everyone else that needed treatment, not me.

Tracy flipped her wet hair over her shoulder, and reached for the oversized thick ribbed grey cardigan that hung on the back of her bedroom door, as she bounced back down the stairs to her waiting parents.

Mr and Mrs Bennett sat on the sofa by the fire, they looked nervous. Knowing the news they were about to deliver, I'd be nervous too. Well, I wouldn't, but then I'd have to care, to feel nervous in the first place.

The news that the Bennett's had to deliver would add to Tracy's depression. Depression and Tracy were firm friends. Personally, I didn't understand the condition. Why let someone, or something make you feel that way? Would it not be easier to just get rid of the thing that was causing you to feel that way? I'd killed a boy once for something very similar. I'd been around fifteen at the time. I remember it, like seeing an old film being played back.

He was the same age as me. As his birthday was the month before mine, he liked to think that he was older. Maybe that one month did make him older, technically speaking. OK, so he might have been older, but he wasn't smarter than me, that was for sure. Mind, there aren't that many people as smart as me. I'm not being egotistical, I'm just saying.

We were supposed to meet on Hob Moor; open fields, with a path leading to a number of streets, and a short cut to and from school. He hadn't shown up. I'd later learnt that he had thought it would be fun to set me up. Oh, they'd had quite a few laughs at my expense. Well, when I'd got hold of him as he walked home from a friend's house, by the side of the River Ouse, he'd soon learnt I'd be the one having the last laugh.

His name had been Brian Thompson. Brian had dark coffee coloured skin, which reminded me of a caramel bar. His thick wiry black hair cascaded around his head like a frizzy hat, which added a few inches of much needed height. For a boy, he was on the short side, coming up to my shoulder. Despite this, I had quite liked Brian's sharp intellect. He seemed more interesting than the rest. Well, that was of course until he had decided to set me up. I'd soon learnt that intelligent or not, Brian was a loser. A loser that was soon to be dead.

79

I had picked up a brick and smashed it over the top of his head before he knew what was happening; serves him right for being a short arse if you asked me. His body had crumpled before me, blood running down his face. When I'd seen the blood, I'd found it intoxicating. The amount of satisfaction I had got from seeing his lifeless body at my feet was so gratifying; I knew in that moment that killing was for me. I had kicked him into the River Ouse that runs through York City Centre. It seemed the easiest way to get rid of the body. I'd stood there for a long time watching the river carry him away, a smile of satisfaction on my lips. I'd felt nothing for Brian Thompson, or the life I had taken, other than a deep satisfaction that it would be the last time he ever laughed at me. His death had definitely given me a lot of ideas. My main thought that day, was that I needed to learn how to kill without being discovered.

The local newspaper reported the death as an 'accident'. Turns out that the blow I'd given Brian had only knocked him unconscious, the river was what killed him. I'd learnt a valuable lesson that day. Always make sure that they were dead and not just sleeping it off.

"Tracy love, why don't you sit down?" Tracy's mum looked like she wanted to be anywhere but in Tracy's living room.

"I'll make us a drink first." Oblivious that was our Tracy. I swear a naked man could do a lap round her living room at this moment, burn his bits on the fire, and she wouldn't notice a thing. She was like an ostrich, burying her head, hoping things would go away. I could tell from the way that Tracy was ignoring the fact that her parents had something to tell her, that she was hoping, rather stupidly, that nothing would change. That whatever brought her mum and dad to her house would somehow disappear, like condensation from a window. The Bennett's discomfort was obvious. They twitched and sent each other worried glances. At some point Tracy was going to have to sit down, and listen to the news that her parents brought. I believe in getting the pain over with, so that I can move on quickly. Tracy liked the slow torturous approach.

Without giving her parents time to comment, Tracy shot into the kitchen, and started filling the kettle. I sighed as she pulled out the white wooden tray and laid a tea towel on top of it, before placing cups and plates on it. My eyes narrowed as she reached over and opened my cupboard door. As Tracy didn't eat much, she never had biscuits or cakes in stock. I, on the other hand, liked to keep a healthy amount of sweet stuff in. I had what people termed as a sweet tooth.

Tracy hesitated, looked around, and must have decided it was safe to help herself to my food. I'd get her for that later. Someone was definitely going to pay.

Tea cups clanking and a good stock of my cakes and biscuits now sitting neatly on a plate, Tracy walked back into the living room.

The sky outside had turned darker, and the rain now forcefully beat against the living room windows. It was only two o'clock in the afternoon, but the darkening sky made it look more like six.

"Mum" Tracy passed her mum a cup of tea, before repeating the process for her dad. I watched as she offered them my biscuits and cakes. I wanted to chop their fingers off bit by little bit, as they began to nibble on my biscuits. Tracy sat down on the opposite sofa, her shoulders tight with anxiety. She had no option now but to listen.

"Did you get Danny's letter?" Mr Bennett asked as he munched on his third biscuit.

"Danny? No why?" I could see Mr Bennett's spirits sink.
"Oh, that's a shame." I couldn't agree with Mrs Bennett more. It was a shame that they had to step up to the mark, and actually act as parents.

Mr and Mrs Bennett placed their cups back onto the tray simultaneously. They reminded me of synchronised swimmers. Only these little fishes were about to drown.

"You see Tracy." Mr Bennett leant forward, a worried expression on his face. I could see Tracy start to waver, her pulse had picked up a bit, and if they didn't tell her soon, she would shrink so far into herself, she would disappear altogether. Not that normally, I would have a problem with this however on this occasion, it wouldn't suit me. I had my own reasons for that which I do not wish to express but just to say, I was beginning to think that the best thing that the Bennett's could have done on the way here, was to have a car accident and be taken to hospital.

Mrs Bennett found her spine. Sat up a little straighter and just went for it. "They've released Uncle Kevin from prison dear."

Tracy sat stock still, frozen in place, hands shaking. Her eyes temporally glazed over. I thought that all things considered, she was taking the news rather well. That was of course before Mr Bennett had to elaborate.

"Tracy love, you're fine, he isn't allowed anywhere near you. The police have him under surveillance. What was it they put on him?" A bit more colour left Tracy's face.

"A tag, don't you remember that film we watched the other night? They put one on that man recently released from prison. I think it was on his leg."

"Ah, yes. You know I don't think we ever saw the end. I must have fallen asleep again."

"You always fall asleep." Mrs Bennett grumbled.

Tracy stood up. "I'll go make us a fresh brew." Her hands were shaking as she reached for the tray, before she could reach for it, there was a knock at the door. Tracy froze, eyes wide, pulse beating hard. She swallowed nervously.

"Are you going to answer it love?" Mrs Bennett asked.

"Yes...I'll...be...right back." My eyes flew to the ceiling, this was not going well.

"Bloody hell Tracy, take your time why don't you," Susie grumbled as she stepped through the front door, Abigail right behind her.

It was still raining, and yet, I was not surprised to see that Susie didn't have a coat on. Her dry hair remained artfully styled as it coiled up on top of her head, the brolly she passed to Tracy, was the only thing that had kept it dry. Her skirt was leather so luckily the rain ran off it. Her white top however had several wet patches on it that now clung to her breasts. The problem (as most of us know) with white when it gets wet is, it becomes transparent. All I can say is, that at least Susie was wearing a bra, albeit a lacy white number which didn't do a good job at hiding anything. Her nipples were standing to attention better than any soldier, their dark shading like two large spots against the wet fabric.

"Pass us a towel Tracy, so I can wipe down my legs, you wouldn't believe how wet they are." Oh, I would, the top told everyone exactly how wet things were.

Abigail put her coat onto one of the hooks and took off her ankle boots. Her black jeans were wet about four inches up from the hem. Unlike Susie who dressed like every day was summer, Abigail wore a thick ribbed orange jumper that did nothing for her complexion, but did at least serve some purpose, in that it kept the cold out.

"Oh, hi Mr and Mrs Bennett," Susie smiled at them, as she began drying off her legs. Unlike Abigail, Susie wasn't prepared to lose the shoes, which increased the length of her slim legs by four inches.

Mrs Bennett shot Mr Bennett a disapproving look, as he watched the towel slide up and down the length of Susie's legs.

In the end, she elbowed him in the ribs, which seemed to shake him from his trance. His cheeks reddened slightly, his eyes wandering around the room, as though to stop himself from ogling Susie again. If he'd noticed the wet top earlier, he didn't show it, his wandering eyes never shot back for another quick peak. That could have been due to Mrs Bennett's hand, which casually gripped his knee.

"Tracy love, why don't you get Susie one of your tops? She's positively wet through."

Susie shook her head. "Don't bother, I'll sit near the fire. I'll be dry in next to no time. Besides, I'd be lucky to get one of these babies in one of Tracy's tops." Mrs Bennett didn't look impressed, but refrained from saying anything else.

"Hi." Abigail sent the Bennett's a wave. "Oooo biscuits! I like it when you two visit. Tracy never gives us biscuits. Were you making a fresh brew Tracy?" Abigail sat down on the opposite sofa and began munching.

"I'll have a cup if you're brewing up," Susie said as she finished off drying her legs.

Tracy lifted the tray leaving behind the biscuits and walked back into the kitchen.

"I'm glad you're both here." Mr Bennett said, his eyes had focused on Susie's legs again. They lingered there longer than they ought to. Mrs Bennett gave his knee another hard squeeze. Mr Bennett coughed to cover the pain as her nails sank in. "We were just telling Tracy that they've released Uncle Kevin."

"Oh God, what awful news, I was hoping that one of the other inmates would bump him off. Do they keep child molesters in separate prisons nowadays?" Abigail looked at Susie, who shrugged her shoulders. "Well I guess that's not going to happen now."

Tracy walked back into the living room and placed the tray down. It hit the surface harder than expected. Tea splashed onto the tea towel. Mrs Bennett shot her a worried look, but didn't say anything.

"No, I suppose not," Mr Bennett said. "Well, look it's getting late, and well the weathers not so good."

Mrs Bennett rose to her feet, the relief that flitted across her face was not missed by anyone. "Yes, you're right we'd better be on our way. It was lovely to see you both. Tracy love, thank you for the drink. I'm sorry that we had to deliver such awful news. Remember, the police have everything under control, and that you're safe. Well you're a good deal older than you were, and it appears that Uncle Kevin liked them young." Now wasn't that reassuring.

Tracy had gone a good deal paler. Abigail reached up to her and gave her hand a squeeze. "It's OK, we're staying."

I watched Tracy as she waved goodbye to her parents. She looked unnerved, but for Tracy she was doing remarkably well.

"Do you have any more biscuits? Fatty here's eaten them all," Susie asked as Tracy closed the front door and walked back into the living room.

"Hmmm, no they were Lauren's. I'd better replace them before she finds out." Tracy looked nervous. She ought to.

Abigail jabbed Susie with her elbow. "I didn't eat them all, Mr and Mrs Bennett helped. Besides, look at it as me doing you a favour, biscuits cause cellulite and with your short skirts you couldn't afford it."

"Do they?" Tracy asked as she hovered by the living room door.

"Do they what?" Abigail asked as she took a long sip of her tea.

"Biscuits cause cellulite?"

Abigail smiled "They do if you're called Susie."

Susie sent Abigail a look. "Sometimes I wonder why we're friends."

"You're not the only one. I've come to the conclusion that despite everything, you can't live without me. Maybe we should get married?" Abigail smiled sweetly at Susie.

"I'm not your type."

"True, but I'd make an amazing bride. I can see myself in a beautiful big wedding dress. I don't think I'd wear white though, off white, ivory or champagne maybe."

"You'd bankrupt me." Susie shook her head. "I can't quite believe I'm having this conversation. Come on Tracy sit down, you're managing to make me nervous, and I'm not the one that has to deal with Uncle Kevin's release."

Abigail patted the sofa next to her. "You know we'd never let anything happen to you. Who'd be our bridesmaid?"

Tracy laughed at Abigail. I tried not to let it irritate me.

"I take it your mum and dad didn't say where Uncle Kevin was living. After all he has to live somewhere, and I'm sure the last thing you want to do is bump into him unaware." Trust Abigail, from the look of horror flitted across Tracy's face, she hadn't really thought about where Uncle Kevin would be living.

"Seriously Abs, you have as much tact as a rhinoceros." I could tell from the look on Susie's face that she felt that Abigail had a point. "Besides I don't think they'd allow Uncle Kevin to live anywhere near Tracy." Susie cocked her head. "I don't really think we should call him Uncle Kevin, after all what he did wasn't Uncle like."

Abigail raised her eyebrows in thought. "How about *The-Bastard-That-Shall-Remain-Nameless?*"

"It's a bit long winded."

"OK, how about just Him or It."

Susie shook her head. "I think we'll leave his name as it is."

Tracy fidgeted. "I think I should go shopping, I don't want Lauren coming home and finding I've raided her cupboard."

"She never seems to be around if you ask me. I've never met her. If I didn't know better, I'd say that she didn't exist."

"Abigail!" Susie sent her a hard look. "What, I was just saying…"

"I know exactly what you were just saying. Let's drop it."

"Whatever."

Tracy went to get her coat, a strange look on her face as she pondered Abigail's comments about me. If she would just open her eyes, she'd notice me. The three of them were just as bad as the other. I was here watching, waiting and they never saw me, never acknowledged my existence. I'm sure you can understand how that can make a person feel.

"We'll come with you." Abigail pushed up out of the sofa.

"It's OK, I can manage on my own." Tracy smiled at the concerned looks on her friends faces. "Seriously, it's just all a bit of a shock, I'll be OK."

Susie stood up. "Tell you what, why don't you go buy the biscuits or whatever it is that you need, and Abs and I will stay here and clean up." Susie elbowed Abigail.

"Yeah. Sure. Why not." Abigail flopped back down on the sofa.

"You don't have to, you know that, don't you?"

"Sure we do, besides my Wi-Fi's crashed, I'll use the time to catch up on some emails or something. It can't take that long to throw a few things into a basket, now can it." Very good Susie, her point was very clear.

Tracy nodded her head, accepting that her time in the supermarket was limited. Otherwise the search party in the guise of Susie and Abigail would come and collect her.

"Do either of you want anything while I'm at the supermarket?"

"I'll have some of those cakes that your mum and dad ate, they looked really nice."

Susie shook her head. "You had to ask." Abigail grinned.

I almost felt like telling the duo that they didn't have to worry, I'd be going with Tracy. Ha, ha, ha, what a joke. I wasn't going with Tracy because I cared. I hadn't killed for weeks and I was starting to get a bit twitchy. Opportunities presented themselves in all kinds of ways, and I wasn't going to miss out, should one come along.

I watched as Tracy got in her car and drove off down the street to Tesco. She kept her speed at a steady thirty. I didn't know many people who were as conscious as she was about keeping her speed within the limits. I didn't. Then you wouldn't really expect me to.

The trip round the supermarket was getting boring. I'd seen a slug move quicker, and show more enthusiasm. Tracy walked around the place in a dazed state. On the plus side, she was at least putting the right things in the basket, my cupboard would soon be back to what it had been before the raid.

The rain had subsided as Tracy left Tesco. She walked to the car in the same dazed state that she had wandered round the supermarket.

"Excuse me." Tracy turned around startled as she became aware of the man at her side.

It was probably as well that the rain had stopped. The guy only had on a long sleeved purple t-shirt that clung to his torso, not that it did anything for me, but he obviously felt that it made him look more attractive and manly in some way. Dark denim jeans that thankfully were a regular fit coated his legs. I wasn't into men wearing skinny jeans. The brown mop of hair that could probably do with a cut, blew into his eyes. I'm positive that he used his hair to come across as more boyish, and a little cheeky.

"Sorry, I was deep in thought." Tracy flipped the boot and placed the bags inside.

"That's OK. I just wanted to tell you. I think you're gorgeous." I rolled my eyes at him. Seriously!

Tracy smiled and for the first time that day the smile reached her eyes. "Thanks."

"Are you attached, you know seeing anyone?" The hopeful look in his dark brown eyes was almost comical. I was starting to get real interested in this guy.

"No."

"That's great! How do you fancy a coffee?" That sounded good to me. I was starting to feel the thrill of a kill tingle along my spine. This one would be good.

"I don't know. I've got some friends waiting for me at home."

"Why don't you text them, let them know you've got side tracked. Come on." Maybe the hair was working, because Tracy smiled and nodded her head.

"OK," Tracy fished out her phone from her coat pocket.

"Tell you what, why don't you send them a Snapchat of us having coffee. They might be more understanding." This guy really liked himself.

Tracy laughed and walked back into the supermarket, the chap at her side had a lazy smile on his lips. Five minutes later with coffee mugs in hand (Tracy's containing tea), Tracy sent Susie and Abigail a Snapchat, because she couldn't just Snapchat one of them, otherwise there would be hell to pay.

Tracy's phone buzzed twice within seconds of her Snapchat. She laughed when she looked at their responses.

"I take it that they're OK with you taking a bit longer." He raised his right eyebrow, in that inquisitive trade mark manner that James Bond was known for.

Tracy laughed. "You could say that."

"By the way, the name's Richard Burnhill." He held out his right hand.

"I'm Tracy Bennett." She placed her hand in his. "Nice to meet you Tracy Bennett," I laughed to myself wild and shrill. Oh, this was going to be just too much fun. I could tell that Tracy really liked this guy.

A smile came easily to her lips as they chatted. Their drinks had been drunk over an hour ago, the food in the boot forgotten. Abigail and Susie could be living in another universe for all she cared. Not waiting at her house like a couple of Praying Mantis' waiting for the gossip. I don't think that even Uncle Kevin got a look in. No, Tracy was enjoying herself, in a way that I had never seen her do before.

Richard was talking about them meeting up tomorrow, and going out for something to eat. That got me thinking. I decided that it would be fun to let this relationship develop a bit more, before I killed Richard. It would give me time to collect the information I needed about him, to get a grip on his routine and such. The impact of his death would also be more significant to Tracy if this relationship developed. This could be the one that tipped her over into the darkness forever. And then I'd be free.

There would be other opportunities for me to kill before I killed Richard. I'd been thinking about Uncle Kevin too, and I was beginning to come to the conclusion that it would be beneficial if he just died.

I'd have to think about the where and how. I didn't want this tailing back to The Yorkshire Slasher. Finding Uncle Kevin wouldn't be that difficult. Killing him would be easy, and I was aware that I would gain no satisfaction from it, well not as much as I usually got. Hmm, it seemed we would both be busy.

I felt energised as I looked at Richard. He could be my best creation yet.

Chapter Seven

Richard Burnhill was spending more time at Tracy's than at his own place. I tried not to let it get to me.

It was difficult.

Tracy was so happy, giddy in fact.

In some respects, I was pleased that they were getting close. It would make the kill all the more gratifying, especially when I thought about the effect it would have on Tracy. She wasn't the most stable person in the world. That said, I couldn't stop her happiness grating on me like a bad itch. Her happiness brought out all my allergies. I was positive that I was allergic to Tracy being happy. It's the only allergy I had.

To take the pain away, I absorbed myself into finding Uncle Kevin. As expected, it really hadn't been that difficult. He'd shacked up on the outskirts of Leeds, at a little place called Meanwood. I thought the name of the place suited him. He was currently living in a rental property on Stonegate Gardens, a small cul-de-sac off Stonegate Lane. The houses were nice, if you liked chocolate window frames and dark bricks. Some of the occupants obviously didn't, as they had replaced theirs with white frames. I had a thing about UPVC chocolate frames. I found them depressing. And I had Tracy for that.

The gardens were adequate. More than Tracy had, if you could call a slab of concrete for a backyard a garden. I'd noticed a small slide, and a scattering of kids toys outside one of the property's' front garden. I was betting that the neighbours didn't know the kind of person that was living next door.

Luckily for them I was about to sort out their little problem.

I was parked out on Stonegate Lane, where I had a clear view of the house that Uncle Kevin was currently residing at. My black Ford Fiesta fitted in quite well with all the other cars in this neighbourhood, unlike Mrs H's. Not everyone round here could afford a new high-end car. I looked at the clock, it was eight a.m. Uncle Kevin wouldn't be returning for another three hours yet.

He worked the nightshift for a mailing company. Not having a car, he was forced to use public transport, and we all know how reliable buses can be. I felt that Uncle Kevin was making this a little too easy for me, not that I was complaining. Still it would make things a little more interesting, if he had put a little bit more effort into his own personal security, rather than putting everything he had into hiding what he was, a sex offender. It would be hard for the police to feel anything but grateful when they found his dead body.

Uncle Kevin's neighbours all worked days, so the place was alive with people hurrying to get to work, or the kids to school. No one would be around to hear him if he chose to scream; just how I liked it.

I'd bumped into him yesterday and taken his house keys. I had wrapped a scarf around my neck and lower face, and my coat hood had been up covering the top of my head, casting a shadow over the top half of my face. Not that Uncle Kevin bothered to look. Still you never know. He'd given a grunt, stepped round me, and moved on. There was a Shoe Repair / Key Cutters Shop up on the main street near where Uncle Kevin worked, and I'd wandered in and had a spare key cut. I'd left Uncle Kevin's set of keys hanging from the keyhole on his front door. Let him think that he had left them there that morning. He probably wouldn't have even noticed they were missing until he'd wanted them.

I'd had a good wander round the house. It's surprising what you can learn about a person by wandering round their home, and looking in their cupboards. You wouldn't think it, but apparently, Uncle Kevin was depressed and didn't sleep so well. The pills in his bathroom cupboard told me that. You could deduce from this, if you wanted to, that he was sorry for what he had done to Tracy. I came to the conclusion that prison hadn't really suited him that much. A bit like when you break your arm, and have the worse itch in the world, and can't get to it because of the pot covering your arm. That's how I viewed Uncle Kevin's depression. He had been unable to act on his true nature, and that had led to him become depressed. But he was free now. How long would it take before the kid next door but one became interesting to him? I didn't really believe that people could change what they were. You are born a certain way, and no amount of therapy can change that. I know I would never be able to stop killing. I liked it too much to want to stop. It was a part of what I was. I could pop all the pills in the world, and attend as much therapy as they thought I needed. Still deep down, I was me; genetically wired to kill. Nope, Uncle Kevin couldn't change what he was, as much as he wouldn't be able to change the fact that in a few hours he'd be dead.

The sun had yet to make an appearance and the sky looked heavy with snow. The temperature outside hadn't risen above two degrees. I'd turned the engine off half an hour ago, and the temperature in the car had fallen quickly. Winter was definitely here. I snuggled a little more into my black down jacket, pulling the beanie hat further down over my head and flipping my coat hood up. I was waiting for the neighbours to leave before breaking into Uncle Kevin's and setting up.

It seemed that Uncle Kevin had become something of a loner. His routine was an easy one, if not boring. Get up, go to work, come home, sit watch telly, drink himself into unconsciousness, and repeat the whole process again. Boring! It was as if he was still in prison. The bars maybe gone, but he wasn't free. No, he was fighting his true nature, and the drink helped remove the ache.

I was rather pleased with my plan for killing Uncle Kevin.

It was a good one. Simple even.

Weren't they the best?

The last of the neighbours were leaving, bundling kids into the back of their car, to take them to school. Horrible things are kids. They shout, scream, and seem to generally go out of their way to be as contrary as possible, much to their parent's chagrin. You would think that getting a kid into the back of a car was easy. Looking at the monster with the bottom lip stuck out, that had rooted itself next to the front door and screamed every time his dad went close to him, it wasn't. I didn't envy dad's task. It was going to be no mean feat getting that kid anywhere. The kids' hands were currently in and out of the pocket of his yellow duffle coat, depending upon how agitated he got. Grey trousers poked out from beneath, and thick socks under black shoes which were badly scraped at the toes, kept the cold from eating at his toes. The kid held a knitted red hat in his right red gloved hand.

Surprisingly, I wasn't the patient type when it came to people, and little people in my opinion were a hell of a lot worse. They were stubborn, to a point where they would rather lose everything than cave in. Compromise, didn't figure in their vocabulary, never mind acting out the meaning of the word.

I looked at the clock on the dashboard and felt peeved. If dad didn't get the kid in the back of the car soon, I was going to rectify the problem myself, permanently. I could be doing him a favour. From the look on his face, he felt like strangling the kid himself. Still, I noticed that he plastered a somewhat strained smile on his face, and began gesturing towards the car. In response, the kid stamped his feet and threw down the hat. The wind caught at it and sent it swirling down the drive. This sent the kid into a fit of screams, tears running down his face in a torrent of frustration. Dad made a mad grasp for the hat; missed. The kid remained screaming. Dad ran after the hat. Determination won, and dad walked back to his kid hat in hand. You would think that this would pacify the thing. It didn't. What a surprise.

I could see the moment that dad gave up all hope, and produced a chocolate bar. If reason fails try bribery. Still the kid wouldn't move. Whether its problem was bigger than a chocolate bar, or that he was enjoying making his dad late for work, I didn't know. But either way, the kid wasn't budging, and my already limited patience was slipping away fast.

Reason and bribery failing, dad stomped over and picked the kid up. Legs and arms flew, hitting dad in all sorts of places that probably hurt, a lot. Within fifteen minutes, dad had the kid strapped into the back of the car. I could still hear it screaming even though dad had closed the car door. I watched as dad straightened out his frazzled hair, and took a number of deep breaths before getting into the driver's seat.

Within ten minutes they were gone and the neighbourhood was at peace once more. My anger at the kid melted away. I took a breath to release the last of it, checking the time. Everything was fine; I could still get set up before Uncle Kevin came home.

I opened the car door and braced myself for the cold. The wind caught at my hood pulling it down. It didn't matter my beanie hat remained in situ. I pulled out the key from my pocket and opened the front door.

I hadn't brought my large handbag with me today. I didn't need it for what I had planned. Fred would have to sit this one out. As I'd said before, I didn't want this kill linked to 'The Yorkshire Slasher' killings. I could do subtle.

Inside, the house was your typical two up, two down. The small entrance foyer led to the living room and fitted kitchen, which was surprisingly spacious if not big. Off the living room was the stairs to the two double bedrooms and bathroom. The house had been painted in magnolia from top to bottom and the carpet was beige. The only colour was in the kitchen where a roller blind rested fully down, the deep yellow a contrast to its otherwise bland surroundings.

The heating had just clicked on in readiness for Uncle Kevin to come home. I walked upstairs making my way to the bathroom. I'd covered my flat boots with blue shoe covers before I'd entered the house, so that I would be sure not to leave any dirt or shoe prints behind. Picking up the sleeping pills and anti-depressants, I wandered back into the living room. I put the pills on the coffee table that sat between the small cast iron living flame gas fire and the off-white two-seater sofa. A matching chair sat with its back to the window. The off-white curtains were drawn. I got the feeling that Uncle Kevin liked his privacy. I'd seen the photos of the little girl, who I assumed must live in the street. It was as if Uncle Kevin had closed the curtains to keep out temptation. It wasn't working.

I walked into the kitchen and opened the fridge door that sat on the left side under the work units. Taking the full bottle of vodka off the shelf, I closed the door. The glass was snug against the black leather of my gloves. I placed the bottle on the coffee table next to the pills and sat down on the chair. The cushions were surprisingly soft, and I sank into their depths. I'd have to plump them up before I left. The house was starting to warm up. I'd swiped down my black jacket, beanie hat, and trousers with a sticky pet hair remover roller before I'd left the car. I didn't want to leave anything behind. I had decided not to wear a wig today, as I wasn't intending to take off the hat. Despite the rising temperature in the room, I kept my coat on.

In some things, I was an extraordinarily patient person. It was a full three quarters of an hour before I heard the front door click open. I didn't move from where I sat. Instead I silently watched as the living room door open. Uncle Kevin came walking in. He made his way into the kitchen in his socked feet, never looking my way, the silly boy.

I watched as he went to the fridge for the bottle of vodka. He hesitated, before getting down on his knees and working his way into the back of the fridge, emptying the contents onto the kitchen floor. Leaning back onto his heels he scratched his head, pushed himself up and looked round the kitchen. Did he think that the vodka bottle had suddenly sprouted legs and moved? Still, I found his confusion amusing.

He must have got changed at some point before leaving work, as he now wore a pair of worn out denim jeans. Holes were appearing at the knees and the colour was now a washed out blue/grey. A thick ribbed loose fitting jumper fell past his waist; the burgundy wool had lost its shape a long time ago. Pulls littered the chest and arms. His hair touched his shoulders and hung in greasy unkempt clumps. The beard and moustache made him look old, and his sallow skin looked unhealthy. Life obviously had taken a downward spiral for Uncle Kevin.

Despite his unkempt appearance, he liked a tidy and clean house, which was as well given the length of time I had been waiting for him. No one liked to wait surrounded by filth.

Uncle Kevin had started to mutter under his breath, and was becoming very agitated.

"The vodkas on the coffee table." Uncle Kevin spun round eyes wide at the sound of my voice. I placed a smile on my face, not exactly welcoming, and not warm either, but it was there.

"What the hell! Who are you? Get out!" Well no pleasantries to be found here.

"I don't think so, not yet anyway. Stop hovering in the kitchen and sit down." My voice was harsh, and I didn't try to hide the evil that lurked inside me.

I watched him as he tried to regain some of his composure. My response hadn't been what he'd expected. He probably thought he could intimidate me with his size at six foot five and twice my width. I shrugged. I'd killed bigger men.

"Get the hell out or I'll ring the police." Now that little comment made me laugh.

"No, you won't." He reached for the phone that sat on the wall by the kitchen door.

I watched in silence as he began to cradle the handset, indecision clear on his face. I decided to help him make his decision. "Go on, call the police, and let them see the photos of the kid that you hide in your bedside cabinet. Does it make you feel like a man to look at them?" I smiled sweetly at him, though the coldness in my voice let him know I wasn't messing about.

"I don't know what you're talking about." His grip on the phone tightened, the whites of his eyes glistening with surprise. He was wondering if he could lie his way out of this.

I rolled my eyes. "Yes, you do, now sit." He spent another sixty seconds cradling the handset before replacing it.

Slowly he walked into the room. I pointed to the sofa. "Sit, we need to talk."

"I don't want to talk."

"I'm not bothered about what you want. Now sit before I make you."

Uncle Kevin sat, he looked nervous, and kept eying the bottle of vodka with some longing. Silently I watched the mixture of emotions crawl along his face. I was so superior to the person that sat on the sofa. I could feel my superiority like a tangible thing, and wondered if Uncle Kevin could feel it too. Did he know he'd soon be dead?

He swung his muddy brown eyes at me. "Do I know you?"

"Nope, and let's face it, I'm not really your type. Too old for you, aren't I?"

I watched the look of desperation that swept across his face, beads of sweat were starting to pop up on his forehead and his hands shook.

"Take a swig, it might help." I offered from where I sat, pointing at the bottle of vodka.

Uncle Kevin didn't hesitate; he took the bottle between his hands, and twisted off the lid. His lips smacked to together as he brought the neck of the bottle to his lips. "What do you want?" He wiped his arm across his lips.

"I want you dead." He coughed up some of the vodka, and then started to laugh.

"I'm glad your pending death amuses you."

He looked me up and down taking in my slender form. "You going to do it?" His chest rumbled as he laughed to himself.

The vodka was giving him confidence. "Nope, you are." That stopped him. He put the vodka on the table.

"Now why would I do that?"

I felt empowered and totally in control as I sat in the chair. I liked this feeling. There was a calmness that came to me before a kill. "Because if you don't, I'm going to make sure that your life becomes a living hell. What do think would happen if these lovely people that you call your neighbours knew what you were? Knew about the photos you keep hidden away. What about work? I bet there'd be more than one person you work with, that would love to beat you to a pulp, just because of what you are. You're scum, your life is worthless, you don't deserve to live. I can't think of one person that wouldn't agree with me. In fact, I can think of a lot of people that would love to see you six feet under. I bet even the earth would shrink upon itself, to cover up such a worthless piece of rotten flesh like you."

Uncle Kevin didn't look so cocky anymore, his hands were beginning to shake, badly, and beads of sweat had started to trickle down the sides of his face. "You wouldn't."

I laughed at him. "Yes, I would, and believe me it wouldn't be the worst thing that I've done."

"I'll move. You won't be able to find me."

I raised my eyebrows at him. "I found you this time, didn't I? You can't hide, not from me."

"Who do you think you are?"

I smiled and my eyes lit up. "I'm death."

He lost all colour. I'd give him his due though, he squared his shoulders and started to rise from the sofa. "Sit!"

He looked across at me. "Get lost. You vigilantes make me sick!" I'd never thought of myself as a vigilante, for one you had to care, and the only thing I cared about was me and what I wanted. And right now, I wanted Uncle Kevin to shut up, take the pills, die and get this over with.

I was on him before he saw me move off the chair. I pushed him back on the sofa, my left hand firmly on his chest, my right arm pressing down on his windpipe, the pressure not enough to mark him, but it had the effect I wanted. "Now let's get this right. You're going to take those pills on the coffee table, use the vodka, they'll go down better. Because if you don't, you won't like what I'll do to you, and believe me when I say, I'm showing a lot of restraint right now." I moved away from him a little.

I gave him a considered look. "Ever heard of 'The Yorkshire Slasher'?"

Uncle Kevin stayed sitting down. "Yeah. So what?" I smiled at him. "Well you're looking at her."

"You're a girl." Uncle Kevin's grey matter couldn't get much use.

"And your point is?"

"The police report says that the killer is a man."

I shook my head. "Really, you make it sound like the police never get anything wrong."

"You're just trying to scare me." Had I wanted to scare him, I would have used a knife. The thought of running a knife down his body, and cutting off some important male anatomy pleased me.

"Believe what you want." I knelt down on him the pressure of my knee went straight into his groin. He choked letting out a small cry. "Do you know why I use a knife? I like to see them bleed. I like to see the blood as drips from their body. I can have this baby out." I dug my knee in a little more. His face turned red at the pressure but he didn't cry out or move. "Cut off, and on the table, quicker than it would take your brain to process what was happening. And right now, that's exactly what I want to do."

I released the pressure. Uncle Kevin took a breath and covered himself with a protective hand. I raised my brows at him, letting him know that it wouldn't stop me. I'd push a knife straight through his hand and into the male anatomy he was so desperate to protect. My need to cut this man up into very tiny pieces, to sever that which he held so important to him, from his body, was so strong. I was fighting my need with every bit of willpower I had. I was beginning to think that subtle was a total waste of time.

Some of my struggle must have shown on my face because Uncle Kevin started to cry, his body shaking. "Why are you doing this?"

I moved away from him back to the chair. "I want you dead."
"Why? What have I ever done to you?"

I sat down and looked at him. "Is that what the little girl asked you when you took her and raped her?" He paled. "You broke her into tiny pieces. At least when I kill, its clean, they aren't left suffering." I paused. "Don't get me wrong, I have little thought or feelings for them, or those that are left behind. I kill because I like it, because it makes me happy." I didn't mention Tracy by name. Making Tracy suffer was only a small part of why I killed, and I'd kill even if Tracy wasn't around. In fact, I was planning on continuing long after Tracy was no more. I really did like it too much to ever consider stopping.

I leant forward. "Take the pills, or I'm going to start carving you up."

The vodka bottle hovered near his lips. He'd drunk a quarter of the bottle. "I'm twice your size, what makes you think you can take me."

I laughed, this chap was slower than I had thought possible. "You might be bigger than me, but trust me, you don't have my training or skill. Think about it; your only escape is to try and get out the front door before I catch you. Think you can move that quick. Run and I'll cut you up." I pointed to where his left hand lay protectively on his crotch. "And feed that to you, while I watch you bleed out." I took the knife from beneath the cushion that I had taken from the kitchen earlier, and showed it to him. "Did you know that the heart creates enough pressure to project the blood thirty feet?" Fear shone in Uncle Kevin's eyes, he watched the knife that sat in my hand, with unbound intensity. I balanced the knife on the edges of my fingers, before wrapping them loosely around the handle. Some people held a knife like they were going to stab someone, Norman Bates style, all knuckles and rigid wrists. I balanced it perfectly in my hand, allowing my wrist to move swiftly, my grip light, yet firm enough that when the blade touched flesh, it wouldn't fall out of my hand. "I took the time to sharpen it when I took your keys. It's not the nicest knife, but then I'm really not that picky, it'll still gut you."

I ran a gloved finger along the body of the knife. I looked at him, my eyes cold. "Take the pills, they really are your best option right now."

His hand shook as he reached for the pills. His eyes never left the knife. "That's a-boy. You know you're getting off real easy taking the pills, a chap like you, doesn't deserve to get off so easy. See you really are a lucky chap."

I watched him as he brought a handful of pills to his mouth. Still he hesitated. I moved my legs as though to move out the chair, the blade of the knife slashing through the air. He emptied the contents of his hand into his mouth and took a swig of the vodka. "And the rest," I nodded my head to the sleeping pills.

In a daze, Uncle Kevin reached for the sleeping pills and put them all into his mouth. He finished off the vodka. Tears ran down his face, his hands shaking. "Don't look so down beaten; I'm going to stay around until you stop breathing. Don't want you coughing them back up once I leave." I didn't want him to think that he could cheat me, cheat death.

Remember Brian Thompson; well I wasn't going to let Uncle Kevin cheat me out of his death. No, I was going to stay to the end.

I watched as he cried, I stopped listening to his slurred voice, his words really weren't that important to me. The temperature in the room began to drop. The heating had clicked off. Outside darkness was falling. People were returning to their homes. I stayed where I was. Uncle Kevin was slumped on the sofa. His body had given out sometime ago.

There was no gratification to be found in today's kill. I felt deprived. There was no high. Euphoria wasn't licking its way along my body. Today had been a waste, and Uncle Kevin's death meaningless. Just like the man himself. I hated people like him, people that allowed themselves to live their lives with the impossible. Uncle Kevin could have accomplished so much more. Instead he hid himself away from public view, while stashing the impossible dream away in his bedside draw. To me the impossible was a puzzle to be solved. I was working at solving my own impossible. I was going to see to it that Tracy Bennett was no more.

I pushed myself out of the chair and plumped up the cushions. Walking back to the kitchen I placed the knife back in the drawer. The fridge light shone, the door propped open by the contents of the fridge that Uncle Kevin had emptied, while looking for his fix of alcohol. I put everything back in the fridge, and closed the door.

The temperature outside was dropping fast, and frost was turning the pavement white. I walked back to my car. I dropped the key I'd had cut to Uncle Kevin's in a grate. I shrugged; no one would come looking for it. Uncle Kevin had quite literally killed himself. Not that technically you could call it suicide. Suicide made it sound like he'd had a choice.

I got in my car and started the engine. I needed to kill, to cut, to watch the blood flow from the body. To watch as life left, as their blood drip, drip, dripped out of their open veins, taking with it the very essence of that which gave us life. Without blood, there was no life. It was such a rich and beautiful thing.

I thought about Karen, Tracy still hadn't been able to pacify her. Maybe it was time to show Karen that she could be made into a very beautiful person.

I smiled.

I liked the thought of that.

Tracy would be distraught; she wouldn't like the fact that she would never have the opportunity to make things up to Karen. Served them both right.

The more I thought about Tracy, and the effect Karen's death would have on her, the more I liked the idea.

I sang along to the radio, leaving behind my discontentment over Uncle Kevin's death.

I would have my blood – soon.

Chapter Eight

Richard was sprawled out on the sofa, feet resting on the coffee table, a lazy arm slung around Tracy's shoulders. His red t-shirt had ridden up slightly, showing off an expanse of pale flesh. The blue jeans he wore were relaxed and misshapen, his feet bare, toes wiggling to the beat of the music. I didn't see what Tracy saw in him.

If I was to compare Richard to Patrick Barnes' perfect body, it would lose. Despite Richard's muscular form, I don't think that Richard had ever seen the inside of a gym. The muscle definition was due to his love of running, and the few weights that he pumped during his strength training. Running seemed to be the main thing that they had in common, that and their music tastes. He did make Tracy laugh, which she seemed to do a lot lately. It grated on my nerves.

I couldn't see this relationship lasting.

I smiled at the thought, he'd be dead soon. Ha, ha, ha.

As far as my plan for Tracy was going, I was starting to move things up a little. I was bored with the waiting, and after the un-fulfilment of Uncle Kevin's death, I had used up what little patience I had had for Tracy Bennett.

I now wanted to be free of Tracy, and I had just the plan to ensure that it happened.

Richard had been an added element that I had not foreseen, however it was working in a good way. The closer they got, the happier she became, the more significant his death would be to her, and the more pleasure I would take from killing him.

The heat from the fire warmed the room and it felt like one of those Sunday mornings when life just was, and you just enjoyed doing nothing. Unlike Tracy and Richard, I had a killing to organise.

Killing Karen would bring the police's attention back to Hopscotch's, with some ferocity. They couldn't afford to miss the connection between Mrs H's death, and the soon to be death of Karen Stillman. They had to be desperate to catch me by now. I was a high-profile case. They needed this win. It could be the break that they thought they needed. Had a pattern developed? They'd be praying that it had. Mrs H's death hadn't fitted in the profile that they were bound to have on me. No, Mrs H's death had taken them onto a different path. It had raised more questions. By killing Karen, they would need to re-hash their profile.

John Douglas, a former FBI agent, had been the inventor of criminal profiling. Profiling was a way to get into the killer's mind, a way to understand them. There was even a list of the ten most common traits of potential serial killers. I didn't see myself fitting into any of the ten. I wasn't into alcohol or substance abuse; neither had I suffered any psychological abuse during my childhood. Nor, were there any sexually stressful events in my childhood, and I didn't feel that I had grown up isolated or lonely. I had chosen not to forge any real friendships. Friends were for needy people. I didn't need anyone to talk to, to support me through bad times. The only person I needed was me. I could rely on me. If I made a promise to myself, I would keep the promise I never disappointed or let myself down.

They had even added bed wetting into the top ten traits, I ask you; can't a kid have a nightmare and wet the bed without becoming a serial killer? To me profiling spelt desperate. Let them try and profile me, and think that they'd made a connection between my other killings, Mrs H's death and the fated death of Karen Stillman.

The more I had learnt about Karen, the more intrigued I had become with her. She was like the mad dog lady. Four dogs in a poky flat, *really!* They were the yappy kind too, which wasn't helpful when you wanted to knock off their owner.

I hadn't identified their breed. Suffice to say, that they were small and fluffy, with white, brown, grey and black coats. Karen was more obsessed about the dog's appearance than her own. Each one wore a different coloured ribbon, and spent more time getting pampered at the groomers than their owner did at a hair salon. I'd go so far as to say that Karen didn't even know what a hairdresser was. She should take a look in the mirror. When your dog's look better than you, you've got a problem.

The dogs I could see to, drop them some meat, with a bit of something to make them sleep. Animals weren't really my thing, and killing them was a total waste of effort. According to the trait list, 99% of serial killers admitted to practising on animals first. I couldn't see the point. Brian Thompson had been my starting point. Animals didn't bleed the same way that a naked human being did. And I wasn't about to start shaving them so that I could see the beauty of my knife work. I'd end up covered in dog hair, and probably an allergy to go with it. Just thinking about the amount of evidence I would be taking with me was enough to put me off that idea. I'd be like Hansel and Gretel, instead of following the breadcrumbs, you'd be able to find me by following the dog hair. Nope, I wasn't that desperate. Anyway, to perfect an art, isn't it better to start with your chosen subject matter. My subject matter was people.

The dogs had a job to do. Once the little pooches came around from their sleep, they would be all over Karen and just think of all the evidence that would get destroyed, as they nudged, licked and pawed at their owner's dead body. Yep, they definitely had a job to do.

"Fancy a refill?" Richard asked as he leant forward to pick up his mug.

"That would be nice." Tracy smiled at him, her long chocolate hair fanned out around them. She wore a lightweight pink sweat top, teamed with a pair of black yoga pants. She looked relaxed...happy, content. The late morning sky had yet to lighten up. Snow had piled up outside overnight and the wind blew and howled down the street. Looking at Tracy, I felt the weather's icy rage. It was as if we were one.

A knock sounded at the front door. "I'll get it, you stay there." Since when did Richard feel comfortable enough to answer Tracy's door? I had obviously been spending too much time watching Karen.

"Bloody hell its cold out there," Susie shuffled her way through the door. A pair of thigh high black boots covered her legs, her short mustard yellow skirt skimmed the tops. A thick woollen cardigan was wrapped around her body, as she tried to fight off the cold. Of course, she could have put on more clothes, tried to cover herself up a little more, but then we are talking about *'show-everything-off'* Susie here.

"Don't close the door, Abs is somewhere." With that the Abominable Snowman came scurrying through the door. Abigail was dressed from head to toe in white. A white down coat fell past her knees, meeting white fur padded boots.

Abigail shook out of her coat sending snow over the floor. Handing the coat over to Richard's outstretched hand she took off her boots and made her way into the living room.

Susie, with no concern over snow fall and puddles, walked straight into the living room, her heels hitting the floor with a tap, tap sound. I had to be impressed with how she had remained upright in the six-inch spiked heeled boots, as she had waded through the snow from the car to Tracy's front door. Lowering herself onto the opposite sofa to Tracy, she shrugged out of her cardigan to reveal a short sleeved, low cut, cross over cream fitted top.

Tracy raised her eyebrows. "There's no wonder you're cold."

Susie arched a brow at her. "I have boots on."

"It's not the boots, Tracy was referring to." Abigail plonked herself on the sofa next to Susie. Now that she had lost her coat and boots, she was very colourful, from one extreme to the other that was Abigail. Her red stretch jeans and bright green jumper made her resemble a Christmas tree. It didn't help that she was sporting a pair of chandeliers for earrings.

Susie ignored them both and looked across at Richard. "I'll have a tea if you're brewing up." She smiled sweetly and tapped her leather clad toes on the floor, bringing attention to the long expanse of leather clad leg on display.

Richard nodded his head and looked at Tracy. Their eyes met in a way that said there's a shared joke going on, and you're either a part of it or not. Their shared joke was all for Susie, and the unconscious and automatic way she used her body to get what she wanted. It never entered Susie's head that not every male on the planet thought she was irresistible.

"I'll have one too, and do you have anything sweet to help the tea go down?"

"I thought you were supposed to be losing weight." Susie asked.

Abigail wrinkled up her nose. "I've decided that this is my shape, why torture myself over it. I'm an apple, and should just enjoy it. Besides, I haven't eaten properly in days."

"You were chewing down a Big Mac when I saw you on Friday," Tracy pointed out.

"Yeah, but I didn't have a pudding or fries or anything."

"Oh, you poor thing, you must be starved," Susie echoed with false sympathy.

"I won't be if there are biscuits or cakes on offer with the tea."

Richard laughed at Abigail. "I'll see what I can do."

"Things look to be going well between the two of you." Susie observed as she watched Richard walk into the kitchen.

Tracy smiled a lazy contented smile. "They are."

"Who would have thought that a trip to the supermarket could turn out to be the best thing you could have done under the circumstances," Abigail said, as she snuggled further into the sofa. "You know maybe Uncle Kevin did you a favour this time round. If they hadn't released him, your mum and dad wouldn't have come over and eaten all the cakes, *without sharing*, and you wouldn't have gone to the supermarket. And if you hadn't, *no* Richard." Tracy and Susie looked at Abigail as though she had suddenly broken out in warts.

"You really do have a strange way at looking at things Abs," Susie said as she looked at her friend. I couldn't help agreeing with her. Uncle Kevin hadn't been on vacation and suddenly decided to move to Leeds. No, he'd been in prison, which meant that by the grace of the jurisdictional system, he had been released after serving his time.

"You know what I meant." Actually, if Abigail wanted to place Tracy's happiness on anyone, it was me. After all it had been my biscuits and cakes that everyone had been tucking into. I include Abigail in this, as I recall she ate her way through more than her share of my biscuits.

Susie turned her attention from Abigail to Tracy. "Speaking of Uncle Kevin, have you heard the news?"

Tracy looked at Susie eyebrows raised in question. "No, we haven't been up that long."

Abigail gave a snort. "I bet you haven't."

"Keep it clean Abs." Susie gave Abigail a long look. "I'm trying to deliver some serious news here."

"I was just trying to lighten things up."

Tracy drew her feet under her body, a look of agitation falling across her face. Richard walked in with a tray stacked full of tea and coffee, and a plate piled high with my biscuits and cakes. I couldn't wait to show this guy what happened when people touched my stuff. The lesson would be permanent, but you wouldn't expect anything less from a person like me.

"What's wrong?" Richard was staring at Tracy. "They're Lauren's." Tracy pointed to the plate containing the biscuits and cakes.

"I bought some the other day and put them in your cupboard. I thought it was time that we started to cater towards Abigail's sweet tooth without risking the 'wrath of Lauren'." Richard cocked his head to one side. "I wouldn't mind meeting this Lauren." No, you would, trust me on that. Because when we do meet, you're going to be dead.

"We all would," Abigail interjected. "Are you going to put that tray down, my tea's getting cold, and my stomach thinks you're torturing it."

"Sorry." Richard placed the tray down on the coffee table. Abigail wasted no time in snagging a biscuit.

Susie picked up her tea. They all spent far too much time together. I found it irritating that Richard knew how Susie and Abigail liked their tea and was now stocking the cupboards for them. "I was just asking Tracy if you guys had listened to the news this morning." Susie asked.

A lazy smile tugged at the corners of Richard's mouth. "No, we were busy."

"I bet." Abigail sent a splattering of biscuit crumbs across the carpet as she spoke.

"Be good." Susie jabbed her in the ribs lightly. Abigail choked on biscuit crumbs. "Serves you right," Susie huffed.

Richard placed a soothing hand on Tracy's legs, patting them in that way that people did, to their loved ones.

"Uncle Kevin was found dead last night. They say that he committed suicide." Tracy paled at Susie's words.

"I thought you'd be pleased. At least you'll never run the risk of bumping into him," Abigail said as she reached across for another biscuit. If they weren't careful, the biscuits and cakes would be gone before anyone else got a look in.

Tracy looked at her friends. "I don't really know how I feel. It just strikes me as odd, that he would kill himself. His wife committed suicide when he used to live next door to us and well, it had quite an impact on him. I remember him saying that only cowards committed suicide."

Abigail shook her head. "Cowardly, really? I don't think I could do it. I'm not so sure that Uncle Kevin was looking at it from an impartial perspective when his wife died. I mean, how does someone get the strength required to kill themselves? I know

I couldn't." Abigail surprised me with this comment. She always came across as shallow. This was very deep for her.

"Well it doesn't matter. The police seem content that it was suicide." Susie sent Tracy a knowing look, as though she had first-hand information on this. "They said that he overdosed on sleeping pills and anti- depressants. And they'd know, wouldn't they. They do all that forensic science stuff, don't they? If it wasn't suicide, they wouldn't be reporting it as one. You need to relax Tracy." I laughed to myself at this comment; the absurdity of her words was just too much. The police hadn't got a clue. There were only two of us that knew the truth, and one of us was dead. See, if you plan things right, you can get away with murder. Ha, ha, ha.

Tracy looked doubtful, and with good reason. "Come on."

Richard tugged her to him, and I saw the comfort she took from his embrace. Yep, killing him was going to send her over the edge and I would be rid of her for good.

"The main thing is that he's dead and as Abigail not so tactfully said, at least there's no risk of you bumping into him," Susie said as she sipped on her tea.

"Do you know where they're going to bury him?" Everyone looked at Tracy, shock mirrored on their faces.

Tracy waved her right hand, as she snuggled deeper into Richards's arms. "I think I'd like to be there when they bury him. It might help to give me some closure." I didn't like the sound of that.

"Well, in that case, if you're going then we will too. Did he have any relatives? I'll make some enquiries for you, if you like." Susie was always the practical one.

Tracy smiled at her. "I don't think any of his relatives would care. But ask mum, she would probably be able to tell you. Thanks, I really appreciate it."

"If we're going to go to this guy's funeral, we should go dressed in bright colours. I've seen this really nice red woollen dress that would be perfect. And there's a coat I've been meaning to get that would look good with it. It not only looks stylish, but it'll also keep me warm." You see what I mean about Abigail being shallow.

"It's not a fashion parade Abs, it's a funeral," Susie reminded her.

"Yeah, I get that, but it's not like the chap's going to be missed, and I can't see anyone stood there crying at his graveside, so why don't we make this a celebration. Like Tracy says, it could give her some closure and well, isn't that worth celebrating."

Richard gave Tracy's shoulders a squeeze. "You know, I think on this occasion, Abigail has got a point. We'll all go out afterwards, somewhere posh. Let's celebrate the fact that he'll never hurt you, or anyone else, ever again."

Susie gave Richard an appreciative glance. "You know Tracy, if you ever want to get rid of him, I'll take him. I never seem to hook a good one."

"It might have something to do with how you dress. The guys you meet aren't getting past what's on display." Tracy laughed as Abigail pointed at Susie's chest.

Susie sent Abigail a sour look and stuck out her chest. "You're just jealous."

"If I were jealous, you'd know about it. At least men like me for my brains and not just my boobs. I can't help being an interesting person, with heaps of good looks. I'm the total package."

"And that's why your single is it?" Susie shook her head.

"Abigail, I think your brains would be the last thing a man would be interested in."

"Yeah, well, let's ask Richard, he's a guy." Abigail nicely turned the attention from her to Richard.

Richard paled under their scrutiny. "Richard's with me, and I'm sure that you wouldn't like to put him in this sort of position, especially with his current girlfriend *and* your best friend present." Tracy smiled at the pair, and I saw Richard relax.

"What a get out." Abigail rolled her eyes, and took a cake.

Chapter Nine

I had asked myself at least twenty times now, whose bright idea it was to attend Uncle Kevin's funeral. Right now, I really wanted to stick a knife into their stupid heart and watch it bleed out. I wasn't even fussed about them being dressed. That's how bad things were.

The icy fog had yet to lift and the temperature was still dropping, despite the fact that it was after one in the afternoon. The wind was building up, throwing leaves, and bits of rubbish around. The cold bit into my face, which was the only part of my flesh on display. The freezing atmosphere sank deeper beneath my flesh. My nose was probably red and my cheeks stung. There would be no let up from the weather today.

Though I had boots on and thick thermal socks, I could still feel the cold and dampness settling in, nibbling at my toes. I'd lost feeling in my fingers some time ago. You'd be wrong in thinking me incapable of wielding a knife in my present condition. I prided myself on being able to wield a knife, no matter what. And I wasn't going to allow my body to let me down.

I had even gone to the extreme of testing out my theory when I'd killed Billy Harper. With a name like that, he deserved to die. He was the ugliest kid I'd ever seen. His eyes weren't level and his nose was too big. Other than that, he was average, for an ugly kid. Billy's dad owned a butcher's shop which had one of those big walk in freezers. I'd dared Billy to go into the freezer with me. Billy hadn't been able to turn down this opportunity. I may have hinted that he'd be getting rewarded if he did as I asked. By the decidedly wicked leer Billy had given me, I had concluded that we were talking at cross purposes; there was no way I was putting out for ugly Billy Harper. When I'd suggested that he strip out of his clothes so that I could admire his body, I may even have suggested that I would warm him up. Billy hadn't needed to be asked twice. When I'd made the suggestion of using one of the hooks to lift himself up so he could get a better position, Billy hadn't needed any further persuasion.

It wasn't until I'd whipped out my knife that Billy had become alerted to the fact that he was going to die. Legs dangling, arms flayed, he wasn't able to stop me. I had been in the freezer for five minutes before I'd started stabbing Billy. Enough time for my hands to feel the effect from the cold. I am happy to say that my experiment with Billy concluded how I had thought it would; Billy dead. The cold had had little effect on my hands. OK, maybe I hadn't been in the freezer long enough for there to be any real effect on my knife wielding skills. Still a girl has to practice, and there was no point in both of us ending up dead. It had taken ages to clean things up and get rid of Billy's body where no one would find him – soon. But it had been worth it. Billy had been my second kill. I'd found out that my need to kill was very strong. A little like needing to breathe.

So, why was I here, freezing to death, in a stupid cemetery. Tracy *Bloody* Bennett, that's why. Tracy was here and I didn't have a choice. My hate for her was flooding my whole essence. I had wanted to kill Karen tonight but the possibility was becoming less likely by the second. The thought made my teeth grind together.

Bloody Tracy, it was always about Tracy. Well soon, there would be no Tracy.

Tracy was all loved up in the arms of Richard, with Abigail and Susie flanking her right. Tracy wore a cream coat that she had bought six years ago and never worn. A bright multi-coloured scarf was wrapped around her neck and lower part of her face, a matching hat sat on the top of her head. This touch of colour was given to Tracy by Richard, who said that Abigail's rule was that colour had to be worn. Tracy had loved it. Of course, she had yet to see any of Richard's faults, like the way he arched his eyebrow in question about fifty times an hour, or the way he left his shoes lying round the house for someone to trip over. And why was it that Richard seemed incapable of picking up his used socks and undies off the bedroom floor? The chap deserved to die just for being untidy, in my opinion. As I was the one that was going to kill him, it was my opinion that counted.

The wind caught Tracy's chocolate hair, sending it into her eyes. Richard moved it away with the softest of touches, his fingers coming to rest under her chin. He looked into the depth of her stormy blue eyes. "You OK?" His words were all but a whisper. They sent more of a chill down my spine than the drop in temperature.

Tracy looked up at him nodding her head, a watery smile on her lips. Richard bent down and kissed her lips, soft and reassuring. She looked at him, the look full of vulnerability and trust. Richard smiled down at her, a look of tenderness falling across his face. The emotions that swept through Tracy's body sent me into the worst mood ever. I wanted to lash out at Richard, to push him away from her, to bury him with Uncle Kevin.

In a fit of rage, I envisioned myself grabbing hold of the lapels of Richard's black coat, hooking a finger through the red woollen scarf and twisting the fabric, drawing it tighter and tighter about his neck, his fingers clawing at the fabric to no avail. I took out my knife and drew it back, plunging it deep within his flesh. I could almost hear his cry as the knife sank into his flesh piercing his stomach. I took out the knife and drew it back into his flesh, this time hitting his heart. I almost heard the interruption in its beat, as the knife sunk further in. I withdrew the knife again and slid it between his ribs. The knife hit his left lung. He gasped. Blood trickled from between his lips. I let go of him and kicked him into the waiting grave like the garbage that he was.

I heard Tracy scream, felt her evaporate into nothing as the walls that kept her sane fell away. Richard's blood stained her white coat. Abigail and Susie were looking at her strangely, their mouths open in disbelief.

Tracy whispered something to Richard, the noise bringing me back to the present with an angry snap. Richard stood there fit and healthy, the wind making his cheeks rosy. Tracy was smiling and happy. I had been so lost in my thought that it had felt very real.

I wanted to scream.

My disappointment clung to the inside of my mouth, sharp and bitter.

I switched my attention to Susie, better to try and ignore the loved-up couple.

For the first time ever, Susie wore trousers. Her red leather clad legs were encased tightly in the fabric. Given that leather had a natural habit of stretching and becoming saggy, which Susie's weren't, I was betting that she had bought a size or two too small for her. There was no give in the tightness of the leather as it gripped at her legs. The pants moulded to her legs like spray paint. The length of her legs offered the observer a taste of what lay beneath. Of course, it would have been too much for Susie not to have a least one, or should that be two, of her assets on display. Despite the cold, Susie didn't wear a coat. The thickness of her grey jumper did little to keep out the cold and the low, low cut of the neckline showed more boob than it covered. Right now, her boobs were lined with Goosebumps, her nipples threatened to poke through her flimsy bra and woollen jumper, like deadly spikes. I didn't think that Susie had considered the fact that processed wool was different to that found on a sheep. Processed wool did not offer the same insulation properties.

The scarf wound round her neck wasn't offering anything in the way of warmth either. Nor did the matching red leather gloves stop the freezing temperature from nibbling at her fingers. Susie hopped from one six inch heeled black boot to the other, the ground beneath did not give and the heels despite their deadly spikes, sat on the top of the frozen soil.

"How much longer?" Susie whispered to Abigail. "They lowered the coffin in ages ago."

Abigail snorted, warm within the confines of her black and red flecked coat. The coat fitted Abigail beautifully, adding height to her short frame. The dress beneath slimmed down her waist and fell to just above the knee. For once I had to admit Abigail looked very classy. The black calf length boots gave her an extra three inches, their block heels looking sensible yet stylish. A black bucket hat with a crochet red poppy flower sat to the right of the hats' trunk, which was placed at a slight angle on top of Abigail's head, keeping in the heat. Her black leather cashmere lined leather gloves helped to prevent the frost from biting at her fingertips. Toasty, was how I would have described her.

"You should have put a coat on."

Susie gave a snort of her own. "I didn't think it would take this long. What do you think she's looking at, surely once you've seen one brown shiny box, you've seen them all?"

"I don't think it's the coffin that's got her attention somehow." Abigail sighed. "I'm getting hungry."

"Yeah, that sounds about right. What did you have for breakfast?" Susie rubbed at her arms. "I'm going to have to go soon, I'm losing feeling in my legs."

"Four Weetabix. I'm beginning to wish that I'd gone for six."
Abigail glanced at Susie as she danced on the spot. "Look if
you're that cold, why don't you go back to the car and get my
down coat out of the boot."

Susie looked horrified at the thought. "What, and appear as
frumpy as you do when you're wearing it. No, I'd rather freeze."

"You're all heart sometimes Susie. I don't look frumpy by
the way, I look warm. Besides I don't think that anyone here
gives a toss about you, or how much is or isn't on display. You're
in a cemetery, not a nightclub."

"Well, if that's how you look when you're warm, I'd rather
be cold and retain my gorgeousness, cemetery or not."

Abigail looked Susie up and down. "If that's what you're
calling it. But right now, your gorgeousness is covered in
Goosebumps, and you look like you're suffering from the Plague
or something equally as revolting. You fit in well with your
surroundings. Plus you look like you need to pee, hopping from
foot to foot like that."

Susie sent her a long meaningful look, but refrained from
saying anything. Instead she moved over to Richard, touching his
left arm to get his attention. "I'm thinking that it might be best if
Abigail and I went back to the car." She nodded her head towards
Tracy who was staring down at the coffin. "It might do her good
to have a few moments on her own."

Richard looked at Tracy and then at Susie's shivering form.
"OK, we'll meet you back at the car in a bit."

The smile Susie sent Richard burned away some of the frost.
"Thanks."

I watched Susie with a stab of envy as she shimmied over to
Abigail. "Come on let's go."

I noticed that Abigail didn't object, but walked with a quick pace back to the car. That left the three of us standing at the graveside.

To occupy myself, I began to wonder what Richard saw when he looked at Tracy. Did he ever see me lurking in the background or was he so wrapped up with loving Tracy that he never noticed the darkness that hovered so close to him?

I thought back to this morning, as Richard had lain naked next to Tracy sleeping, his breathing even and soft. I had run a long painted fingernail down his back, wishing that it was a knife. His skin had tightened under my touch as he'd slumbered gently.

The thought gave me an idea. I smiled as I drew on that thought. Richard naked and all cut up, blood spilling over the bed sheets and carpeted floor. His dead body growing cold and stiff, Tracy waking, to find Richard's lifeless body, blood covering her skin, Tracy screaming, Tracy losing control and fading away into nothing. I had closed my eyes as excitement increased my heartbeat, and blood flowed through my veins, like a happy song.

I had shown a lot of restraint this morning and left Richard to sleep and Tracy to wake up happy and comforted in Richard's arms.

Karen was first.

I had spent too long planning to suddenly let her live. I couldn't control my need to kill, it was as necessary as breathing to me. Besides, I wasn't so sure that killing Richard now would benefit me too much. A month, two tops, and I'd kill Richard. That would be the right time.

Tracy shifted, Richard looked down at her. "You ready to go?" She nodded her head and together they walked away, arms around each other's waists. Tracy's black heeled boots left a small pin mark in the frost next to Richard's sturdy flats. I looked down at the footprints, their stride was a perfect match. I'll admit it scared me to see them. I didn't like Tracy happy, didn't like to think that quite possibly Richard could be her salvation.

No, I wouldn't let it happen. I had worked too hard to be free, to lose it all to Richard. His killing would be personal and I would let the police know just how personal it was. It could possibly be my last kill for a while so I needed to make sure that it counted, that I could feed off the memory of it for some time.

"I thought you had frozen to the spot out there," Susie said as Richard opened the back door to the cherry red Vauxhall Mokka. The heat in the car dropped as the cold wind rushed in. Susie gave a shiver as the car door slammed shut. The car was two years old and had been a birthday gift from Abigail's parents who were loaded. It was alright for some.

Abigail slipped the car into gear. "Don't mind her, she's just grumpy." Abigail cocked her head to one side in thought. "Come to think of it, she's always grumpy lately. You missing out on a little action?"

Susie pushed at Abigail's arm. "I don't want to talk about it."

Abigail laughed. "You going through a dry spell?"

"I don't want to talk about it."

Tracy sat forward. "I think it's a little late for that, you know what Abigail's like. She won't give up until you tell her."

Abigail nodded her head in agreement. "Sherlock Holmes has nothing on me. I'm like a bloodhound."

Susie looked at Abigail. "Now you mention it, I always wondered where that snout of yours came from. Well, now I know."

Abigail patted Susie's knee, a smile on her lips. "I'm not biting, so don't try and change the subject."

Richard chuckled. "I don't think you've got a choice Susie, and if we're going to make it to the restaurant in time, you'd better tell Abigail everything she needs to know." Susie shot Richard a dirty look.

Abigail's stomach gave a groan, she looked pointedly at Susie. "OK playtimes over, spill before my throat feels like it's been cut." Oh, don't give me any ideas.

"OK, OK, just start driving." Abigail put her foot on the accelerator a little too hard, and the car lurched forward, skidding on ice. They came to a slippery stop, four inches from one of the oak trees that lined the drive at the cemetery.

"I said I'd tell you, no need to try and kill us all."

"Sorry." Gently Abigail set off again, at a slower pace.

Susie sighed. "I'm trying to attract a different kind of male attention."
"Not dressed like that you're not," Abigail interjected.

"Do you want to know, or are you just going to sit there and be derogative?"

"Oooooo, look at you and your BBC 2 word, you been eating a dictionary?" Susie slapped Abigail on the arm. "OK, OK, I won't say anything else."

"I've decided that I want a more long-lasting relationship. Fun is nice but at twenty-six, I'm starting to think that there's more to this relationship lark than a quick fling."
Abigail looked at Tracy in the rear-view mirror she was snuggled up to Richard, their hands entwined. "I wonder what brought that on."
Susie ignored her. "It's an age thing."

"Yeah, right," Abigail snorted. "So, the real reason for your grumpiness and making us suffer, is because you've put yourself on a sex free diet. We'll let me tell you, you weren't meant to eat lettuce, you're not a rabbit Susie, you're a carnivore, face up to it and start sampling the beef again."

"We're talking about relationships not food."

"It's the same thing. You're starving, and taking it out on your nearest and dearest."

Susie shook her head. "I never had you pinned as the romantic type, just as well really."

"I can be romantic. If you want wining and dining, let me know, though you're not really my type, I'm willing to be adventurous."

"I think what Abigail is trying to say, is that it might not be good to take away all the fun." Tracy lent forward and patted Susie on her arm. "Twenty-six is still really young."

"You're right but still, I have to grow up at some point, and I think I'm getting tired of the same old, same old."

Abigail put the car into neutral and pulled on the handbrake, as they sat in traffic, crawling into York city centre. "You, know, if you want to attract a different kind of male attention, then you're going to have to change the way you dress. We could go shopping on Wednesday."

Susie looked down at her leather clad legs. "I like the way I dress. Besides I've got to work on Wednesday."

Abigail shook her head at her friend. "Just give it some thought. What if we buy just one new outfit, something different, and see what attention you get? If it pays off, then it could be worth it. Besides, I think men like a little mystery, rather than it all being on display for everyone to see."

"I don't put it all on display, if I did that I'd walk around with nothing on."

Tracy laughed. "You do leave little for male imagination."

"I'll think about it." I tried to imagine Susie dressed classy, and gave up.

Abigail parked the car and turned off the engine. "Come on, food awaits."

I watched them as they climbed out of the car, all smiles.

They had no idea how their lives were going to change.

Chapter Ten

Karen had taken a sleeping pill.

In some ways, this was a good thing. My only problem at this moment in time, was getting her over to the kitchen chair. She was as helpful as a sack of potatoes, and about as giving.

I pulled back the duvet to reveal Karen's naked form. I'll admit, it had come as some surprise to find that there was no winceyette nightie covering her sleeping form. Karen always came across as sensible, with her sturdy flat shoes and skirts that fell to her calves. Her shirts or jumpers were loose or misshapen, and most definitely did not reveal any feminine curves.

Not that I was complaining. Naked worked for me, and saved me the trouble of trying to remove clothing from the un-giving form in front of me.

I placed some slippers on her feet. They were the old person's type. We all have a granny or old relative that wears them, so you know the type I'm talking about. I did this to protect her heels. The last thing I wanted was some forensic clever clogs pointing out how 'the victim' had been dragged. I'd make the bed as soon as I got her on the chair, nailed down her feet and zip tied her hands to the wooden frame. I wanted to ensure that I had easy access to the inside of her arms, easy to cut into the radial or ulnar arteries that way. I ran a gloved hand over Karen's skin where the arteries lay hidden. Hmmm, I could almost sense the blood. Hear its eager cry to be free. I knew all about wanting to be free.

The floor in the kitchen was wood. Oh, the joy I'd felt when I saw it, sweet, sweet joy. There is a special type of pleasure to be gained from nailing a person's feet to the floor. The feel of the skin as it breaks, the blood that swells in response, the bone that crunches and scrapes against the nail. Hmmm, beautiful.

I looked at Karen, it wasn't as if she was going to just sit there strapped to the chair and let me work my magic. Not Karen, she'd fight like a tiger caught in a trap. The thought of the fight ahead made me smile. The best bit was when they realised that they were going to die and it didn't matter how hard they fought, they were still going to be dead soon. The emotion that filters across a person's face at that very moment was spellbinding. Magic!

Anticipation is such a lovely feeling.

The thick furry fabric that ran around the slippers had slid along the oak flooring in the bedroom and the hall. In fact, all the floors in the house were wood. Karen was not the artistic type and her lack of vision showed.

From the magnolia walls to the grey unrelenting sofa and flower duvet set, that wouldn't have looked out of place in the Castle Museum near Clifford's Tower in York. If you wanted a look into the past, from furnishings, home electrical items to toys, then this museum was the place for you, that or Karen's flat. However, I got the feeling that Karen wasn't going to be around that much longer, so maybe you'll just have to stick to the Castle Museum.

It had taken quite a bit of effort to finally get her on the wooden chair, but with persistence I'd gotten there. The dogs snored softly in their baskets under the kitchen window. I had

placed the chair near their basket. I wanted to ensure two things:
-

One: that when they came around, their owner was the first thing that they saw.

Two: that the blood spatter reached them, coating their fur.

I could almost picture the joy on their furry faces when they saw her lifeless form. Of course, the dogs wouldn't know she was dead. I cocked my head to the side, contemplating how intelligent dogs were. Would Karen's dead body smell different? Would they realise that something was off? That they would soon be headed for the dog's home? Aw, poor things, ha, ha, ha.

Karen opened her mouth and let out a loud snore; it rolled from the back of her throat and echoed round the small kitchen. I palmed one of the balls of socks I'd taken from her drawer and shoved it into her mouth while I had the chance. Tape in hand I placed it over her mouth as her lips smacked together.

I looked at my watch she'd be starting to stir soon – hopefully. Sleeping pills weren't always the best things in the world when it came to timing. I think it had something to do with how the body processed them, and the dosage. Everyone was different, though I could be wrong. I didn't really care, so long as she didn't keep me waiting too long. I walked over to my large black bag, and took Fred out. A few big puffs, well, OK, a lot of puffing, and Fred was as inflated as he was going to get.

I looked around the kitchen, space was tight. I decided to put him near the door facing Karen. There wouldn't be much blood splatter in that direction but there would be enough to create a void, giving the impression that two people had been here.

I'd selected a knife from Karen's kitchen draw. The thing had been blunt so I'd had to sharpen it over the sink, washing away the tiny shavings once I'd done. I couldn't really see the shavings but I knew a group of people that would wet themselves when they found them. CSI's, they get *sooo* excited over the smallest of things. I always carried a double-sided knife sharpening block with me for such reasons. People never seemed to appreciate the beauty of their knives. I had lost count of how many times I had come across unloved kitchen knives that would be hard-pressed to cut into an overripe tomato cleanly, never mind make a nice clean cut to a person's skin. I had taken the time to sharpen a couple of other knives. My knife wouldn't look out of place that way. Didn't want those pesky CSI's getting ahead of themselves.

I'd just finished setting up when Karen started to stir. Nice timing Karen.

I leant forward bringing my head level with Karen's. I wanted to see the emotions reflected in her eyes when she saw me. My deep purple, sharp cut bobbed wig fell along my jaw line. My tight fitting black jeans and snug long-sleeved top, made me look something of a cat burglar. I particularly liked the way that the outfit made my body look slinky and yet muscular, without the bodybuilder *'I've been pumping weights and eating protein shakes most of my life'* look. Mysterious is how I saw my outfit.

The deep purple wig and violet contacts was the only colour, and they made quite a dramatic impact. I always liked to make an effort in the way I dressed when I went out killing. To me it was as important as the act itself.

Karen opened her eyes. They widened as they looked straight into mine. "What the hell?" I think was what she was trying to say. It came out more like 'mm, mmmm, mmmmmm." That's a sock in your mouth for you and tape to keep your lips together; they create a definite lack of conversation.

"Hello Karen." I whispered the words, my lips almost touching her left ear. She tried to rock back from me. Instinct, an involuntary reaction, caused when the body senses danger. I watched as the initial shock wore off and Karen started to become aware that her feet wouldn't move. I stepped back allowing her to look down. I laughed as she went into spasms of shock at the nails. There were lots of 'mmm, mmmm, mmm, mm's' emitting from her. Her body began shaking. Karen shot a look of horror at me. Bet her feet really hurt now. Funny how cuts and such never hurt until you become aware of them; they're like a bruise that you don't remember how you got, but press it and, *ouch.*

"Oh, Karen, don't be like that," I said ever so sweetly, batting my eyelashes at her.

Karen answered me by trying to move her upper body off the chair. Really what did she expect to happen? "Your neighbours are starting to leave for work. Soon you'll be the only one left. The only one not going anywhere. Not that it would matter, because as we have established." I pointed to the zip strips holding her body to the chair and the nails sticking out of the tops of her feet. "You aren't going anywhere. And conversation for you is very limited. But please feel free to scream as loud as you want." I brought my head back in line with Karen's. "Oh, wait, you can't can you." Ha, ha, ha.

Karen thrashed a bit more, such a waste of energy.

I picked up the knife that I'd sharpened from the work surface by the sink. That seemed to stop her. Her eyes widened, following the knife as I moved it slightly in one direction, and then the other. I liked the way that her eyes travelled along the blades edge. Did she see the beauty in its cold glistening surface? How the fluorescent light in the kitchen caught and glistened along the steel edge? I doubted it.

"You will be pleased to know that I've sharpened it for you." I tilted my head looking at the knife. "You know, you should really have taken better care of it."

Karen started 'mmm, mmm, mmmm-ing' at me. I took that to mean, *'please stab me.'* So, I did. Blood sprouted from the cut in her upper arm. Karen 'mm, mmm, mm-d' again. I sent her a wide smile.

Very lightly I ran the knife down the length of her face, starting in the middle of her forehead and curving it round the

133

right side, following her hairline and coming to a stop at her jaw line. Blood ran down her face, and she paled. Beads of sweat sat on top of her forehead.

I liked it when panic set in. Karen knew that this was it. She was going to die.

Everyone seems to have a different look for death. Some just shut down and stare at you with flat eyes, their brains unable to cope with what was happening to them. Some, like Karen, seemed to come to life. They fought with everything they had, their need to survive, to keep on fighting for life driving them on. Karen's eyes were lit with anger, and fear, and determination. I had to admit to being impressed with Karen.

Not that it was going to change my mind.

I needed this kill.

I moved the knife closer to her face, lowering myself so that I could look into her eyes. "I'm going to make you look pretty Karen. All those people at Hopscotch's never paid you enough attention. To be fair you are rather crabby. Still, we both know that true beauty is on the inside, and I'm going to ensure that everyone can see how beautiful you can be on the outside. Let the inside shine, Karen."

I ran the knife with just a little more pressure along her collar bone and down the centre of her chest. I think she was screaming at me. I closed my eyes. In my head a melody had started, and I began to dance to its tune, swinging the knife with swift light pressure as I drove it across Karen's body. I could no longer hear her muffled voice from behind the tape.

I danced around Karen's body, careful not to bang into anything, running the knife down her back, sides and front, finishing at her feet. Blood began to spray as I applied more pressure, sinking the blade deeper into her skin, removing it and then whipping the knife across her flesh. Her body soon became coated in her own blood. Blood; so precious, so beautiful. I sighed as my pleasure grew. Blood was my fuel and the more I cut, the more I wanted to see. And the more my pleasure heightened, until euphoria hit me.

When I stopped Karen's eyes were full of fury. I blinked, there was no fear. She knew she was going to die and still she looked at me with complete and utter loathing. No longer was she thrashing in her seat. Her body was still. Hate radiated from her. I felt swept away, riding the high from her emotional state. I closed my eyes and through my eyelids, Karen's hate filled eyes burned into me. Beautiful – truly beautiful.

Karen may not realise the gift that she bestowed upon me. I accepted it and promised never to forget her. Never to forget the passion that slowly boiled beneath her unkempt surface. She was the most beautiful person I had ever killed. Patrick Barnes might have had the perfect body. But Karen had strength; fire ran through her very core. Pure fiery hate and it was all directed at me – all for me.

For the first time in my life, I felt truly appreciated.

I smiled. I couldn't remember ever feeling so happy, so noticed. No longer was I a shadow lurking in the background, no today right now, someone was seeing me. *ME!*

I placed a gloved finger on Karen's lips and smiled; there was acceptance in my smile, of the gift she gave me. There even might have been a little warmth where my lips curled. "You take my breath away." I whispered the compliment as I took the knife and with a swift jab, I sank it deep into her stomach. Karen's eyes widened in shock, it was a natural reaction to the knife sinking into her flesh. Quickly I removed the knife and slid it between her ribs and punctured a lung, before sinking it into her heart. Karen's body jerked involuntarily. Blood fell from her mouth. Her heart beat out her blood, splattering it over me, Fred, the dogs, onto the work surfaces and cupboards. Karen's body began shutting down as the blood made its way onto the wooden floor. Drip, drip, drip. Still her eyes blazed with hate.

I patted her head and breathed deeply. "You've been the best Karen." She deserved the compliment.

Moving away I sat on the floor and watched as life left Karen. Her eyes full of hate and staring right at me, right up until she drew her last shallow breath. I wasn't worried about the blood trail I'd be leaving behind as it pooled around me. After all it was only fair that I leave the police something to hypothesise over. If the dogs didn't ruin it first that is.

I waited over an hour before I left Karen's apartment. I found it hard to pull myself away from her sightless eyes. Karen's hate seemed to still linger in the room. It thrilled me, took me on a ride so far and high, that I never wanted to come down from it. Outside the sun had made an appearance and the frost had started to subside a little.

A small part of me realised that I'd been sat in Karen's kitchen for too long. I just couldn't seem to stop appreciating Karen's beautiful bloodied body. My clothes had started to soak up Karen's blood, becoming stiff. A good job I'd brought an extra set of clothing. Finally, I forced myself to pull away from Karen's hypnotic stare. I'd changed into a pair of grey joggy bottoms and a pale pink sweat top. My shoes were now a vibrant purple trainer with lime green laces, rather than the oversized black loafers I had used while killing Karen.

There would be no blood trail leaving the apartment.

I looked at my watch. The dogs would soon be awake, spreading the blood further into the apartment, in a frenzy of confusion. *'Why did Karen not pat them? Why did she just sit there not moving or blinking?* There would be no morning cuddle for them today. No one to feed them or let them out to do their business, no, from today, they were on their own. I smiled; still they had each other– for now.

My large bag had been replaced with a large lime green backpack, which I'd thrown over my shoulder. The black bag and contents were wrapped in a plastic bin liner which sat snugly in the backpack. My clothes would go in the wash when I got home, so I wasn't too worried about the blood. I'd been thinking about throwing Fred in the wash, for ease. He was made of plastic so it wasn't like he was going to shrink. I'd put him on a cold wash so the plastic wouldn't become misshapen. Fred could always be replaced if something went wrong. As silent partners went, you couldn't get better than Fred. No demands and easy to dispose of. That was Fred.

My shoes and black bag, I had decided to get rid of. I was planning on dumping them in someone's black bin down the street. It was dustbin day judging by the line of bins along the street down from Karen's. By the time, Karen's body would be discovered, the dustbin wagon would be coming towards the end of its shift. No way would the police be able to tell which street my bag and shoes had been collected from, should they find them.

I'd ensured that there had been nothing left behind that would lead the police to look in my direction. The knife I'd used I'd left by Karen's feet, after all what could it tell them, and it saved them a job with all the *'let's identify what kind of knife had been used'* analysis work that they liked to do. I had considered that maybe I was taking away some of their excitement, over evidence collecting and analysis etcetera. They'd get their chance when I was ready. I was the one in control here not them, and they needed to know that.

I looked at my watch. The dogs would be awake now.

I let the thought of the damage the dogs would be doing to the evidence entertain me as I jogged over to the car. I had on a pair of purple leather gloves, my black ones had been badly bloodied and while I could have cleaned them down at Karen's, again I had decided to clean them when I got back home. They now sat in a plastic bag along with my bloodied clothes and Fred, inside the backpack. I'd just brought the backpack, no point in covering it in evidence.

I started the engine and looked at the clock on the dashboard. It was ten o'clock, by the time I got home and cleaned up, it would be nearer dinner time before I made it into work. Well that was just life.

Chapter Eleven

"You're late!" Tracy flinched.

I stifled a snigger.

Mr Orange stood tapping his left shiny black brogue at her. "Sorry Mr Andrews."

"Sorry might have worked on your previous manager but it won't wash with me. I want to know exactly why you find it *'OK'* to turn up…." There was a dramatic pause as Mr Orange looked at his watch. "Three hours and twenty-two minutes late for work." Did nobody notice the big clock on the wall above Tracy!

"I had a migraine." I raised my eyebrows at her words. That was pretty quick thinking for Tracy, given that she had no idea why she was late for work. I did though and I wasn't about to let anyone know what had happened. I didn't want to incriminate myself.

All Tracy knew was that she had gone to bed alone last night, and woken up at eleven this morning to find that she was running late. I did note however, that Tracy had lied to Mr Orange. It was unusual for Tracy to lie with such ease. I took another look at her. I noticed a confidence about her that hadn't been there before. I cursed softly under my breath. *Bloody Richard.*

I'd kill him, I really would.

I laughed at myself. Of course, I was going to kill him! That had been my plan all along. Simmer, simmer, I told myself, and took a few deep breaths as I tried to get my rage under control.

I had been exercising a lot of patience lately. It wasn't in my nature.

Here's a joke for you, which I'd read on the internet one day. It got me laughing, tears rolling down my face. Do you know the difference between a sociopath and a psychopath? One of them will kill you! Ha, ha, ha. I'd have to remember to tell that one to Richard as I stuck a knife into his heart.

The thought lightened my mood.

Mr Orange gave Tracy a long look. She didn't back down, which again was not the Tracy I had come to hate. "Make sure it doesn't happen again."

"Yes, Mr Andrews."

I watched him as he gave Tracy the once over. "Your figures may be up but you still have a long way to go to make up the shortfall. No slacking."

"Yes, Mr Andrews."

Together, Tracy and I watched Mr Orange walk back to his cupboard. He wore a pair of dark grey slim cut trousers that seemed to accentuate his lack of butt, and made his legs look extra twiggy. A pink shirt poked out from a brown knit tank top which had a purple diamond on the front.

Mr Orange swung round to look back at Tracy as he reached his office, hand on the cold metal of the door handle. His mind had obviously been festering over something. "And do something with your appearance, you look like shit." All the other girls looked over at Tracy, she sent them a shrug.

"Yes, Mr Andrews." Tracy stood, still waiting for Mr Orange to make a move inside his office.

As Mr Orange closed his door, she let out a sigh of relief. So, she wasn't as confident as she'd come across, nice to know.

Abigail took that moment to come running across the shop floor. The customers parted quickly as she sped through them. At one point, I thought she was going to take out the granny, shuffling to the till with an arm full of thick denier tights. Lucky for the granny, Abigail changed course at the last minute.

Tracy unaware of Abigail's approaching form, began straightening out her uniform and applying some make- up. Tracy didn't need much which was probably as well, given the hurricane known as Abigail, which was fast approaching. Abigail hit the counter, hands flat on the glass surface, at top speed. It was as well that the counter was made from safety glass. It wouldn't have withstood the impact otherwise.

Tracy paused, lipstick hovering near her lips. "Everything OK?"

Abigail shook her head with vigour, gasping for breath. Susie sauntered over, hips swinging, legs on display, brown skirt swishing the tops of her thighs. Her low-cut cream top rippled across her chest, struggling to keep her boobs hidden. Susie flipped her long blond hair over her shoulder. "What's got you all riled up?"

Abigail caught her breath as she straightened out her grey skirt and boxy jacket. "Karen didn't come into work today."

Susie raised her eyes to the ceiling. "Not over reacting then, Abs. For a second I thought it might be something interesting."

Abigail shook her head, sending her bobbed hair flying into her face. "You don't understand. Karen is never late and she always turns in when she's supposed to. I have a bad feeling about this."

Tracy's face lost some of its colour. "What do you think has happened to her?"

"How should we know?" Susie pulled out one of the faux leather chairs by the counter and sat down, crossing one slender leg over the other. "You know Abs, her *'bad feeling'* has probably got something to do with her needing a pee than anything to do with Karen not turning in for work." Susie idly swung one of her legs as she leant forward, arms leaning on the glass counter, her boobs hanging dangerously close to escaping the flimsy fabric.

A man walked into Helen's counter with force, eyes locked onto Susie's swinging leg. Lipsticks went tumbling to the floor in a clatter of plastic. Helen shot Susie a hard stare. Susie smiled at her. The man's cheeks reddened and he began muttering and picking up the lipsticks, trying hard not to look at the length of leg that Susie was showing.

Abigail ignored Susie's comment. "I've tried ringing her and she's not picking up. Maybe she's fallen. She could be laid in that flat of hers hurt, desperately waiting for someone to come and help her." Nope, I could guarantee that Karen wasn't waiting for anyone to run to her rescue, and most definitely didn't need any assistance.

"Seriously Abs, she's probably taken the day off and forgotten to mention it."

"Come on Susie, I know you don't like her but at least admit, this is out of character for Karen. Put your dislike for her to one side for a moment, and try and be a bit more understanding. I really think something's wrong. I've asked around and Karen hasn't booked any time off. She's AWOL."

"She's not in the army." Susie muttered, more to herself than anyone else.

"Do you really think that something has happened?" Tracy asked putting the unused lipstick down on the counter top.

Abigail nodded her head. "Yes, I do."

Tracy looked at the closed door to Mr Orange's office. "I can't leave, I've only just come in." Susie and Abigail looked at her. "I had a migraine."

Susie cocked her head at Tracy. "You OK now?"

"Yeah, thanks."

"What do you think we should do?" Abigail asked. Blank stares met her. "About Karen; I can't go on my own. What if she needs medical attention or something?"

Susie rolled her eyes. "Then you call for an ambulance. It's just three little numbers 9-9-9. Dead easy." Oh dead, yep, that would be Karen. Ha, ha, ha. Abigail had no idea what beautiful artwork she would find at Karen's. The thought made me smile.

Abigail sent Susie a flat look. "Come on, we've got to do something."

"Why do *'we'* have to do anything?" Susie put her hands in front of her, palms facing Abigail as if warding her off as Abigail lightly punched her on her arm. "OK, OK. As Tracy can't leave early as she's just come in and I've got a stocktake to do before I can leave, why don't we all go after work?"

"What happens if she's laid on the floor with a broken leg and unconscious or something? It seems a really long time to wait for someone to come to her rescue." Karen wasn't conscious that was for sure. I was getting more enjoyment out of this conversation than I thought I would. Usually I switch off when the three of them get together. Boring!

"If she's unconscious, she's won't know what time we turn up. So, what's the point in rushing? If you ask me, Karen should be grateful that we're going in the first place."

"You're all heart sometimes Susie."

"Look I can't help being the caring kind." Susie got off the chair. Her skirt lifted up, exposing part of her bum cheek. "I take it you're working through afternoon break?"

Tracy nodded her head. "I'd better make up some time. He's worse than Mrs H ever was."

"Do you think it's because he's single?" Susie and Tracy looked at Abigail.

"What makes you think he's single?" Susie asked eyebrows arched.

Abigail shrugged. "I saw him chatting up some fella, that didn't seem at all interested in his advances."

"That doesn't mean that he's single."

"True, Susie, but it would explain his bad moods. Look how you were when you went on your *'I'm-sick- of-attracting-the-wrong-type'* thing."

Susie gave a snort. "I wasn't that bad and besides, it's good to try different things now and again."

"Says the girl that won't try being a little bit more conservative in her dress."

Susie looked at Abigail. "Do you know how they spell conservative? B-O-R-I-N-G, that's how, and kiddo I'm anything but boring." Susie flipped her blonde hair back, stuck out her chest and winked at Abigail.

Behind her, the man who had just finished helping Helen with her lipsticks, got distracted again, his arm hit the lipsticks and down they went – crash.

Susie laughed at Helen's exasperated sigh. I was betting that Helen wished she was free to do a lot more than sigh. "Leave them, I'll get them." Helen ground out at the poor man as he began picking up the lipsticks again.

The man fled on instinct, at the undercurrent of tension in Helen's voice. Whether he intended to or not, he followed the swishing of Susie's skirt to hosiery.

"Why can't she wear skirts like the rest of us?" Helen bit out from the floor, lipsticks in hand.

"I think you'll find she *was* wearing a skirt," Abigail helpfully pointed out as she watched Helen on her hands and knees, grabbing at the lipsticks.

Helen looked up. "That wasn't a skirt. I get to see her knickers more times in one day than I do my own."

"At least they're clean," Abigail said in a sweet voice. "I'd be careful Helen, you're starting to sound jealous."

Tracy leaned forward, touching Abigail's arm. "I think you'd best go." Just when it was starting to get interesting.

Abigail shrugged, however Helen was now annoyed to the point that she was forgetting where she was. I smiled, this could get real interesting.

"Jealous? What of? Slutty Susie?"

Abigail turned, face pinched. Abigail was like a lioness protecting her cubs when it came to her best friends. Tracy made a grab for Abigail's arm. Missed. "She's only trying to wind you up, don't let her."

Abigail took a small step closer to Helen and leant down. "You take that back. Susie might have a unique way of dressing but she's no slut. If you want to see a slut, I suggest you look in the mirror Helen Black. You've had more guys than I've had hot dinners, and I like my hot food."

Helen gave a shriek. Tracy flew round her counter grabbing Abigail's arm. "Come on, I'll walk up to accounts with you." Tracy went for a better grip and casually but firmly slung her arm around Abigail's shoulders, steering her towards the escalator.

Helen made a lunge for it and raising her right arm she threw a lipstick at Tracy and Abigail's retreating backs. I looked on and smiled. Mr Orange took that moment to open his cupboard door and step out onto the shop floor. The lipstick went sailing towards him at quite a speed. I caught the panic on Helen's face as she noticed Mr Orange. Her face lost its colour. Even with all the layers of make-up she had on, there was a definite pallor to her skin.

The lipstick came to an abrupt stop as it hit Mr Orange right on the ridge of his nose. It must have gathered some speed, that or it hit his hyper sensitive nose at just the right angle. Blood spurted from his right nostril quickly covering the tank top he was wearing. Tracy didn't stop, she kept leading Abigail towards the elevator. Abigail let out a giggle, quickly covering her mouth with her hand in case Mr Orange heard her.

I stared at the blood gushing from Mr Orange's nose. My pulse quickened, and for a second I could see Hopscotch's painted in beautiful red blood. Glorious! I'd never killed more than one person at one time. It was definitely something to think about.

"Helen!" The cosmetic floor went deathly quiet at the sound of Mr Orange's voice.

Helen regained some of her composure and went running up to him with a box of tissues. "Sorry Mr Andrew's, it just sort of flew out of my hands. A customer knocked all my lipsticks on the floor, I was picking them up." Helen grabbed the lipstick from Mr Orange's feet.

Mr Orange resembled a blood orange. I liked the thought; red really did suit him. Maybe I should take the time to show him how much the colour suited him. "This is a department store not a playground, Helen." He sounded like he had a bad cold.

Tracy came back from the elevator leaving Abigail to travel up on her own to accounts. A satisfied smile settled on Abigail's lips as she watched the scene below as she sailed up to the first floor. Say what you want about Abigail, she was a very loyal friend.

Tracy walked over to Mr Orange and Helen. "I'll get you an ice pack. Why don't you wait in your office, I won't be long." Tracy guided Mr Orange back to his cupboard. Helen huffed and went back to her counter, muttering all the while under her breath.

Depositing Mr Orange in his two by two cupboard, Tracy ran to the café and into the kitchen for an ice pack. Luckily Hopscotch's café was situated just past the cosmetics department on the right-hand side, so she didn't have too far to go. By the time Tracy got there, word had spread and an ice pack was already waiting for her. There was a lot of sniggering going on, not only on the part of Hopscotch's staff. I noticed a few customers hiding their smiles, covering their giggles with coughs.

Hilary Lambert, the café supervisor held out an ice pack to Tracy, closing the freezer door. "He had it coming, if you ask me." Tracy nodded, taking the ice pack. Hilary rubbed her cold hands together, warming them up.

"Thanks," Tracy said, as she rushed back towards the closed door of Mr Orange's office.

Tracy didn't bother to knock on the cupboard door but went straight in. Mr Orange sat at his desk, nose wrapped in a once white hanky. "Here you go." He grabbed the ice pack without a thank you, and indicated with his left arm for her to leave. Well, no one ever said Mr Orange was the grateful type.

Helen gave Tracy a hard stare as she placed the lipsticks back where they belonged but refrained from saying anything.

After the lipstick incident, the day became boring, and I settled back waiting for the trio to meet up and go round to Karen's.

This was going to be one of those occasions I wasn't going to miss. In fact, I was really, *really* looking forward to it. Maybe it would take away some of that new confidence Tracy had gained over the last few months. I smiled, now that was a nice thought.

I wondered if anyone had found Karen yet, or if Tracy and her party would be the first to find her.

That was an interesting thought.

It made me happy to think about how they would react when they saw Karen's bloody body.

My pulse leaped against my skin.

This was very exciting. I had never been around when someone discovered my artwork before.

I found that I was looking forward to going back to Karen's.

Thinking about the possibilities of the trio discovering Karen's lifeless body, I couldn't help but reiterate what I had said to Karen. She had truly been the best.

Even in death she was still giving.

That type of thing shouldn't go unnoticed, or forgotten.

Chapter Twelve

"Come on," Susie urged. "It's bloody cold out here."

The early evening sky had darkened and the cold was starting to settle in as the temperature dropped to freezing. Abigail shuffled, zipping up her long down coat. "You could try wearing a proper coat," she grumbled.

Susie looked at her. "I am wearing a coat and I've got boots on." She pointed to her black spiked heeled thigh high leather boots. The dark brown coat was more of a waist length jacket and only had one button, which allowed Susie's ample chest to make an appearance.

"That's not a coat, *this* is a coat." Abigail snuggled deeper into her down coat.

"Yeah, my granny had one just like it."

Abigail nudged Susie with her elbow. "Bet she was warm, unlike her granddaughter."

Tracy walked out of Hopscotch's, the hood up on her red duffle coat. Like Susie, she had swapped her court shoes for a pair of black boots. Unlike Susie, the boots had a sturdy heel and a good grip. "We ready to go?" Tracy asked.

"How's Mr Andrews doing?" Abigail tried to hide her smile and look concerned.

"His nose has swollen up a bit, but it's not that bad. Who'd have thought a lipstick could do so much damage." Tracy couldn't stop the smile from spreading across her lips. "Helen's quite a shot." Tracy and Abigail began laughing.

Feeling grumpy and cold, Susie huffed next to them. "Come on, let's just get this over and done with. I'm telling you, Karen better have broken at least one of her legs after all this."

"Susie!" Abigail scolded.

"I'm only saying, we're going to a lot of trouble for absolutely nothing. She's probably snuggled up in front of the fire with those god-awful dogs of hers."

Tracy threaded her arm through Abigail's. "She's just grumpy because she's cold."

"She could try putting a coat on."

"I heard that Abigail." The trio trudged over to Karen's. Fortunately, given the cold and lack of coat on Susie, Karen didn't live too far away from town and Hopscotch's.

Within fifteen minutes at a brisk pace, the girls made it to Karen's. I was pleased to see no flashing blue lights or yellow crime scene tape, which meant one thing. These three were in for a discovery of a life time. I wondered how they would react when they first saw Karen.

Would they take the time to appreciate the beauty of my artwork?

Well, I was about to find out.

The flat where Karen lived had been a large town house at one point. Now it held three flats on each of its floors. A large plastic carport covered the parking area which was situated to the right of the house. Parking was at a premium so close to the city centre, not that Karen had a car, however she still maintained her own parking spot, placing her push bike where she would have parked a car. The bike was grey and what I called a trolley dolly bike, with big upright U curved handlebars so that she didn't have to stoop over and could maintain an even straighter spine. A brown wicker basket was perched in front. It reminded me of the bike that the nasty neighbour who turned into the witch in the Wizard of Oz rode. A long thick silver chain was wrapped around both wheels and tied to one of the supporting metal poles that held the plastic roof of the carport up. The chain was secured with a very sturdy, very large silver lock. Talk about overkill. It would ensure however that the bike didn't go walk about while not in use.

"Look." Abigail pointed at the bike, "Karen must be home."

Susie shrugged. "All that the bike tells you is that she's not using it. Still doesn't mean she's not propping up a bar somewhere, all warm and cosy, unlike us."

"I can't imagine Karen propping up a bar," Tracy said.
"True, but I'm still cold." Together they approached the front door to the flats.

Karen's flat was on the third floor. I'd had a key copied which had enabled me to come and go as I pleased without disturbing anyone. These three weren't that lucky and as they pressed the buzzer for Karen's flat, they beat the soles of their shoes and boots on the pavement outside, trying to prevent the cold from seeping through. Susie stood in the middle of them, trying to absorb as much warmth from Tracy and Abigail's bodies as she could.

One day Susie might cotton on that warmth was preferable to chattering teeth and a good covering of Goosebumps. I looked at Susie, I'd seen what she had to offer on more than one occasion, and quite frankly even the thought of her naked body covered in blood, didn't excite me. Not that it would stop me from killing her, should the timing be right.

151

"I don't think anyone's home. We should go." Abigail and Tracy looked at Susie, frown lines creasing their brows.

"We're not here for a social chat, we're here because Karen didn't come into work or pick up her phone." Abigail pointed out.

"Good, because the thought of eating biscuits and drinking tea with Karen isn't doing anything to warm me up."

"You're not funny, you know that don't you."

Tracy ignored their exchange and pressed the buzzer to the first floor flat. "Hello?" Abigail and Susie jumped at the sound of the female voice over the intercom.

Tracy lent closer to the intercom. "Hi, sorry to bother you, but we're trying to get in contact with Karen Stillman who lives in the top flat and she's not answering."

"And?" Don't you just love helpful people?

"Well, we were wondering if you could let us in so we could check on her. She didn't turn into work and she's not picking up the phone. We're just concerned about her." Tracy added the last bit in the hope that it would provoke some type of sympathy. Hopefully the person in the first floor flat was more sympathetic than Susie.

"I don't know. You could be anyone." The voice over the intercom didn't sound uncertain about letting them in, just annoyed that she'd been disturbed.

Susie rolled her eyes. "Look its freezing out here, and all we want to do is check on Karen and go home so just let us in so that we can get this over and done with." The intercom went dead.

"I don't think the person on the intercom felt your concern Susie. Maybe there was something missing, like warmth and genuine concern. You should have just let Tracy handle it."

"Yeah, right." Susie snorted.

"At least she wouldn't have been rude."

"I wasn't rude."

Abigail raised her eyebrows at Susie questioningly. "If that wasn't rude, I wouldn't like to see you when you're *trying* to be rude."

Footsteps sounded behind them. "Excuse me ladies." The three of them swung round to see a man standing behind them.

He wore a black bomber style down jacket, the hood was up sending his face into the shadow of the fabric, the faux fur round the outside of the hood moved slightly in the wind. Black smart slim cut trousers and a pair of black dress shoes that shifted as he moved lightly from one foot to the other waiting for them to move.

"Sorry, we were trying to get in. Our friend Karen didn't make it into work today and we were unable to get an answer from her on her mobile." Susie all but purred, thrusting out her chest.

"Come on, I'll let you in." Susie shot the stranger a blinding smile.

Abigail rolled her eyes and Tracy smiled at Susie.

"You just returning from work?" Susie asked as she pushed out her chest a bit more, removing her coat as they entered the warm hallway.

The man looked at the expanse of flesh on display and licked his lips. "Yeah." His eyes never left the two mounds of flesh.

Abigail grabbed Susie's arm. "Karen, remember!"

Susie protested as Abigail pulled her along the foyer and up the stairs. Tracy looked across at the man, his hood still hiding his face. "Thanks."

"You're welcome." The man shuffled and unlocked the door to the bottom flat as the trio marched up the stairs.

They stopped at Karen's white door. "What now?" Susie asked. "There's no point in knocking, if she didn't answer the intercom or the phone, I'm betting she's not going to answer the door either." No, she definitely wouldn't be answering the door. I smiled a rather smug and satisfied smile.

"Why don't we try the door?" Tracy said, though I noticed that neither of them made an attempt to reach for the door handle.

"Oh, for Pete's sake!" Susie reached for the door handle. It gave, and the door opened a crack.

I hadn't locked the door behind me because I'd thought it might give the Police something to titter over.

You know the type of thing; the victim must have known her attacker and all that. Now as the trio watched the door open, I was even more pleased with my decision.

I'd read this book once in which a CSI identified where the killer had been prior to killing their victim from soil left behind from their footprints. I'd found this idea quite interesting. Looking at the dirt forming on the floor from the trios of shoes, I felt it would give the CSI something else to mull over as they tried to distinguish between theirs and mine. The thing is, I knew that there wouldn't be any dirt left behind by me that would tell the CSI anything.

The shoes I had worn, had been scrubbed clean from the last time I had used them, and all I had done was walk on the pavement containing the usual dirt that clings to the streets. Nothing different, no particular insect that only settles in certain areas, or dust from a disused warehouse. In fact, the dirt I had left behind was positively ordinary and boring. I shrugged; there was nothing wrong with that. The CSI crew would need to work that little bit harder to find their incriminating evidence.

"Come on, we can't just stand here," Abigail said; she didn't move from where she stood.

"You first, it seems only fair as it was your idea." Susie put an encouraging hand on Abigail's back.

"It feels like we're breaking in."

Susie rolled her eyes, at Abigail. "Do you want to see if Karen is OK or have I just been freezing my assets off for nothing?"

"You know I do," Abigail moaned.

Tracy leant forward. "Sorry Abs, but we're going to have to go inside to do that."

Abigail sighed. "Karen!" She shouted as she stepped over the threshold, closely, if not a little hesitantly, followed by Tracy and Susie. Their forms were instantly absorbed by the darkness as the sun faded away for the evening. There was no answer from Karen. The door closed softly behind them and I almost laughed out loud, as they all jumped in union.

"Can you see a light switch?" Abigail asked. "I can't see a bloody thing." Susie muttered.

Tracy, hands stretched out in front of her as she had been the closest to the door, feeling her way back to the wall near the door she pressed on the light switch. Light instantly filled the room. A low growl filled the space between where the girls stood in the living room and the kitchen.

"Shit the dogs! I'd forgotten about them," Abigail said as she looked at the little balls of fluff with razor teeth, bouncing on the spot and yapping like mad things. "What have they got on their coats? It looks like a really bad dye job."

Susie poked her head over Abigail's shoulder. "I think that could be blood. Maybe they've eaten Karen."

Abigail's face lost some of its colour. "That's a horrible thing to say." It might be a horrible thing to say, however Abigail didn't sound like she was convinced they hadn't.

The dogs started barking in earnest and Tracy took a step back. "I don't think they like me."

"They probably know that you stood Karen up and that you weren't *'friends'* anymore." Susie raised her hands and bent her index fingers as she said the word 'friends'.

"You're being mean Susie," Abigail said, her eyes never leaving the bouncing dogs.

Susie shrugged in answer. I got the impression she wasn't sorry.

"Why do you think they're covered in blood, *apart* from them eating Karen I mean?" Tracy asked, giving the dogs a nervous look.

"I don't know, maybe Karen slipped, broke her leg on the way down and hit her nose, which then started to bleed. And the blood covered the dogs as they went over to see if she was OK." Wow, that was some imagination going on there. I couldn't help but wonder why no one had thought that maybe Karen hadn't come in to work as, let's say, she'd been murdered by a serial killer that was on the loose in York. Connect the dots girls. Come on work it out. It's not that much of a stretch.

"Well, I guess there's only one way to find out, come on, if we ignore them they might leave us alone. They don't look like they're going to take a chunk out of our legs." Abigail took a step forward.

Susie snagged Abigail's arm. "Chucky looked cute, but it didn't stop him going around killing people."

"Chucky was a film. It wasn't real," Abigail said as she shook off Susie's hand.

"Sometimes we can learn something from films and I'm saying those dogs right now might look cute, but they still have sharp teeth."

"We don't have a choice if we're going to find Karen. She's got to be here somewhere and if she has fallen, she's going to need help." Go, Abigail. "What do you think Tracy?"

"I guess we can't stand here all night."

Abigail looked at Susie. "See, come on." The dogs gave a low growl but stayed where they were as Abigail began slowly moving forward, looking round the flat for Karen's fallen body. The door to the kitchen was open. The dogs must have pushed it open when I'd left.

Another tentative step forward from Abigail sent the dogs into a frenzy of high pitched barking. They never left their spot near the kitchen door. Their paws beat against the wooden floor and they jumped up and down on the spot in earnest now. I was quite impressed at how high they could jump. And all the while leaving more evidence behind and destroying other evidence. I just had to appreciate the job they were doing.

Abigail turned and looked through the kitchen door. I wished I could have seen her face when she'd seen Karen but the angle was all wrong. Her scream echoed round the tiny flat. I closed my eyes and absorbed the terror that accompanied that scream. Hmmm, beautiful.

Susie and Tracy unglued themselves from their spot and ran forward to Abigail; from the looks on their faces I was betting that they wished that they had stayed where they were. Their eyes were wide with shock and I could almost hear their brains whirring as it fought to make sense of the message their eyes were sending it.

Karen's lifeless body was slumped in the chair where I had tied her. Bloody paw prints ran all over the kitchen floor and Karen's naked body. I gave my work another once over. I smiled. I had done a beautiful job. Lacerations covered Karen's body. The blood had congealed and the pattern left behind was pure gold. The light from the living room cast a shadow along the length of Karen's bloodied body. A dark pool of blood lay

157

beneath her. Her head was tilted on her chest to her right. Her hair fell across her eyes. I thought about those eyes, hard and filled with hate. They sent shivers of pleasure running down my spine. I looked at Abigail and Susie; there was no appreciation of my work. Instead they looked ill. That made me angry. The colour had drained from their faces. Anger rose swift and true. How dare they look at my artwork with such loathing.

Stupid, stupid people, never seeing the beauty of what was in front of them.

Never appreciating pure art.

Abigail gave a deep breath and moved closer to the kitchen. "What are you doing?" Susie clung to Abigail's arm.

"She might not be dead."

"She's dead. No one could go through that and live." Susie took a laboured breath fighting back the bile that rose in her throat.

Abigail took another look at Karen's body. One of the dogs leapt forward racing across the floor to Karen. It nudged a wet nose against her leg. Karen's head moved, angling towards them, her cold sightless eyes staring at them. "I think I'm going to be sick." Abigail put a hand to her stomach and took a breath.

Susie however was already losing the contents of her stomach on the rug in the living room. Tracy stood there, not saying anything, or moving. I could feel her shutting down as the full horror of what she was seeing began to hit her brain.

Abigail reached for her mobile, hands shaking so badly that she nearly dropped it twice.

I sensed the moment that Tracy's brain started to crack. The very moment when she could no longer process what her eyes kept telling her.

Tracy took a deep unconscious breath of air, her brain now working on instinct. And she started to scream. Her scream echoed round the room, it was like a continuous long high pitched sound that never stopped.

The mobile fell out of Abigail's hands. She turned to Tracy and wrapped her in her arms. "*Shh, shh,*" she whispered into her ear.

Footsteps sounded on the stairs, heavy and urgent. The door to Karen's flat was flung open. A man's form covered the entrance to the flat. Susie rose from her squatting position, wiping a hand across her lips. Her face was pale and tears fell down her cheeks. Her eyes fell on Karen and she turned and began vomiting again.

Tracy was still screaming; her whole body shook as a thin layer of cold sweat appeared on her forehead. Her eyes were wide as though her eyelids had been pinned opened. I knew that she no longer saw Karen's lifeless body; her brain had removed that image and shut down. My beautiful artwork had been too much for it.

"Get her out of here," the man said.

Abigail complied without argument and led Tracy out of the flat and onto the small landing. The dogs ran at the man their tails wagging as they jumped up at him. He bent down his hand poised to ruffle their coats. The blood lining their fur stopped his hand before it made contact.

His grey sweat pants were quickly turning red and he reached inside the pocket of his navy-blue hoodie and took out his phone. Tracy had finally stopped screaming and was slumped against the wall, her body spent. She rocked back and forth, her arms hugging her body tightly and her hands shook uncontrollably. Her legs finally gave out and she sank to the carpeted floor taking Abigail with her. Her lips quivered as they parted to take in deep shaky breaths of air.

Abigail unwound herself from Tracy long enough to snatch her mobile and tuck it in the pocket of her coat. Sinking to the floor next to Tracy, she placed a reassuring arm around her shoulders. Tracy's head naturally fell onto Abigail's shoulder and a tear ran down her cheek and dripped onto Abigail's down coat where it started its journey down to the floor. Tracy's eyes were as sightless as Karen's. I thought the look suited her.

Susie came to stand next to her friends, her arms wrapped around her stomach. For the first time, I don't think Susie thought about her appearance and the fact that there was a man in the room. Her breast seemed to cave in on her as she began to pull the sides of her jacket together, covering herself up.

The man stood alone in the apartment as he rang in the incident to the police. His words somehow seemed to bounce off the walls as the dogs calmed down, sensing that this was it, Karen wasn't going to wake up. They sat at the man's feet, their big sad eyes looking up at him with longing.

Time lost all meaning and purpose.

I took in the emotions that littered the room like small dust particles.

This was better than I had thought it would be. I liked Tracy scared and lost.

That would teach her, and stop her getting all cocky because she's with Richard.

Tracy was back to being fragile.

Her screams still echoed round the room. I had liked the sound of them, enjoyed watching her crumble. It had been such pure raw emotion.

Tonight's events would live with her for a long time. Let's see if Richard could mend this.

Tracy was a mess.

I was back on track and that's all that mattered.

Who would have thought I could have achieved so much with just one kill?

Chapter Thirteen

The street outside was filled with flashing blue lights.

It turned out that the chap downstairs who had let the trio in was a policeman. Ha, and I'd killed Karen right under his nose. His professional title and whether he was uniform or detective didn't interest me, so I didn't bother trying to find out. Plod was as stupid as the rest of them and not worth my attention.

Judging by the dog's reaction to him, he'd known Karen and yet had suspected nothing. He had never noticed me hovering around watching her, making a note of her schedule. He hadn't even missed the fact that Karen hadn't walked her dogs at six this morning, or had he simply not been interested enough to want to notice? And that was going to cost him. He could have been the one that caught me, taken the glory and the fame. And now he would always be nothing; he would simply be the one that had let me kill Karen Stillman. I could have changed his career, I could have elevated him through the ranks. He would have been famous, simply for catching me.

The press were gathering, their flashes going off at high speed, jostling each other as they tried for a better angle, looking for that perfect shot. You never know they might even get a picture of the serial killer milling amongst the crowds, or say, sat with the police within the taped off perimeter. Ha, ha, ha. They wouldn't know what they'd got even if they did catch me on camera. Journalists shouted, each one vying for attention, firing off questions quicker than anyone had a chance to answer them. They were all so desperate for the scoop. Unlike Plod they knew that I could be the start of a very lucrative career. The problem was that they were so busy, busy, busy doing their job that they were failing to do them at the same time. Worthless fools.

They were all blind.

Not one of them saw me. Not one of them noticed the killer that sat within the ring of flashing lights and police tape, watching them, as they looked for me.

Ha, ha, ha.

I will say this for Plod and what had got my interest peaked, was how quickly he got the crime scene secured. Given all the evidence that had been destroyed, I thought it a waste of effort. Still procedure was procedure and had to be stuck to.

The intercom woman on the first floor flat had not been impressed by all the racket being created and seemed to blame Plod for disturbing her. This I felt was rather ironic, as Tracy had been the one making most of the noise. Still why blame someone like Tracy when there was a policeman around to lash into. I was beginning to think that this woman was a sociopath and therefore she had no feelings for the dead woman found in the apartment above her; tied to a chair and all cut up.

Apparently, the intercom woman worked nights and this was her one day off or would that be night off? I could understand where she was coming from. Still, I did feel that she should take a minute or two to appreciate what had happened while she had been doing her sleeping and shopping. My artwork needed the time to be really appreciated. Maybe if she'd seen Karen, she would be showing more appreciation, rather than stood arguing with Plod about noise levels and being disturbed. Being a psychopath, I had some very similar traits to that of a sociopath, so I guess you could use the old saying *'it takes one to recognise one'*, or in this case, someone with very similar traits.

Remember as destructive and abusive as a sociopath is, they aren't going kill you because they feel like it, say on a whim, just because it's going to make them happy, or because they want to. Anger is a very important emotion to a sociopath and is linked to their actions, unlike me. I don't need to be angry to kill. Sociopaths still hang onto some of the constraints issued by society. They might get extremely angry and throw things around. They might even hurt you, throw the odd punch or two and feel no remorse. They would however never be as free as me.

I like being a psychopath, my actions are boundless, my desire to kill limitless.

Tracy was sat in the back of a police car, a blanket wrapped around her shaking form. I didn't think it was the cold that was making her shake. Her reaction to Karen's body had been priceless. The fact that she had still to come round and process what she had seen, told me that Tracy was still very fragile.

Just wait until I killed Richard.

A pang of joy hit me as I contemplated this. Tracy broken.

Tracy going to that quiet place where time has no meaning, life is no more.

Tracy dead.

I gave a giggle, and quickly covered my mouth to stop it from coming out. I looked around, no one had noticed. I sat quietly and absorbed my joy.

The police had tried to talk to her. No one had been home and instead all they had got was an empty stare. That was Tracy for you, weak, vulnerable Tracy. The police were hapless creatures. Really, here I was, sitting here watching them, and they never saw me. They never really bothered to look for me. My hiding place was a good one. No one would think to look for me here. Still, it showed how mindless the police were. They should have known better with all the resources they had. It probably

wouldn't have helped them that they were looking for two people.

Suddenly I felt annoyed. Angry.

Did I have to do everything? Could these stupid people not do anything right? This is the problem when you create boxes to put people in. They had put me in a box and labelled me, Caucasian male, medium build, Etcetera, Etcetera; it all spelt, stupid, stupid, stupid. Sometimes you couldn't categorize someone, because they didn't fit nicely into your box. I was different; they needed to see that, to truly understand what drove me.

The evidence they were using to profile me was corrupt. I had planted too much evidence and falsified a lot too. The weights I had used in my shoes, Fred, none of it pointed to a woman of my build. In fact, the police were that busy looking for a man, that I bet that they had never stopped to consider that these killings were actually being made by just one person; a woman.

Abigail and Susie made up for Tracy's lack of vocal ability. For once Abigail didn't feel the need to elaborate and kept to the facts. It could be that it was because she was talking to the police and not the captive audience at Hopscotch's. Or, and I preferred this scenario, I had done such a splendid job, that there was no need to elaborate further. You can't beat perfection.

The sun was coming up by the time that the police dropped the trio home. They had all decided to stay at Tracy's given the mess she was in. Susie had mentioned ringing Richard later in the day.

I couldn't wait for that conversation.

I was now taking a lot more interest in Richard.

Tracy was in a bad way, what better time to kill Richard, strike before she had time to recover properly.

I looked at their sleeping forms. They made quite a little puppy pile, all snuggled up in Tracy's big bed. The sun was now high in the sky; the blackout blind and heavy cream curtains kept the sun out of the bedroom. I let my imagination take me, as I contemplated what it would be like to kill them as they slept. Would one of them wake up and start screaming, as they watched me slice my way through their friend. Maybe then they would notice me, by which time it would be too late for them. I had become quite clever at hiding myself from everyone. The only ones that saw me were the ones I wanted to see me and all of them were dead. I was a true ghost, communicating with a select few.

My eyes ran across the thick pile carpet. Its beige density took on a dark stain as the blood ran across it. I shook my head; no, the bedroom would be out. I liked to see the pool of blood form, to watch it as it spread out its sticky dark fingers. A carpet would absorb it and stop its journey long before it had begun. Blood once it left the body deserved to run free. I smiled, just like me. I deserved to be free too.

Abigail began snoring. Unconsciously Susie gave her a push. Abigail rolled over onto her side, her short-bobbed hair fell across her face. Lucky for all of them, they spent that much time together that they had spare clothes and a toothbrush at Tracy's. Some may look at the trio and see good friends, friends that truly cared for each other. Me, well, all I saw was stupidity. Tracy was like a noose around their necks. Right now, they could be sleeping in their own beds. But no, because of Tracy they were here, with me.

I smiled. I could be their liberator.

Saving them from Tracy and her pathetic needy ways.

I thought back to how they would react if they woke and saw me watching them, knife in hand. I could almost hear their screams. Karen's kill had been the best. I wanted to feel that way again. I needed to feel that way again. The problem was, that I didn't think that either Susie or Abigail would be able to show the same strength of will that Karen had. They would scream and blubber. No hate. Just fear. Borrrrringgggg....

I tapped the cold steel against my palm. Lightly I ran the flat side of the blade along Susie's exposed leg where the duvet had fallen away. Susie wore a pair of check pink pyjama shorts and a vest top with support. I didn't think that the support was doing a good job. Her blonde hair fell over the end of the bed. Her leg twitched as the cold steel softly touched her skin. Goosebumps formed where the flat edge touched. No blood spurted to the surface but still, I felt a certain satisfaction at the way the skin tightened under the steel.

Abigail threw an arm over her head and snorted. Susie pushed her again. This time Abigail stayed where she was. I retreated back into the shadows as Susie pushed at Abigail who continued to snore. "Stop it." Susie's harsh whisper echoed into the semi darkness.

Abigail didn't react; instead, if possible, she began snoring louder. Susie gave her a swift kick, tucking her leg under the duvet to ensure that she met flesh. "Stop it."

Abigail's eye flew open. She sent Susie a hard look. "Stop kicking me, I'm not doing anything."

"Yes, you are, you're snoring." Abigail had closed her eyes again, sleep claiming her. One loud snore came from Abigail's open mouth. Susie, now wide awake gave Abigail a big shove. Abigail rocked onto her side and snored again at full throttle. Susie followed thru with a kick, as Abigail's body began to rock onto her back. Snore, snore, snore, it filled the bedroom like a fog horn warning others to be careful, to be safe. From the look on Susie's face, I was beginning to get concerned for Abigail's safety. Susie nipped Abigail's arm as she let out a long loud snore.

"Ow!" Abigail was now awake, and looking at Susie, annoyance painted across her sleepy face.

"You were snoring," Susie announced.

"I don't snore."

"Yeah, you just keep telling yourself that."

Tracy stirred. "What's wrong?"

"Abigail was snoring."

"Was not!"

"How would you know, you were asleep." Good point Susie.

"I've never had any complaints before."

Susie sent Abigail a pained look. "I've told you loads of times."

"Yeah, but that's only you, no one else has complained. Tracy never notices. I think it's all in your head."

"I could think of a ton of things I'd rather have in my head than your snoring."

"What time is it?" Tracy asked.

Susie leant back to look at the clock on the bedside table to her left. "Eleven."

Abigail flopped down on the bed with a groan. "I'm knackered."

"Yeah, well you want to try being knackered and being woken up by someone snoring in your ear."

"I wasn't *snoring.*"

Tracy climbed out of bed. "I'll go put the kettle on and light the fire." Grabbing the towelling dressing gown from the bedroom door, she tied the pale blue ties tight across her body.

The bedroom was a decent size; the super-king bed didn't look out of place. A triple sized white painted wardrobe with a set of three drawers underneath sat across the back wall, and in the corner near the window sat a white dressing table, cluttered with make-up, creams and perfume. There was a textured cream and pale gold wallpaper at the head of the bed, making a feature wall. The room was feminine without the flowers. The bedding where Susie and Abigail still laid wrapped up, was a soft cream, a gold faux fur throw that would normally have sat at the end of the bed now lay on the floor.

"What do you have in the way of food?" Abigail asked, hopefully.

"Richard's just been shopping so there's all sorts of things." Bloody Richard, was Tracy ever going to wake up and see how irritating he really was. He was way too thoughtful and full of crap.

"Do you have any crumpets, or teacakes? How about bacon? A bacon butty would be good."

"I'll go look." The door closed softly as Tracy made her way downstairs.

It took her thirty minutes to get the fire lit and the bacon under the grill. Her fingers still shook a little and I could tell from the dark circles under her eyes that she'd had little sleep.

I liked seeing her like this. It made me happy.

Susie and Abigail came into the living room as Tracy walked through from the kitchen. The tray she carried was stacked with bacon butties, and steaming cups of tea.

Abigail reached across and snagged a butty, she moaned with joy as she bit into the soft bread bun. Susie wasted no time in snagging her own butty. No one had eaten last night and I could hear their stomachs groan as the smell of bacon assailed their nostrils and food finally found its way into their tummies. Abigail licked her lips, and looked longingly at the last butty. You couldn't afford to dither if Abigail was in the room with food. Tracy sat down on the opposite sofa closest to the fire, and drank her tea.

"You not going to eat that?" Abigail asked as she pointed to Tracy's butty.

Tracy shook her head. "I don't feel hungry."

"You've got to eat," Susie mumbled as she chewed on a mouth full of butty.

"It's OK, I'll eat something later." Abigail didn't need any more encouragement and picked up the butty.

Tracy's hands began to shake as she raised the mug to her lips. "You OK?" Susie asked as she watched the tea spill onto Tracy's hand.

I felt like shaking the wreck of a woman and telling her to get a grip. I had no patience for such emotions. Regret was for fools. The only thing I ever regretted was waiting so long to end Tracy's miserable existence. Still, I couldn't call it true regret, because sometimes waiting made everything worthwhile. It built up the sweet anticipation, the thrill of the kill.

Since killing Karen and watching Susie and Abigail sleep, I had decided to kill Richard in three days' time. Why three days, well Richard had developed the habit of staying over at Tracy's on a Thursday. I didn't have any research to do, I'd watched the pair of them for so long that I knew their routines.

A knock sounded at the front door. Tracy stiffened at the sound.

"I'll get it, you stay there. It's probably Richard. I sent him a text while you were getting breakfast." Susie swung her legs off the sofa and walked towards the front door.

I heard Richard's voice and tried not to let it irritate me. He walked into the living room. Tracy sent him a small strained smile as he glided over to her, arms open wide.

"Come here you." Tracy lent into him as he sat down, his arms snaking round her back and hugging her tight. Tracy began to cry softly into Richard's chest.

Richard was dressed in his work clothes. Dark grey pinstripe trousers with a deep purple shirt and black striped silk tie.

Susie came back into the room after hanging Richard's black down jacket on the peg with the rest of their coats.

"How are you two doing?" Richard asked as he held Tracy tight. Tracy snuggled deeper into Richard, sniffing. My eyes reduced to slits as I watched Tracy take strength from Richard's embrace.

"Fine. Tired. It was a long night after we'd given our statements to the police. I think we were lucky that there was a policeman living in the ground floor flat. He confirmed our story," Susie said as she sipped on her tea.

"It was awful, poor Karen." Abigail added. "Susie's right, if it hadn't been for that policeman chap, we could be sat in a cell right now."

"I think you're stretching it a bit there Abs." Susie snorted into her mug.

"No, I'm not." Abigail shook her head venomously. "Without that chap, I don't think they would have believed us."

"They wouldn't have locked you up because you found Karen. They would have taken your statement, much like they did last night and then checked your story. Let's face it, we don't really look like serial killers now do we?" I looked at them and wondered what Susie thought serial killers looked like. Big and mean, with beefy arms and a scar along their cheeks; someone should alert the police to this. Ha, ha, ha.

"Since when do you know so much about police procedure?" Abigail asked as she swallowed the last of Tracy's butty.

"I don't but a little common sense helps."

Richard looked at Abigail and Susie as though he was watching a Ping-Pong match. "Anyway," Abigail said. "I don't think that serial killers go around with a label on them saying, *'hey, I'm a serial killer, watch out!'*" Abigail sighed. "It would really help if they did, wouldn't it? The police wouldn't suspect us of anything then, would they?"

"Oh, come on Abs. Karen had obviously been dead some time. We'd only been there a matter of minutes. I don't think that constitutes murder. Nor, were we covered in blood." Susie shook her head. "I think you watch too many movies."

Their constant bickering seemed to soothe them, made everything seem normal. As though they hadn't walked in to find Karen's bloodied dead body strapped to a chair. I'd have felt annoyed; however, I had become accustomed to the pair, so I ignored their bickering and took note instead at what they weren't saying, like the fact that this was the second person at Hopscotch's to be killed.

Susie gave a shudder, her eyes lost focus and for a split second, she was back in Karen's living room. Susie didn't say anything but from the look on her face, it was obvious where her thoughts had drifted to. I drank in the emotion.

Susie's eyes were still a little unfocused when she spoke. "I rang work earlier, told them what had happened. The police were already there asking questions. They seemed OK with us having a few days off. You know, to come to terms with everything."

"I don't know how we're supposed to come to terms with it. I don't think I will ever forget seeing Karen in that Kitchen. And those dogs, covered in her blood, it gives me the creeps just thinking about it," Abigail said as she sipped her tea. "It was awful, just awful. Tracy's not been right since." Everyone looked at Tracy. Her eyes had glazed over and it was obvious to everyone that she was trying hard to forget what she had seen.

Richard gave Tracy's shoulders a squeeze. "It's OK, love," he whispered into her ear, as his hand gently moved her dark brown hair away from her face.

"You know what I don't get. Why Karen? What did she do? It's freaky. How did she get chosen?" Abigail pondered.

"I don't know. I guess that's what the police will be looking at right now." Richard said. "This is the second person from Hopstocks to be killed by this Slasher chap isn't it. I assume it can't be a coincidence."

"You're right." Abigail nodded her head in agreement. "Do you think that Slasher is targeting us?" I raised my eyebrows at the intimate way that my serial killer name was being bandied about. Someone would think that we all knew each other. I knew them, knew their stupid little routines, knew what made them happy, what made them sad. I knew everything about them. They knew nothing about me. *Nothing.* Not one of them had bothered to recognise my existence, never paid me any attention. I lived in this house with Tracy, and they never even saw me.

"We could be next on his list." Abigail paled. "Do you think we should hand in our notice, go work somewhere else?"

"I think you're getting ahead of yourself, Abs. There's nothing to suggest that the staff at Hopstocks are being targeted. Karen and Mrs H's death could just be a matter of circumstance, a coincidence. Maybe, there's something else linking them together rather than Hopstocks." I smiled looking at Tracy, yeah, you could say that.

"The other killings weren't related to Hopstocks. This could be a new development. Susie's probably right; something else probably links them all together." Richard said.

"What, like they all attended the same step class or something?"

Susie sighed. "You're being silly now, Abs. No matter how hard I try, I just can't see Mrs H and Karen in a step class together. Actually, scrub that. I can't see either of them attending anything together." Susie tilted her head to the left in thought.

"It's up to the police to find the link. Till then I think we should all stick together, safety in numbers, and all that." I didn't like the sound of that. The only thing I wanted right now was to get the next few days over with so that I could kill Richard.

"What, we move in together?" Abigail raised the question that interested me the most. "You said that Slasher wasn't targeting staff at Hopstocks, so why do we need to start living together?"

Susie put her empty mug down on the table. "I don't. But there has to be a link somewhere. All I'm saying is it wouldn't hurt for us to stick close to each other for a while, just until the police can look into this. Besides, would it be that bad?" Susie looked at Abigail's horrified face. I felt her pain. "We were the ones that found Karen, Abs, who knows what the fallout from that will be. Would it really hurt living together for a few weeks?"

Silently I screamed *YES!*

"We have locks on our front doors for a reason." Abigail grumbled.

Susie sent Abigail a stern look. "So did Karen and look what happened to her." Silence filled the room.

"OK, so, if we move in together, how long are we going to be together for? Tracy only has one bedroom as she lets her second room out to the mysterious Lauren."

"Careful Abs, you're starting to sound bitchy." Susie warned. "I don't know what your problem is."

Abigail slumped in the sofa. "I just don't like the idea of having to give up my freedom."

"I'm not your mother."

"I know, I know, I guess I'm just scared. That's probably it. The thought of living together, it's like admitting that it could have been one of us, not just Karen. Is it wrong to think, thank God her and not me, or you, or Tracy?"

Susie reached across the sofa and squeezed Abigail's hand. "It's OK Abs, if we're honest, we're all thinking the same thing." Abigail gave her a watery smile. Personally, I couldn't understand how Susie had made the leap, connecting Karen's death to them all living together. I'd only killed Karen. I hadn't left a note, saying you're next Stupid Susie. I just couldn't understand why Susie felt that I was interested in either of them. Well, that's not true. I was very interested in Tracy but at the moment, had no intention of killing Susie or Abigail. It just made me mad that they couldn't see this and was now about to scupper my plans to kill Richard on Thursday. My hands shook as rage filled me. Could nothing go right with this lot? Could they not just go back to living their stupid lives and leave my plans alone.

"I'm in a one-bed flat," Susie said. "Which isn't what you'd call spacious, so my place would be worse than Tracy's. The only other place is yours, Abs. You've got two rooms, Tracy and I could bunk in your spare."

Abigail shook her head. "Na, that's not going to work. The roof leaked in the spare room and the rooms a mess. I'm waiting for everything to dry out. I guess Tracy's is the best place for us all to bunker down in."

They both looked at Tracy. "Are you OK with this?" Susie asked.

Tracy looked at them. Whatever she saw on their faces seemed to shake her out of her stupor. "Sorry, yes that's fine. I'll slip a note under Lauren's door so that she knows you'll be staying over for a while. I can always sleep on the sofa down here to give us a bit more room." As bad situations went, Tracy sleeping on the sofa would give me a little more wriggle room. It wouldn't help me in killing Richard. That one would have to wait. I'd have to find someone else to kill while I waited for things to get back to normal.

Tracy looked down at her hands, they shook a little. "You know, you're both right about Lauren. If the money didn't keep going into my bank account each month, I'd start to wonder if she really existed." Tracy rose. "I'll make us all another drink. Then we should start to get things sorted. If you're both staying here for a while, then we need to pick some clothes up."

"I'll get some more food in for the three of you." Richard said, though I had the feeling this was more directed at Abigail.

Tracy smiled at Richard. "You OK with this."

"Don't worry about it, it's not forever and we'll be back to normal again soon."

Tracy leant over and placed a soft kiss on his lips. "Thanks."

"Did you say you had some crumpets or tea cakes?" Abigail asked.

"You've only just had breakfast." Susie pointed out.

"That was hours ago." Susie held up her hands and mouthed ten minutes. "And worry makes me hungry."

"Everything makes you hungry."

"There's nothing wrong with a good appetite." Tracy laughed, "I'll see what I've got."

Richard stood up. "Come on I'll give you a hand."

"Shouldn't you get back to work?"

"No, they're not expecting me back. I explained everything to them." I watched Tracy and Richard as they walked into the kitchen.

Mad didn't even come close to how I felt right now. I wanted to kill them all, stick my knife into their flesh and make sure that none of them had the opportunity to scupper my plans again.

There was no such thing as safety in numbers. I could drop them all a pill, send them to sleep and kill them before they woke up. And right now, that is exactly what I wanted to do.

I paced like a tiger trapped in a cage, my rage bouncing off the iron bars that held me.

I'd be free, I would.

Chapter Fourteen

"You've got Susie, and her *'let's stick together'* plan to thank for this." I looked at the man in front of me. His hands were zip tied to the black faux leather office chair. The man's arms sank into the soft leather arms, the leather acting as a cushion. It didn't stop the plastic zip strips from digging into his skin. One of the best inventions ever were zip strips. They were easy to use, kept the victim in place and I could tighten them real tight, letting the plastic bite into the skin with ease. I wonder if the person that designed them liked killing people too. I'd used rope and silk ties and anything else I could find to tie a person down. Zip strips were my favourite. They were light to carry around and not at all bulky, unlike rope.

Wide cherry brown eyes stared at me in fear. I'd stuffed a sock in his mouth and taped his lips together, other than the odd muffled mmm, mmm, nothing was coming out. At six-foot something and as wide as a tank, the office chair on casters had been a real find.

The pill I'd slipped him had sent him into darkness quickly and I had wasted no time in appraising and assessing my surroundings. I couldn't afford to be sloppy, besides it wasn't my style.

Opportunity had presented itself and since I wasn't in the best of moods, I wasn't going to pass it up. The man in front of me had been drooling over Tracy for some time. He had been way too subtle in letting her know how much he liked her. The odd stumbled comment as Tracy had gone to the gym with Susie and Abigail. Susie had once mentioned it to her, but Tracy being Tracy had laughed it off as nothing.

Since Tracy had hooked up with Richard, the poor sod didn't even get a look in. I felt it only fair that I remove his misery and kill him. Who wanted to see someone they really liked, going out with someone other than them? No one, that's who. Well, there was no need for this chap to put on a brave face anymore when he saw Tracy. *'Brave face'*, such a stupid expression, bravery if you ask me, was doing something about your situation, not putting a smile on your lips and saying look at me I'm happy; *no, really I am.*

Stripping him out of his black jogging bottoms had been easy, made easier as the guy didn't wear underwear. The loose fitting purple t-shirt and green hoody had taken some working at but I had got there in the end.

Leaving the discarded clothes on his bedroom floor, I'd pushed him like a baby in a pram into the kitchen, which was stacked high with dirty pots and pans. This guy obviously didn't have any objection to living in a slum. It was like walking into a student flat. The apartment smelt of stale food and sweat. Judging by the amount of clothes lying around the place, the washer must be broke, either that or personal hygiene wasn't important to him. I hated people like this. It was as if they had given up on life. No self-respect. What kind of life was it? I was doing him a big favour today.

"All I wanted to do was kill Richard, and watch Tracy crumble but *nooo*, Susie had to spoil things. I can't just sit around and wait for them to decide the threat's over and they can all go back to their own homes. It could take forever, especially as I've

179

already killed two employees from Hopscotch's." I waved the knife in the air as I spoke; his eyes followed the steel blade back and forth. "I have to tell you, I was not happy with Susie's decision. Why did she think that I was going to kill them? Well I might, but that's beside the point. I wasn't planning on killing them *now*, maybe later." I shrugged. "You could consider yourself a diversion." I smiled at the man in front of me sweetly. From the sweat trickling down his forehead, he didn't look comforted. Ah well.

I watched as he tried to push the chair back. "That isn't going to work." I pointed at his feet. "Wooden floor boards, you've just got to love them, I know I do."

The man was tied to the chair good and tight and was unable to appreciate the fact that his feet were nailed to the floor. Still I could appreciate it.

"Henry Watts, isn't it?" He nodded his head. I'd got his full name off the unopened mail sitting on the kitchen work surface. "Henry, today you're going to die." I liked the sound of that. Henry however didn't, and started struggling and mumbling in earnest. I stood back and watched him. My glance slid to Fred who I had positioned at the back of Henry. I'd had time to blow him completely up so he matched Henry in height and stature.

I shook my head. "Henry, Henry, Henry, you aren't going anywhere. All this energy, it's such a waste. Why don't you try a different emotion?" I thought back to Karen and the hate that burned in her eyes. Henry wasn't a patch on her, and I knew long before I touched the blade of my knife to his flesh, that Henry would be whimpering like a baby – hence the sock and sticky tape. I didn't want anyone hearing his pathetic screams.

"You're such a disappointment. Where's the fight, the need to survive, to succeed." I looked round his flat. "Yeah, there isn't any, is there. I knew that when I walked into your flat." I spread my arms wide. "You invited me in, into this mess and expected me to be what, be grateful?" I shook my head at him. "It wasn't going to happen Henry, not the way you wanted it to."

I bent so that our noses almost touched. "Henry, life left you a long time ago. What happened to you? Was it some girl? Or was it mummy and daddy, didn't they spend enough time with you? This isn't living Henry."

The flat was pokey, made even more so by all the clutter of dirty clothes and unwashed pots. The kitchen and living area shared a space. The one bedroom fared no better. There was no need for a wardrobe given Henry's need to throw his clothes around, so I hadn't been surprised not to find one. The bed took up all the room there was in the bedroom. The sheets were dirty, the bed unmade. The fact that Henry hadn't seen a problem in trying to get me into that bed, even in its current state, told me he had very low self-esteem. Still, there was no need for him to think that I would stoop to his level. Henry may not have standards but I did.

Giving him the pill had been easy. I'd put it in the wine I'd brought with me. Henry had been so desperate that I don't think he even stopped to process what was really going on. His intentions were plain he wanted my knickers off, legs spread. Getting him to drink the drugged wine was effortless. No drinky, no sex. He'd slugged the large glass of wine down his neck so fast, that I had taken the opportunity to re-fill it for him while not touching my own. By the time the drug hit him, it was all too late. I had remained fully clothed and untouched. Worthless piece of shit wasn't getting his hands on me.

Without warning I raised my left arm and brought the blade slithering down his head. Henry was bald and I have to admit, I hadn't really thought about how much of a turn on it would be to see the trail of blood as it ran from all angles down his head. Within seconds Henry looked like a bloody waterfall.

It was gorgeous.

Perfect.

Maybe he wasn't so worthless.

Henry whimpered and I shut him out as I began my dance, feet moving blade cutting. Blood flew everywhere, splattering on Fred, the walls, the ceiling, falling onto the floor, droplets merging, becoming one. The sheer beauty of it caught me, and my dance and my tempo increased. At some point, Henry had lost consciousness. Irritation seized me and I stopped my dance waiting for him to wake up, before I made my last cut.

It took Henry nearly an hour to wake. I watched as the light faded and darkness encroached. His eyelashes fluttered. He looked dazed, confused, as he looked around the room. His eyes fell on me and in a split-second reality came rushing back. There was no escape. Today really was going to be his last. Fear gripped Henry, eyes wide, darting wildly around the room. Silly, silly, boy, hadn't worked out yet, there was no escape.

Henry wiggled that much that the nails in his feet started to rip his skin. Fresh blood came rushing to the surface. I wasted no time. I took the knife and ran it along his left forearm in one long deep slice. Blood came quickly. I spun the knife and repeated the cut on Henry's right arm. Again, blood came thick and strong, as though it had been waiting for this opportunity to escape. Henry looked at the blood and started whimpering. Rage filled me. Henry, like the others, didn't appreciate me.

Without thought I took hold of his head bending it back against my chest. I took the knife and slit his throat. Blood poured and flew around the room, coating, dripping, sticking to each and every surface. Henry lost consciousness and I watched the blood as it ran like a river down his body, over the chair, onto the floor.

I took a shaky breath. Henry might not have been able to give me what Karen had, but his blood was just as beautiful. My blood cooled; my rage dissipating. I was spent.

I took a deep breath. My eyes never left the blood. It seemed to speak to me, to thank me for releasing it. I nodded my head in acknowledgement.

When the blood stopped flowing I sank to my knees. The blood within my veins slowed down, as my heart rate returned to normal. Time slipped by and I became conscious of Tracy. It was time to start cleaning up.

An hour later I had everything packed away. I turned to Henry, his lifeless body slumped on the chair. His life hadn't been a complete waste after all. Thanks to me, he would be remembered.

I picked up my large black handbag and made my way to the door. I'd taken longer in the clean-up than normal; it wasn't easy cleaning and making the place look dirty at the same time. Before I closed the door on Henry, I took a minute to envisage the CSI crew in their white overalls and little booties, putting down markers, taking photographs. With a smile, I decided to leave them a little something. I took off my right glove and picked up Henry's water bottle, the one he took to the gym. I wrapped my fingers around its body before setting it back on top of his gym bag. Let the CSI make something of that.

I smiled, oh Tracy, you haven't got a clue what's coming, do you.

Silently I closed the door behind me and walked down the stairs. The blackness of the night sky enclosed around me, with my long black curly wig, and black workout leggings and fitted coat, I blended nicely into the night. My black trainers' silent on the damp pavement.

Henry's death had brightened my mood, however the closer I got to Tracy's the darker it became.

Within three quarters of an hour, I stood outside Tracy's house. No lights were on, which meant that everyone would be asleep. Quietly I opened the front door and slipped inside.

Without thought I walked upstairs and opened Tracy's bedroom door. Abigail and Susie were fast asleep in Tracy's bed. I looked at the pair, so cosy, so secure that nothing would hurt them while they were together.

Such fools.

There was no such thing as 'safe'. Why did they not see the monster that lurked in the shadows? Feel death as it stretched out its fingers towards them. I snatched my hand back as Susie stirred. One day; one day, they would see me, and then, well by then, it would be time for them to die.

Freedom was coming, I could feel it. It was no longer laughing in my face. Now, now it was beckoning me, welcoming me.

For the first time in what felt like weeks, I smiled, really smiled.

I looked at the sleeping friends. Yes, soon very soon there would be no need for me to hide. I would be free.

Richard would soon be dead and Tracy would be gone, and then Susie and Abigail would soon find out just exactly who had been following them around.

Ha, has, ha. I walked into my bedroom and closed the door.

Chapter Fifteen

A knock at the door woke Tracy.

I watched her as she pushed the hair out of her face and stumbled off the sofa, sinking her feet into her sheepskin mule slippers and rearranging her striped pink and purple pyjamas. The knock on the door increased its intensity.

I could hear Susie and Abigail moving around upstairs; from the sternness in Susie's voice, I would say that she wasn't too happy about being woken up on her day off, at nine thirty in the morning.

Tracy opened the door to find the police standing on her doorstep. This could be interesting. I thought back to the finger prints I had left behind on Henry's water bottle and smiled to myself.

Susie came stomping down the stairs in her short pyjamas and flimsy top. Her boobs bobbed about out of control as she made her way to the door. Whatever she was about to say died on her lips as she saw the police standing outside.

Abigail followed like some Hollywood vision. Her black silk lace nightie and silk black dressing gown fell to her feet in a pool of ink. Her hair swung about her jaw line, her eyes widening in shock.

"Sorry to disturb you. I just have a few questions." The detective said flashing his ID. He was the only one not dressed in the age old black uniform of a policeman, but wore a long navy woollen coat. His patient black shoes shone in the dim morning light.

Tracy looked at the man, her stunned silence continuing past what would be thought comfortable.

Susie reached across Tracy. "Would you like to come in?"

"Thank you." Susie took the door out of Tracy's numb fingers and opened it further, allowing the detective and his crew to enter Tracy's house.

The front door closing seemed to wake Tracy from her stupor. Abigail leaned into her. "What do you think they want?"

"I don't know?" Tracy's voice was unsteady, as she and Abigail followed Susie and the police into her living room.

Quickly dashing round everyone, Tracy picked up the duvet and pillow off the sofa. "Sorry, would you like to sit down. I can put the kettle on, make you a drink, if you would like that."

"I don't think they're here for a social chit chat Tracy," Susie said dryly as she stood watching the police take a seat on the sofa. Automatically Susie, Abigail and Tracy sat on the opposite sofa, their bums perched on the edge.

"We had another murder three weeks ago," the detective said, his beady blue eyes watching for a reaction. He had undone his coat to reveal dark grey pants and a light grey shirt, with a navy blue tie. His brown hair stuck out at all angles and would have benefited from some styling gel. Stubble shadowed his jaw line.

"Oh, my God!" Abigail breathed, if not a little too dramatically.

"What does this have to do with us?" Susie asked, recovering from her shock at seeing the police standing on the doorstep. Her voice didn't sound too friendly. "It's not that I'm unconcerned, but I'm just wondering. Was it someone from Hopstocks?"

"No, the latest victim didn't work at Hopstocks." Judging by the sullenness in his voice, the detective here wasn't happy about my killing Henry. It took away the precious link they had formed to Hopscotch's.

"So, what's it got to do with us?" A scowl was beginning to line Susie's forehead. She was probably thinking about going back to bed.

The detective shot Susie an unfriendly stare. Susie stared back. This act of defiance made me think back to Karen. I could feel a sweep of joy take hold of me; could it be possible that Susie would be just like Karen? Hate and anger radiating from her eyes as I dug the knife into her flesh. Suddenly I felt very interested in Susie.

"We're just checking into a few things, eliminating people from our enquiries. It's all standard procedure, I assure you." Susie didn't look reassured, in fact she looked put out. She was not known for her morning cheerfulness.

"Who was it that died? Do you think it was Slasher?" I think Abigail was misunderstanding the process. The police asked the questions. "Oh, my God, was it someone we knew? Do you think that we'll be next?"

Susie gripped Abigail's arm. "OK, OK take a breath and calm down." Susie shot a look at Tracy. "You'd better get the biscuits out, if she's eating she's not hyperventilating."

"Good idea." Tracy shot off the sofa and before the detective could say anything, was in the kitchen grabbing packets of biscuits.

As soon as the biscuits hit the table, Abigail grabbed at one of the packets tearing open the packaging. The detective watched and waited, a look of impatience had fallen across his face. I couldn't blame him; he was the one that was supposed to be in charge here.

"The victim was Henry Watts." Empty stares met him.

"Never heard of him." Abigail spat biscuit crumbs at the detective. "What about you two?" Susie and Tracy shook their heads, indicating that the name didn't sound familiar to them.

The detective reached into the pocket of his coat and took out a photo. "What about now?"

Susie lent forward and took the photo. "That's Tanker."

"Tanker?" the detective asked.

Abigail opened her mouth to speak and biscuit crumbs began to rain down on everyone. "Yeah, Susie calls him that coz he's built like one, and when he starts lifting weights he makes this click, click sound. Susie says it's like the gun thing on a tank moving. Not that we've actually been in a tank, or seen one. But Susie's brother had this toy tank that made the clicking noise, when the gun on the tank moved."

Susie patted Abigail's arm. "Have another biscuit, you've only eaten six."

"Is that who was killed last night?" Tracy asked, her eyes never leaving the photograph.

"No, it was his brother, that's why the detective here is showing us Tanker's photo."

"I think you're being bitchy, Susie." Biscuit crumbs covered Susie.

"Sorry, just irritable. It's lack of sleep." Susie shot a look at the detective.

"How do you know Henry Watts?"

"He goes to the same gym as us," Susie said.

The detective turned to Tracy. "Your fingerprints were found on his water bottle." Tracy paled.

Abigail shook her head, letting out a sigh. "See Tracy, I told you to leave it where it fell. But you had to pick it up and give it to him. Sometimes you're too nice. Before you know it, the detective here will be accusing you of killing Tanker and being the Slasher." Abigail reached for another biscuit. "My throats getting dry; I think we should have a cuppa."

Tracy stood up. "I'll put the kettle on. Is that OK with you, Detective?"

The detective nodded his agreement, not that he had much of a choice.

Susie's voice carried across the room. "We named Tanker, Tanker for a reason, Abs. I don't think for one second, that Tracy or either of us would be able to move him, never mind lift him anywhere. I bet he'd be a dead weight." Susie blanched. "Sorry, I didn't mean…well, you know…that cuppa nearly ready Tracy?" I shook my head. It may come as quite a surprise to Susie and Abigail, what people are actually capable of. Looking at the expression that crossed the detective's face, he'd seen enough to know what people were more than capable of. Even people like vulnerable, likeable, fragile Tracy.

The kitchen door opened and Tracy walked in with a tray filled with chinking mugs, a jug of milk and an overflowing teapot. The detective hadn't seen her as a flight risk and had allowed Tracy to enter the kitchen, without being accompanied by the uniformed policeman that had begun to wander around the room. Even I had a hard job envisaging Tracy racing out the back door, throwing her cotton pyjama clad body over the five-foot brick wall, and running for escape in her sheepskin mules. The ice and the thin layer of snow that covered the ground could have had something to do with it. Either that or the detective felt that her cotton pyjamas were no match for the sub-zero conditions.

Abigail played mum and began pouring out the tea, offering a steaming cup to Susie and Tracy. "Sorry I don't know how you take yours, so I'll leave it up to you." The detective didn't move. Instead he sat silently watching them, assessing them. Maybe eliminating them from his enquires. Stupid policeman. Did no one see Tracy was the key to all the killings? Stupid, stupid, stupid. I could tell from the way he was looking at them, that he had already discounted them.

Susie leant back against the sofa, her boobs swayed against the fabric of her thin sleepwear. I watched the detective as his eyes slid across Susie to her breasts. If he wasn't careful, he'd end up with sea sickness, with no boat or water to blame it on, just Susie's boobs swaying back and forth.

Tracy walked over and picked Susie's cardigan up off the floor near the kitchen door where she'd left it. "Here I think you should wear this, it'll stop you from getting cold."

"I'm fine thanks."

Abigail took the cardigan. "I think Tracy was being tactful. Here put this on before one of those enhancements makes a beeline for freedom. We wouldn't want to embarrass folk." Abigail nodded her head toward the detective.

Susie grumbled but took the cardigan. The detective seemed to draw himself back to the present as Susie covered up. "Where were you all three weeks ago?"

Abigail gave a dramatic sigh. "Here. We're living together at the moment, you know, because we found Karen. Do you remember Karen Stillman? Yeah, of course you do. Anyway, Susie thought it was a good idea that we all stick together for a while, and Tracy's was the best place. I had a water leak upstairs so my place was out, and Susie's is a bit on the bijou side.

We got in from work at about six thirty. Didn't we?" Susie and Tracy nodded their heads.

'It was Susie's turn to make tea', so Tracy and I chilled in the living room. We watched a bit of TV then went to bed. What time was it? I'd say about eleven, that about right? Or was that the night that we went to bed early because you weren't feeling too good, Susie? No, let me think, yes, I helped Tracy with the laundry while you tended to your headache. So, we did have an early night. Susie doesn't like to be disturbed, so I had to go to bed when she did; apparently, I make a lot of noise when I go to bed. I can't help it if I have an electric tooth brush. "Got to look after them." Abigail tapped her teeth.

"My granddad has all his teeth and he's coming up to eighty-eight in September."

Susie looked at Abigail who had yet to draw breath. "That was insightful, Abs, if a little O.T.T."

The detective remained professional, but I could tell that he couldn't wait to leave. I found it interesting how Abigail's waffling had inadvertently removed them from the detectives' list of suspects.

"We'll be in touch if we need anything else." The detective stood up. Tracy followed him to the door, the policeman in uniform followed. As the uniform hadn't said anything the whole time he had been here, he had been forgotten. I knew how he felt.

Tracy walked back into the living room, a look of concern painted across her face. "What do you think?" She asked as she sunk down onto the sofa where the detective had sat.

"I think that despite Abs' obvious regret, I was right for us to stick together for a while. Do you know that this is the third person that Slasher has killed that we all know? I mean knew." Tracy's face lost some colour.

Abigail gave a snort. "Do you really believe that we're in danger? We didn't know Patrick Barnes. I would say that our link to Tanker is tenuous at best. There must be hundreds of people that go that gym, and many that knew him better than us." Abigail looked down at the table. "I've eaten all the biscuits."

"You sound shocked." Susie mumbled. "Well, it's not going to do my diet any good."

"I thought you weren't dieting anymore; you're an apple remember. You been lying to yourself again?"

Tracy smiled at Abigail. "I don't think it's that bad, maybe you're burning more calories, due to nervous energy."

Abigail pointed at Tracy and looked at Susie. "Just for the record, that's why I like her more than you. Tracy's always nice to me."

"No, it's because I always tell the truth and you don't like it. Truth is always best, remember Abs."

"Yeah well, on this occasion I'm going with nervous energy. Do you have any bacon or anything in? I could do with a butty right now."

"You know she's got some bacon, we all went shopping together. That said, if you're making one, I'll have one."

Tracy laughed. "Yeah, sure."

Abigail sat back against the sofa. "Do you want a hand?" Isn't it strange how words and body actions can be in such conflict?

"No, you're OK, I've got it."

"We'll get the fire sorted. Funny, but I don't feel like going to the gym today." Susie shouted at Tracy's retreating form.

"Me neither," Abigail echoed.

Tracy popped her head through the kitchen door. "Why don't we go out for the day? I know it's cold out there but if we wrap up warm? We could go out walking."

Susie sniffed. "You know I don't have any walking gear."

"You could borrow one of my down jackets," Tracy said.

Abigail looked from Tracy to Susie. "I don't think Susie would get one boob in one of your jackets, never mind two. She can have one of mine. We apples are more of the right size to accommodate Susie's enhancements."

"Why do I get the impression that I'm going walking whether I want to or not; I'm going to end up looking like you, aren't I?"

Abigail pushed herself off the sofa and started to clean out the fire. "You never know, you might just like it."

"What walking or looking like you."

"You'll be warm for the first time, since forever." Susie snorted a response to Abigail.

Tracy had propped the door to the kitchen open. "We're about the same shoe size, so you can borrow a pair of my walking boots. It'll be fun. I think we could do with it right now." Tracy turned the bacon over on the grill tray and put it back under. "Why do you think that Slasher killed Tanker?" That was easy, I had killed him because of Susie and her stupid idea, not that I think she would let that bother her, so long as they were safe.

Safe, there was no safety to be found, not when I was around. Maybe it was about time that I let them know that.

"Don't you think it's weird how the detective came here asking questions. Surely my finger prints couldn't have been the only ones on the water bottle."

"To know why Tanker was selected, I guess you'd have to be Slasher. Personally, I don't know." Susie was still sitting on the sofa. "I think you're over thinking the water bottle thing. If the detective is stupid enough to think that one of us could be Slasher then he needs to get a new career. Do we look like we belong to the bulging muscle brigade? And you would need a hell of a lot of muscle power to overcome Tanker." Not really; just some sleeping pills and a hell of a lot of determination. "I think they're just clutching at whatever they can, and since our fingerprints are on record since we found Karen and all, the police, would have had to have come here to question us, just so that they can get a picture of Tanker and all. They didn't need to come at this ungodly hour though."

"Aren't you supposed to be helping clean the fire out?" Abigail asked.

"I am helping."

"How?"

"I'm supervising. Come on, you need to speed up, the butties are nearly ready." Abigail muttered into the fire, as she scrunched up newspaper and added kindling and firelighters before putting a helping of coal on top.

The fire roared to life as Tracy walked into the living room with a tray stacked with butties. Abigail trailed behind her, a towel in her hands which were now free from soot.

"Do you think that they'll ever catch Slasher?" Abigail asked as she sat back down on the sofa with her butty.

"Eventually," Susie answered, grabbing her own butty.

"I hope you're right," Tracy whispered, more to herself than anyone else.

Susie looked at Tracy. "Don't worry they all get caught in the end."

"This isn't a movie Susie; this is for real. People we know are being killed."

"Thanks Abs, I hadn't worked that one out." Susie put down her butty. "Look, things are what they are; so long as we stick together we'll ride this out until the police find Slasher and lock him up." I laughed secretly to myself.

Don't you just love naivety?

It took Abigail and Tracy a further two hours before Susie agreed to go walking. They had more patience than me. Tracy had got her a pair of her spare walking boots and put them by the door in a plastic carrier bag, along with her own, ready to put in the car. Abigail was driving, more because all her walking stuff was already in the boot than for any other reason. It saved on the argument of who was crawling between the seats into the back. I don't think that Susie was into three door cars; too much effort. She was top heavy which didn't help. Considering Susie didn't have a car, and couldn't drive, you would think she would be grateful for the lift. Not Susie.

"Good grief, I swear it's getting colder out there." Abigail complained as she came trotting in with a down jacket for Susie slung over her arm. Susie had yet to make an appearance, and was probably still upstairs sulking.

"Come sit down by the fire, while Susie finishes getting ready," Tracy called.

"Susie does know that we're going walking, right? She's not decking herself out to go clubbing." Abigail grumbled as she walked into the living room.

Tracy sat on the sofa, a pair of dark grey fleece lined waterproof trousers on, and a long sleeved purple thermal top and matching fleece. Her hair was tied at the nape of her neck, a bobble hat sat on the coffee table along with a pair of thick thermal gloves and scarf. A light blue down jacket was laid across the arm of the opposite sofa with an extra pair of socks, to be put on when she put on her walking boots later.

Abigail shrugged out of her down jacket revealing a similar pair of trousers to Tracy's, her fleece was a vibrant pink. She flopped down on the sofa opposite Tracy and huffed. "How long can it take to put on a pair of trousers and top?" Abigail looked at her watch.

"I don't think it's getting the clothes on that's the problem, Susie has to come to terms with how she looks. And what can no longer be seen."

"It will do those enhancements of hers good to have a day off." The stairs creaked and both Abigail and Tracy turned their attention to the living room door, waiting for it to open.

Susie appeared; the look on her face told the world that she was unimpressed. The black waterproof fleece lined trousers Tracy had lent Susie were a couple of inches too short, but did the job. Abigail had added her own mark to Susie's attire, lending her a soft green fleece and matching thermal top. Clasped in Susie's hand was a pair of black thermal gloves and scarf. Her blonde hair hung loose down her back. She looked different, very different. Everything was covered up and for the first time Susie didn't look like she should be standing on a street corner earning a living.

In union Abigail and Tracy's eyes travelled down Susie's body. When they got to Susie's feet they broke down into fits of laughter. Susie's feet were clad in a pair of six-inch spiked ankle boots.

"That's it, I'm not going."

"S-s-sorry!" Abigail managed to say through her giggles. Tracy couldn't even manage that.

"It's not funny."

"Oh, but it is." Abigail wiped at the tears running down her face, grabbed her phone and took a picture of Susie.

"Don't you dare post that on Twitter!" Susie made a grab for the phone.

"I don't think that the shoes go." Tracy giggled.

Abigail showed Susie the photo. Susie looked at it, then down at her boots. "Oh." She started to laugh. Soon the living room was filled with the sound of laughter.

My mood suddenly turned very dark.

Chapter Sixteen

I hadn't killed anyone for four months now. I was betting that the police thought I had gone to ground. Well, I hadn't. I was exercising control which, let me tell you, was starting to slip. I needed Susie and Abigail out the house. Things were getting way too cosy, and I was finding it increasingly difficult to refrain from killing them all. That had never been part of my plan. Yes, Abigail and Susie's death would affect Tracy deeply, but Richard would still be there to pick up the shattered pieces.

No, Richard had to go first. His death would be more significant.

Tracy loved Richard.

She might not have acknowledged this feeling herself, still it was there. And well, what is it that they say about the *'power of love'*? Don't ask me, I don't get it. Still, I'd seen enough to know that it had a big impact on most people's behaviour.

Observe and learn; that was me.

I wanted Abigail and Susie to see me, to know what they had slept so close to, without knowing. To know that at any time I could have killed them. In living at Tracy's, they had put themselves in harm's way, in my way, in the way of Death. I wanted them to blame Tracy and leave her, severing their friendship.

Tracy would be alone. No Richard.

No Susie.

No Abigail.

Without them she would shatter and crumble. Tracy's family wouldn't be able to save her. They hadn't even been able to protect her from Uncle Kevin. Nor had they been able to put Tracy back together after Uncle Kevin had raped her.

I was going to kill Susie and Abigail together; one killing, one mess to clean up. It would be easier to compare their deaths that way. Would they try and save the other? Or was their friendship just for show. I was hoping that they would fight. I liked it when they fought back. My mind cast back to Karen. Yes, it would be good to kill like that again, to feel the hate, knowing that that was the last emotion they felt before they died.

Hate was intoxicating, and knowing that their hate would be for me, for what I was forcing them to go through, to experience. Knowing that they were going to die and yet never giving into their fear. It would be all for me, every little bit, all for me. I won't lie, it was empowering.

Mr and Mrs Bennett had tried to get Tracy help, tried to make her well again, '*normal*', but they hadn't been able to put Tracy back together. No one had. They had sent her to a psychiatrist when their love and support was what she had needed most. At some point, Tracy's mind had shattered into a million pieces. I don't think that even Tracy knew just how bad things had become in her head. Slowly she had found friendship and love. Abigail and Susie had given her the type of support and care that her mother and father hadn't been able to. And then along came Richard, with his easy smile and understanding ways.

Yes, I had a plan and as cranky as I felt right now, it would all be worth it. I just needed to keep control of my inner killer, for a little longer.

"This feels weird. I feel like I'm leaving home again." Abigail stood in the living room, her suitcase set to one side. I don't think that she had intended to blend in with her suitcase but she did. The maroon woollen jumper was the perfect match, her black jeans a twin in colour to the little wheels of her case and the handle.

"I thought you'd be relieved; you were never keen on my idea in the first place," Susie said from where she sat on the sofa. Unlike Abigail with her thick knitted jumper, Susie wore a thin jersey print top. The rose pattern with its soft reds and pinks, suited her complexion and the cut of the neckline was low enough that it showed off the soft swell of her breasts. The hem of the black leather pants rested on a pair of six-inch black ankle boots. It made her legs go on for miles. Still the outfit was not fit for the cool spring climate. But then, Susie hadn't worn a jumper when snow had fallen, and ice had coated everything it touched.

England was not known for its soaring temperatures. We were now heading into spring, having left winter behind with its heavy snowfall and freezing temperatures. England was an island blessed with a lot of rainfall and interchangeable weather. We were a very green county for a reason. Susie dressed like she lived in Melbourne, Australia, where the temperature rarely reached freezing.

I liked the change in seasons. I always felt as though I was shaking off an old coat as winter changed to spring. Colour was everywhere and it made me want to paint my own picture, add a splash of red.

"Yeah, well I've got used to it now."

"You do know you're hard to please, right?" Susie asked.

Tracy laughed. "Come on Abs, you'll get back into that house of yours and this will be a distant memory."

"Well, I for one won't miss your snoring."

"You're so mean Susie, you know I don't snore. I think it's you that snores and you like to blame it on me."

Susie rolled her eyes. "Oh, if only that were true."

Abigail stuck her tongue out. "Anyway, moving on, so where is Richard taking you tonight?"

Tracy's face lit up like she had been plugged into an electric socket and someone had exchanged her head for a two-thousand-watt light bulb. Sickening, that's what it was. "I don't know; he wanted it to be a surprise. He just said to wear something nice."

"Something *nice!* That could mean anything." Abigail looked horrified at the thought of *'nice'*. "Men, it's OK for them. All they have to do is put on a pair of trousers and a shirt and the jobs' done. Something *'nice'* to us girls could mean anything. Do you wear a dress, a little black halter neck sexy number, or go for something a little more classic, like a shift dress? Then, do you wear a dress at all? Maybe trousers would be better, something fitted with a chiffon shirt. Or do you wear a skirt, and then there's the problem of what to wear on top. Nice, really doesn't say a lot, does it?"

Tracy lost some of her colour. She sat down on the sofa next to Susie and looked across at Abigail. "I was going to wear the red LK Bennett shift dress I bought last year. Now, I'm not sure."

Susie patted Tracy on the legs. "The LK Bennett dress is fabulous and you look great in it. It's a classic, and will fit in well for whatever *'nice'* Richard has planned. Anyway, I remember the last time you wore it, I don't think Richard could take his eyes off you. What do you say Abs?"

"I guess that could fit the bill as *'something nice'*." I could tell that Abigail wasn't so sure. If it was up to her, she would have Tracy trudging round the shops buying several outfits, so that whatever *'nice'* turned out to be, Tracy would have an outfit to suit.

Susie rose from the sofa. "Come on you, we need to get going. Tracy needs to start getting ready."

Abigail looked at her watch. "Richard isn't due for another four hours."

"Yeah, and your point is?"

Abigail opened her mouth to say something, and then changed her mind. "OK, come on then."

The house felt strangely quiet when the front door closed behind Abigail and Susie. For a start, I could hear myself think, without the constant stream of chatter that emitted from Abigail's mouth. It got me thinking about tonight. Was there more going on here than I thought? This was the first time that Richard would be staying over at Tracy's in months, and while Richard had come round, staying over was different. The more I thought about Richard, the more I began to notice certain changes in him. Hmmm, what to do?

Was Richard going to dump Tracy? That would definitely spoil my plans and I'd been so patient. This thought raised another question; should I kill Richard tonight? I could wait and see what he was up to. But what happened if I waited too long. That made me mad. I wanted to be the one to destroy Tracy, not Richard. If Richard was going to walk away from Tracy, then striking now would be best. I couldn't blame Richard if he was going to dump Tracy, still he had a lot of bad habits, real annoying ones, but Tracy seemed to put up with them.

Maybe Richard wasn't going to dump Tracy. Maybe he was going to ask if they could start living together. That would fit in more with the *'wear something nice'*. That made me happy, because Tracy would be euphoric and I had just the thing to bring her book down to earth, with a crash

So, do I kill Richard tonight or not? Decisions, decisions...

202

Four hours passed quickly for one of us; me, not so quickly. I watched Tracy busy herself washing the bed linen, cleaning, spending an hour in the bath, painting her toe nails, then deciding to paint her finger nails as well. I was quite intrigued by it all and not in a good way. My earlier indecision about killing Richard tonight surfaced again. This evening was a big deal for Tracy. And I didn't think it had anything to do with the fact that Tracy and Richard would have some alone time for the first time in what felt like years, rather than a few months.

No, something was happening and it made me feel very uneasy. It would be good if I could just open up both their heads, have a quick look inside, see what they were thinking. Apparently, that would lead to death. Well, given my present mood, I was all for it. I wasn't in control here and I didn't like. You can understand, I'm sure, how much a person like me likes to be in control of every aspect about their lives and the lives of those around them.

When the GHD's came out and Tracy started to curl her hair in soft waves, my unease increased and so did my anger. The thick layer of dust that she blew off the flat irons told me it had been forever since she had used them. I took a closer look at Tracy.

The red LK Bennett dress moulded to Tracy's body, hugging and nipping in her waist. Susie had been right, the dress was a classic, falling just above her knees and skimming across her hips, highlighting their slenderness. Little cap sleeves with a vent running along the centre allowed Tracy to move her arms freely. The six-inch black patent stiletto court shoes elongated Tracy's bare legs making them appear even longer. She didn't seem to care that the cold would eat at her bare skin. No, this was not normal behaviour for Tracy. I hadn't even realised that Tracy owned a pair of six inch heels; they were so un-Tracy.

Tracy's make-up was impeccable, subtle and yet it drew attention to her stormy blue eyes which had been enhanced with smoky black eyeliner. Her red lips were turned up into a soft smile of anticipation as she turned to look at herself in the mirror, her hair swayed around her waist like a chocolate waterfall shimmering in the light. Tracy gave a giggle. My teeth ground together.

The doorbell rang and Tracy grabbed her handbag and faux fur black jacket. When the front door opened, Richard stood looking at Tracy in stunned silence. The look on his face said a million things; how much he wanted her, how sexy he thought she was, and how happy he was that she was his. Desire flickered in his eyes and his mouth rested open slightly in amazement. Nope, that look told me Richard had no intention of dumping Tracy. For the first time that day, I began to relax. I wouldn't have to change my plans after all.

Tracy giggled. "Will I do?"

Richard shook himself. "Do?! You're gorgeous." He grabbed her, his arms pulling Tracy into his embrace. His lips sought hers and his hands moulded her to the length of him as he deepened the kiss.

Personally, I felt sickened by this display of happiness. But what concerned me the most, at this moment, was the designer grey suit that Richard wore, with his black and grey thickly striped silk tie. The black shirt he wore underneath the suit looked good on him, bringing out the light tan of his skin. He'd made a real effort to smarten himself up.

Richard was planning something and I was betting I wasn't going to like it.

Richard let go of Tracy, and shot her a big smile. "Shall we?"

Tracy laughed, running her thumb across Richard's lips, removing the thin layer of red lipstick. "I think we should." She linked her arm through Richard's and they climbed into the waiting taxi.

Richard had booked a table at The Ivy restaurant in The Grange up on Bootham, which was situated just outside of the

Bar Walls that ran round York's city centre. The Grange had been a Regency Town House, built in 1829 by two brothers called Richardson. The entrance was grand with a sweeping staircase. A bar sat to the far left of the front doors and a reception desk sat to the right. Richard guided Tracy down the stairs to the Ivy Restaurant. I noted that Richard had requested a table in the corner, set apart slightly from the rest, offering them a little privacy.

The dim lighting added to the romantic feel of it all. The mid grey walls and dark wooden tables gave the restaurant a modern twist, whilst remaining sympathetic to the decade in which the property had been built. A bottle of champagne sat chilling in an ice bucket next to their table. The waitress picked up the bottle and the cork popped with a loud bang. Tracy giggled and Richard took her hand in his. She leaned forward and kissed him. Neither noticed the waitress leave them to their champagne or paid any attention to the menu that sat on the table.

Richard sighed. "I love you, Tracy Bennett." My back stiffened. Tracy's face lit up once more. I felt angry. Not because Richard loved Tracy, or because Tracy loved Richard. No, I was angry because Tracy was happy.

Really happy.

Tracy touched Richard's cheek, her eyes shone with happiness.

"I love you too," she breathed. I wanted to reach for the nearest ice bucket and lose the contents of my dinner.

Richard's hand slipped into his jacket pocket and I watched intently as he drew out a small black box. Something told me there wouldn't be a pair of earrings in the box.

Richard slid from his chair onto one knee and I wanted to kill him then and there for his embarrassing display. Tracy however beamed like a lighthouse on a dark night.

"Will you marry me?"

Well, I hadn't seen this coming. If I could have clapped my hands and danced round the restaurant I would have. This was just too much. What a punch Richard's death would have on Tracy. A glittering diamond ring on her finger and one dead fiancée; at least he wouldn't be asking for the ring back.

How perfect.

"Yes. Oh Richard, yes." Tracy threw her arms around Richard's neck and kissed him soundly. If I was the romantic type which, surprise, surprise, I'm not, I would have said that Tracy packed all the love she had for Richard into that kiss.

Richard's hands shook as he took the big shiny diamond out the box. I recon it weighed about a carat. Tracy looked at the diamond on her finger, mesmerised.

The ring was platinum, with tiny princess cut diamonds running along the centre of the band as they met the big diamond in the middle. The princess cut one carat diamond looked expensive. It caught the light of the candle on the table and a million tiny sparkles appeared.

Richard, thankfully, was back on his chair. He watched Tracy as she looked at the ring on her finger. "It's gorgeous Richard, simply gorgeous."

Richard looked happy. His heart rate had slowed back down. "I'm glad you like it."

Tracy looked at Richard. "I can't believe it, we're getting married." Her voice squeaked as she said the word *married*. It made me want to put earplugs in my ears.

"We sure are." They reached for their champagne glasses, the crystal clinking as they toasted their coming marriage, to their love and all that crappy stuff that people in love like to drink to.

There would be no wedding of course, so maybe it was as well that they celebrated now.

I'd made up my mind.

By tomorrow, Richard would be dead.

The night dragged on and on. The pair was so loved up that I don't think that they noticed what they ate or their surroundings.

"Let's walk home," Tracy said as she shrugged on her jacket.

"OK." Richard threw his arm over Tracy's shoulders and she leant into him, content as a cat snuggled on a bed in a warm house on a rainy day.

I battled with myself. Should I kill Richard when they got back to Tracy's or should I wait? Let them sleep on it for a little bit. Let Tracy pass on her news to Susie and Abigail as she showed off her ring.

Oh, dilemma, dilemma.

The high Tracy was on would mean that she would have a longer way to fall. The thing was, I wasn't so sure I could wait too long. Rage wound around my chest making it difficult to breathe. My rage was a very familiar friend; I always felt this way when I was ready to kill and with a four-month abstinence, I was more than overdue this kill.

Tracy rang Susie and Abigail on the way home to tell them her news which worked well for me. The excited squeals down the phone line nearly shattered my eardrum. Richard laughed. At least he would die happy. Ha, ha, ha.

"We can't wait to be bridesmaids, can we Susie? We'll need to make plans to go shopping. Have you thought about what colour you want us in? I guess we need a theme first. Have you thought about a theme? Don't worry we'll come up with one. This is so exciting." Abigail sang down the phone.

"I don't think that Tracy's had chance to think about anything, they've just got engaged." Susie's voice came down the line.

"Never mind, I'll hit the newsagents early tomorrow, get lots of magazines. It'll give us plenty of ideas."

"It's Tracy that's getting married Abs?" Susie interjected. Tracy laughed.

"I know, I know. I was just saying. We'll bring a bottle of champagne too. We'll crack it open and start celebrating. There's a twenty-four-hour Tesco near me, so we won't have to wait for the newsagents to open at eight."

"Calm down Abs. Tracy, we'll be at yours late morning, early afternoon. You've got to give them chance to celebrate Abs."

"Oh! Yeah." Abigail giggled. "Sorry."

Tracy looked so happy; her cheeks were flushed, the light of the full moon reflecting in her eyes.
That sealed it for me.

I wasn't going to wait for Tracy to show off her ring.

Tonight, Richard would die.

Tracy would wake tomorrow to find Richard's dead body and her world would come crashing down.

I laughed to myself. Maybe Richard's proposal had come at just the right time.

Bless him, ha, ha, ha.

Chapter Seventeen

I waited in the corner of the living room as Richard turned off the lights. His jacket was slung over the sofa, where he and Tracy had sat wrapped in each other's arms. An empty champagne bottle sat on the coffee table next to the spent glasses.

Tracy walked forward as the moonlight spilled through the thin curtains. She reached for the zip at the back of her dress and the fabric spilled to the floor. Unconsciously her tongue snaked out, moisturizing her lips. Richard's eyes darkened. I'd dropped a pill into Richard's last drink; he needed to act quickly if he was going to take Tracy up on her offer.

Richard raced forward and picked Tracy up, her legs swinging into the air. It was as if he had heard me.

I sighed.

I didn't need to see this.

An hour later and Richard was snoring his head off, just like a little piggy. His right arm was slung over Tracy. I knew I wouldn't be able to get him back downstairs and into the kitchen. I wasn't that strong. Instead I decided to set him up at the foot of the bed. I looked at the carpet with irritation. Well, I would just have to make the best of it. On the plus side, under the carpet hidden away were wooden floor boards! And if that wasn't enough to cheer me up, then there was always the fact that Richard's lifeless body would be the first thing that Tracy would see in the morning. I'll be honest the thought pleased me no end.

I'd moved the white wooden chair that lived in front of the dressing table into position, and was now trying to get Richard's resisting body on to the chair. It took me a full half hour before I got him into position and all tied up. I'd started to sweat a little. I wasn't concerned about what evidence I left behind. I wanted to be discovered. I wanted Tracy to know who she had let in.

Richard started to stir, earlier than planned. It didn't matter I was ready, perched on the end of the bed. I didn't have a stitch on just like Richard.

I wanted to feel Richard's blood on my skin. I'd never felt their blood on my body and I wanted to know how it felt. To be covered in red.

Richard looked at me his eyes slightly out of focus. "T-T-Tracy?"

"Nope, Lauren." I bent over him, my face close to his. "You did want to meet me, didn't you Richard?"

Richard shook his head, trying to shake off the effects of the drug.

"I'm going to kill you." I watched for a reaction.

His forehead wrinkled into a frown. "What?"

I sighed heavily. "Personally, I haven't got a clue what Tracy sees in you. Yeah, I'm sure you've been good to her. But, I can't let you mend her. She's broken Richard, have you not noticed. Well, by the time I've taken everything away from her, there will be nowhere for Tracy to go. Her grip on reality will slip, until there is no coming back from it. Then Richard, then I will be free."

I slashed the knife across his chest before he had time to think, to act on what I had said. A grunt left his lips. His brain was too foggy with the drug to allow him to feel the sharp coldness of the blade. As soon as the cold steel tore through Richard's skin and the first drop of blood escaped from under the safe protection of his skin, and the veins carrying his blood around his body gave, I felt a rush of euphoria. I licked my lips and started to dance around Richard's body.

I hadn't used Fred; this was all about me, about Tracy losing her touch on reality. About breaking Tracy into so many tiny pieces that there would be no coming back from it. I wanted the police to know exactly who they were dealing with. For them to know that had I wanted, I would never be found by them. The police were idiots; I was so much better than them. Better than Tracy.

I didn't stop sinking the knife into Richards's flesh.

I couldn't.

My control had slipped and I gave into it, feeling alive for the first time in a very long time. In a frenzy of movement, I danced and danced around Richard's body, my knife lightly caressing the skin in some places, and digging deeper in others. If Richard said anything, I couldn't hear him. Blood fell to the floor, some flying into the air and landing in wanton disarray across the bed linen, coating the walls, the carpet, the furniture and me.

A splattering of blood covered my body and I looked on in wonder at the pattern it created. By the time I finished, there would be nearly as much blood on me as there was on Richard. I liked the feel of his blood on my naked body. Richard may not have given off the same emotion as Karen but his blood on my skin took me to the same place that Karen's hate filled stare had, and I enjoyed it so much. I was made for this feeling, and everyone was made to give me this feeling.

Made to make me feel alive. Made to die, for me.

I made the final cut, tilting Richard's head back and slicing deeply across his neck. Blood flew out and I felt the wonder of it as it landed, sweeping out its sticky fingers, reaching far beyond the other blood splatter. It soaked into the carpet and bed linen.

In this moment, there was just me and Richard. No Tracy.

I had given the police enough evidence to lock me up for a very long time.

They just had to find me first. And I was very good at hiding.

It was three hours later when Tracy woke. She reached out a sleepy hand into the empty space where Richard had slept. I was looking forward to this. Her arm moved around the space, her fingers touching the empty linen. A frown marred her forehead. She pushed herself up and looked at the empty space next to her. I leant forward, interest taking hold, as I waited for her to realise what had happened last night. The diamond ring on her left hand sparkled in the sunlight that spilled through the open curtains. They had been too lost in each other last night to think about closing them. It was late morning and the sun had been up for hours now.

It promised to be a sunny dry day outside. Inside, it was going to rain tears of despair.

Tracy looked round the room. Her eyes widened as they rested on Richard's lifeless form. Her hand shook as she pushed herself off the bed and ran around to Richard.

"Richard?" Her voice trembled as she reached out a hand to him. Richard's head fell forward. Tracy gasped. "No! Richard, no." Her arms circled round him, tears falling down her face. Told you it was going to rain inside. "No, Richard, wake up baby, wake up." She rocked him as much as the zip strips allowed his body to move. Funny, but Richard didn't wake up. I sat back and enjoyed the show. This was far better than when the trio had discovered Karen's body.

Much better.

The first scream bubbled from Tracy's lips.

She fell back on the bed. Her body was coated in Richard's blood. She looked at it in horror and grabbed the bed linen to wipe down her body. The blood just smeared itself over her skin. She quickly threw the linen down, disgust causing a groan to break from her lips as she looked at the blood that stained the duvet. Bloody footprints lined the carpeted floor; they circled round Richard's body. Tracy whimpered. Raising a fist, she put it into her mouth and bit down. Falling back onto the bed, her eyes never left Richard's lifeless form. Without thought, she pushed her body back, away from Richard, her eyes transfixed on his body, my beautiful artwork. Her back hit the headboard. "No, no, no, no, Richard, no."

Tracy started screaming and screaming, and I lapped up the terror that shook her body. I felt her brain shut down a little bit at a time.

Sweet, sweet, ecstasy.

It was a testimony to the times that we were living in that not one of Tracy's neighbours came to see what was wrong. Tracy had been screaming now for a full twenty minutes and showed no signs of stopping. It was quite impressive how her vocal cords kept giving. A couple of Tracy's screams had sounded a little hoarse, but they were still loud and very clear.

The front door banged open and footsteps sounded on the stair carpet. The door to the bedroom swung open and Susie stood there, Abigail at her side.

Abigail gasped at the bloody room. Susie gripped her arm, her blonde hair swinging across her shoulders. "Don't you dare start screaming!"

Abigail swallowed back the scream that hung in the back of her throat. Her eyes kept darting to Richard's body.

Susie ran forward grabbing Tracy. "Come on, baby, let's get you out of here." She looked across at Abigail, wincing as

Tracy's screams threatened to burst her eardrums. "Call the police. I'm going to get Tracy into the shower." Tracy's body had seized up, her legs stiff.

Her hands and legs were shaking, tears running down her face and merging with the snot that dripped from her nose. Not a pretty sight, I'll tell you. Susie tugged her harder.

Abigail looked at Susie. "OK," she hesitated. "Do you think it's a good idea to…" Abigail swung an arm in Tracy's direction, indicating the blood. "You know, clean the blood off, the police might need to see it, you know, for evidence, or something."

"I don't give a shit about the police, I'm not leaving Tracy covered in Richard's blood." With that Susie dragged Tracy's shaking, screaming form out of the bedroom.

I heard Abigail's retreating footsteps as she went downstairs.

Susie turned on the shower drowning out Abigail's voice as she rung the police. I would have liked to be privy to that conversation, but I was busy right now watching Susie manhandle Tracy.

Susie pushed Tracy into the shower before the water had a chance to warm up. The cold water had an effect on her and she finally stopped screaming. Her face was red, her eyes looked sore and snot ran unchecked from her nose.

"Blow." Susie directed as she held out a tissue, like a mum would do to a toddler. Tracy blew and Susie wiped away the snot, dumping the tissue on the floor outside the shower. "Let's get you cleaned up." Without hesitation, Susie stripped off her clothes and walked into the shower with Tracy.

Armed with a sponge lathered with soap, Susie scrubbed Tracy's body, cleaning the blood off and washing her hair. I looked at the water as it left Tracy's body. The water ran red. I couldn't stop the shiver of pleasure that ran through me.

Tracy stood motionless, allowing Susie to scrub away the blood; every now and again her eyes filled with tears and she made small hiccupping noises. Susie poured shampoo onto Tracy's head and began working it into her hair. "*Shhhh, baby, shhhh.*" Susie kept saying over and over to Tracy, as she washed off the shampoo and then the conditioner. Turning off the water, Susie led Tracy out of the shower and towelled her down.

The bathroom door opened and Abigail stuck her head through. "The police are on their way."

"Right, get me some clothes for Tracy." Susie asked as she combed Tracy's hair back. She gripped Tracy's arms lightly and looked into her eyes. "It's not going to be alright Tracy so I'm not going to lie to you and tell you it is, because it isn't. But you will get through this." Tracy's eyes looked almost as dead as Richard's. Susie shook her. "You hear me girl, you will get through this. You aren't on your own. Not this time."

I took another look at Susie. It was as if I was seeing her for the first time. She was strong and steadfast in her attempt to pull Tracy back to the living world. Hmm, maybe I should kill Susie now. One swift cut across the throat.

Tracy recovered enough to nod her head. I shrank back into the darkness, a frustrated cry echoed in my throat that never made it to my lips.

There would be no more killing today.

Abigail came back with a pair of navy joggy bottoms, a pink t-shirt over one arm and a dark pink hoody, knickers, bra, and socks over the other. "I can't find her slippers."

"I don't think it matters, come here and help me get her dressed before the police get here." Together Susie and Abigail worked at getting Tracy dressed.

"You'll need to put your own clothes back on." Abigail pointed out, once Tracy was dressed.

"Right," Susie picked up her clothes and went to pull on her short powder blue skirt and white sleeveless low cut blouse. Blood had transferred from Tracy to Susie's clothes. "Crap!"

"Don't worry. I'll get you something else," Abigail said, disappearing momentarily. Susie dropped her bloody clothes to the floor. She caught Tracy watching her. Tears fell from Tracy's eyes. "Come on Tracy, they're only clothes." Even as Susie spoke the words, she knew it wasn't the clothes that got Tracy crying again; it was the blood and everything that it represented. Susie hugged her.

Abigail ran back into the bathroom armed with clothing. Susie raised an eyebrow at the joggy bottoms and long sleeved, modestly cut top.

"It's the only one I had here that doesn't need washing. The joggy bottoms are Tracy's." Susie nodded her head at Abigail and put the clothes on. She didn't mention the drawer in the bedroom that contained her own clothes.

"Come on, let's get you downstairs." Susie placed an arm around Tracy. "Abs?" Susie whispered. "Get rid of the magazines and flowers and stuff will you. Tracy doesn't need to see them."

"I'm on it." Abigail called as she ran down the stairs.

You can see now why I had to destroy their friendship.

Watching Susie, I was starting to think that killing Susie first was my best option. Well no, it wasn't, if I was honest, I wanted to kill Susie first. The more I watched her, as she mothered over Tracy, the more I began to admire her strength. Each time I looked at Susie, the more I saw Karen staring at me, eyes full of hate, fighting me with all the emotion she could summon, all the while knowing that I was going to kill her.

Karen had stood up to death, stared it in the face and let it know true hate. It was sweet joyous fulfilment, the best high I

216

had ever experienced, with the exception of Richard's blood as it had coated my bare skin. I wanted to reach for that feeling again. Susie would give me that, and so would her blood. I could tell.

Tracy started to slip away and I began to wonder again if I had time to kill Susie before the police caught up with me.

I hoped so.

Hmmm, maybe not.

The police sirens sounded down the street. Blue flashing lights filled the living room from the window. Susie sat on the sofa, her right arm slung round Tracy's shoulders as she hugged her to her. Abigail had lit the fire. Still the room felt cold. "You'd best open the front door and let them in," Susie said.

I watched as the police stormed into the house, like ants round a sugary sweet. Abigail spoke to them, telling them how they had found Tracy covered in Richard's blood. I watched as she pointed upstairs. Susie stayed on the sofa hugging Tracy. Tracy cried softly into Susie's side. I could hear the sharp pitch of tape being pulled, and knew they were sealing off the crime scene for the forensic team. Time ticked slowly by.

There was so much going on that I didn't mind the fact that Susie's heart still beat. It had been a long stretch to expect I'd be able to kill Susie before they got here. Still a girl can dream.

The detective from a few months back walked into the living room. Tracy looked at him and burst into tears, her sobs muffled by Susie chest as she rocked her slowly back and forth. Susie sent the detective a hard stare. They hadn't really hit off the last time that they had met. It was obvious that neither liked the other, despite the fact that the detective here should hold himself detached from such things and do his job.

"You've cleaned her down. Tampering with evidence isn't a smart move." The detective's voice sounded hard.

Susie looked him in the eyes. "Lock me up, I don't care. There was no way I was leaving Tracy covered in Richard's blood. I wouldn't treat a dog the way you seem to want me to treat Tracy. You can see how upset she is. How much worse do you think it would be, had I left her in that room covered in blood? You're an unfeeling bastard."

The detective cocked an eyebrow at Susie, her hard gaze never left his. "I understand your feelings towards your friend; however, you've done her no favours. The evidence you have washed away could have held the key to finding out who did this." The words were spoken softly, carried by a sigh that escaped his lips and Susie hugged Tracy closer to her.

"You know who did this, Slasher, that's who. Slasher is still out there, and there's plenty of evidence still upstairs so don't you dare try and tell me that my decision to clean Tracy up hinders you in anyway." Susie was breathing heavily. An assortment of emotions ran across her face; despair, uncertainty, anger, sorrow. She hugged Tracy to her. I could tell that she was worried that she had washed away some vital evidence. This could have quite possibly been the first crime scene which hadn't been tampered with. No dogs around or cat, just Susie.

What have you done girl? Ha, ha, ha.

Without being asked, the detective sat down on the sofa. "At the moment, we don't know if the Yorkshire Slasher is responsible. We need to keep an open mind." Abigail came into the room, sitting down next to Tracy. Her face was pinched and concern hung heavy in her eyes. Without thought, Abigail's hand rested on Tracy's back, patting her softly. Round them the police were a hive of activity as they sealed off upstairs. Two policemen stood guard at the front door forming a barrier around the house outside. People had started to gather, like vultures over a rabbit carcass. Funny how no one had been concerned when Tracy had started screaming. Now the neighbours couldn't seem to get enough as they stretched their necks to get a better look. It wouldn't be long and the press would be here. Everyone was interested in me, interested in my latest creation.

It was nice to be popular.

The detective was asking a whole host of questions. You know the stuff, when had Susie and Abigail last spoken to Richard and Tracy? What time had Tracy and Richard got home? The detective was trying to find a timeline, a timeline between happy and alive Richard and dead not so happy Richard. Susie and Abigail did their best to answer the detective's questions while Tracy sobbed. I could tell that the detective wanted to speak to Tracy but wasn't getting anywhere with her. Frustrating isn't it.

Tracy sniffled, and cried her way through it all, muttering under her breath *'why Richard'*. The only thing that was apparent was that Richard was dead, and that's all that Tracy could focus on. I could tell the detective wanted to know how Tracy had slept through Richard's death. Why she hadn't woken. Why she hadn't been killed. Why leave her to discover the body? Had the kill been personal? Was this more about Tracy than Richard? Was she the important link that they were all missing, in the Yorkshire Slasher Killings?

The detective's gut probably told him that the Yorkshire Slasher had killed Richard. I'd always wanted to look at someone and say that. 'My gut told me'. My gut only told me when I was hungry.

Well, I could confirm what the detective wasn't willing to say, this was no copycat, yes, I the Yorkshire Slasher – aka Lauren Michaels, had killed Richard. The police had the little job of finding out why, and me. You'd think that that wouldn't be too taxing for them, wouldn't you?

I knew that they would take Richard's body away, examine it, look at the differing depths of the knife wounds. Look for similarities between my other killings, and Richard. By the time, they got around to confirming that I had killed Richard, I would be well on my way to killing someone else. That was the problem with the police; they were just too slow for me.

I knew it was the circumstances of Richard's kill that was puzzling them. There had never been anyone else in the house before. No one, who would be in a position to describe the Yorkshire Slasher. And here was Tracy, too wrapped up in her own little world of pity and despair, to recognise how important she had become to the police.

I enjoyed the questions that hung in the air without a voice. I craved solidity, to be seen and recognised. I was a ghost, even now as I lurked in the shadows, no one saw me. No one took note of the killer that was in front of them.

No, even now, it was all about Tracy.

My anger surfaced as I looked at Tracy, and the amount of attention that she was receiving. I had to claw it back, swallow it away. I had a plan to stick to. The problem was, I was becoming aware that I might not have time to kill Susie before they caught up with me. I would have to add it to my 'to do' list. The thought made me feel better. They couldn't lock me up forever. I'd make them think that I was better, that I had changed. I could do that. I was that good. Better than the police and their psychoanalysts.

I had it all planned.

Tracy's demise.

My escape.

Everything.

And I wasn't going to let anyone spoil it.

I looked at Susie, yes, I would kill her. Susie's death would give me something to look forward to. Was it in part insanity that drove me rather than my true nature? I stopped and thought about this. I laughed to myself. Insane. Yep, I was. And in that moment a new plan formed. They couldn't charge me with killing if I was insane, could they? It was a condition, wasn't it? Non-Compos

Mentis, that was me. Definition insane, not sound of mind, yeah, I could do insane. After all, in this world of *'normal'*, all the killings I had done, wasn't what added up to a sound mind, was it?

There was the 'Act for the Custody of Insane Persons Charged with Offences'; that had to go some way to protect me from being banged up behind bars, with a load of halfwits. Or what about the Mental Health Act 1983, surely that could be of assistance to a person like me. I was aware that the plea for mental instability had not gone so well for the likes of Billy Joe Harris, known as the 'Twilight Rapist'. But then the idiot had allowed his conversation with his girlfriend to be recorded as he'd bragged about his performance in court, and what a good show it had been. I wasn't Billy Joe Harris and wasn't about to go bragging to anyone. Let's be honest, I was a loner, and therefore didn't have anyone to go bragging to. Don't get me wrong, I liked being a loner, I didn't need anyone. The other difference between me and Billy Joe Harris was that I really was insane, and no one was going to prove any different.

Hmm, so would they lock me away in some padded cell? In this modern world in which we live, with so many 'do-gooders', did they still lock people up in padded cells and say 'it was for their own safety'? Would they throw a few pills down my neck? Declare that I could be cured. That's what they would think – pathetic. As if a person like me could be cured. Remember the lesion on the amygdala, if they were right about this, it wasn't something that could be undone. Still, I would let them think that they had cured me. I was strong, stronger than their drugs and their therapy. I would survive, I'd give them what they wanted and once released, I would go for Susie.

Yes, the thought of killing Susie would keep me going while I was being looked after at her Majesty's Pleasure in some place they sent the insane.

Admittedly, I didn't know what the police procedure was, to know exactly what would happen to me. But I was sure that they wouldn't be able to lock me up in prison if I was found to be medically certified insane. That was why they had set the 'Act for the Custody of Insane Persons Charged with Offences' in the 1800's, to protect people like me. Ha, ha, ha.

I just had to make sure that I was certified. It was almost laughable to think of me wanting to be labelled insane. Well, if it meant some dimwit thinking they could heal me, I could go along with that. Remember, I have spent an awful long time hiding, watching and waiting. I knew I could act my way through the mental health process as well. Just watch me.

I would still have an opportunity to kill Susie and anyone else I chose to.

It would fill my time.

It didn't bother me that I was going to get caught. I had planned it that way.

It was my final move against Tracy Bennett.

By the time that they came to understand why I had allowed myself to be caught, it would be too late and I would be killing again.

Chapter Eighteen

Tracy stood by her make-up counter in a trance like state, her eyes resting on a fleck of dirt on the wall in front of her. Mr Orange had given her a wide berth since she had returned three weeks ago. It was as though she had an incurable disease and it was highly contagious.

The other girls that worked in the cosmetics department seemed to be of the same opinion as Mr Orange. It was probably because they couldn't think of anything to say to her, apart from 'sorry' and really what did *'sorry'* mean?

Sorry, didn't change things. Richard was still dead.

Tracy was single again.

And I was feeling almost happy. To feel full happiness, I needed Tracy out the way. Still I had to give myself credit for the well thought out and executed death of Richard.

The diamond ring on Tracy's finger was a constant reminder of everything that she could've have had; love, happiness, a life, a family. All of it, all gone like the blood that had dripped, dripped, dripped from Richard's body. I smiled, Richard's body was as cold as the diamond on her finger and yes, visually to strangers, that ring might say Tracy was taken but she wasn't. I'd seen to that.

All in all, I have to admit things were going better than anticipated. You might think that it's wrong for me to derive pleasure from Tracy's sad and pitiful state. But then we psychopaths are a selfish, egotistical lot. One girl's despair is another girl's pleasure. It's the yin and yang of it all. Ha, ha, ha.

I watched Susie as she clip-clopped over in her six-inch heels and very short deep brown skirt with bare legs. Given that she worked on hosiery, she wasn't what I would call 'showing off the merchandise'. Today she was dressed for the weather, in a sleeveless cream silk shirt that was unbuttoned to the swell of her breasts. Her long blonde hair caught the sun as it shone through the wide expanse of the shop window. Had her skirt been eight inches longer, Susie would have looked sophisticated, classy even; as it was she still maintained that trashy quality that followed her around.

I had been taking a lot of interest in Susie lately. She had never been on her own, so I hadn't got the opportunity to use my knife on her. Bloody frustrating! Tracy, Susie and Abigail were altogether again, staying at Abigail's who had finally got the spare room sorted, redecorated and now inhabited by Susie and Tracy. Tracy's house had been sealed off by the police as 'an active crime scene' and Tracy evicted as the forensic folk moved in. If only Susie and Abigail knew that I had moved in with them as well. Ha, ha, ha. Now that would give them something to keep them awake at night, other than Abigail's snoring.

New houses; it was as if the walls were made of paper. And Abigail's snoring penetrated through the walls flimsy structure, as though it wasn't there. I was starting to think that if I couldn't get the opportunity to kill Susie, then I might kill the snoring little piggy in the neighbouring room. Put it out of its misery.

"Hi there." The smile that spread across Susie's pink painted lips wobbled with concern.

Tracy picked up the cloth and glass cleaner and started to wipe away the fingerprints from yesterday's customers. "Hi."

"So, how about we go out for lunch?" Susie asked as she pulled out one of the faux leather chairs from the counter.

Tracy shook her head. "I don't know, my figures are down and well, I'm just not sure."

"Well, in that case I take back the question, and now I'm telling you, we're going out for lunch." Susie caught a light hold of Tracy's arm as she swept it over the glass. "Come on, Tracy, you've got to start moving forward. Get back on the horse, as so to speak. I haven't said anything these last few weeks, I've left you to work it out on your own, and I'm sorry to say you're not doing a good job."

"I'm trying, really, I am." Tracy removed her arm from Susie's. Tears made her stormy eyes glisten.

Susie slid off the chair and hugged Tracy. "I know. You just need help. And that's what Abs and I are for. So, then, it's settled, we'll go out for a long lunch and hang the rest of them." She pulled Tracy away from her, and gave her a long look. "You have to do this for Abigail, she's wasting away. If we aren't careful we won't be able to see her sideways on." Tracy laughed. It was one of Susie's favourite lines from Andrew Lloyd Webbers and Tim Rice's 'Joseph and the Amazing Technicolor Dream Coat'.

Abigail rounded the corner. The grey skirt suit she always wore for work was minus its jacket, and the white blouse tucked into her skirt helped to show off her waist and give a little more height to her than the boxy jacket did. The four inch chunky heels of her black shoes probably helped more than the shirt to add height. Still for once, Abigail looked a little less round.

"What's so funny?" Abigail asked as she pushed herself up onto the unoccupied chair, and put her hands on the newly cleaned glass counter.

"Tracy's just cleaned that." Susie pointed at the glass.

"Right, yeah, sorry." She kept her hands where they were. "So, what were you laughing at?

"Would you take it the wrong way if I said you?" Susie asked.

Abigail shrugged her shoulders. "I guess that would depend on what it was."

Tracy smiled at Abigail; it was a little strained but a smile none the less. "We were just saying that you looked like you've lost weight."

Abigail beamed. "Not that I think that's funny, you understand. But I've lost a full two pounds these last few weeks."

Susie leant back and gave Abigail the once over. "See, we have to go for lunch. Abigail's wasting away before our eyes."

Abigail tapped Susie with her foot. "You're so funny, I think I might fall off my chair."

Mr Orange passed by the counter. He shot Susie and Abigail a stern look but didn't say anything. Susie and Abigail giggled at his retreating back.

Tracy watched Mr Orange as he strode over to Helen. "I don't think he knows what to say to me."

"I get the impression no one knows quite what to say." Abigail looked across at Helen and Mr Orange. "It's quite strange really. You're still you. If they're stuck for something to say, why not talk about the weather, its England after all."

"I don't think it's that easy Abs," Susie said. Helen's face had started to redden slightly. Whatever Mr Orange was saying, it was clear that Helen didn't like it.

"Right, so back to lunch..." Abigail swung her gaze away from Helen. "What time are we going?"

"I'm on second lunch today and I don't think it matters what time Tracy takes her lunch."

Tracy nodded her head in agreement. "They just let me be at the moment."

"Bloody hell you're lucky. I get no peace up in accounts. Karen's replacement thinks she's got something to prove. When I reach forty, I'm hoping I'll be a nicer person than she is. I think it's probably got something to do with her name. I mean, what parent would name their kid, Patsy Green! Pea Green that's what we call her, well, actually that's probably the nicest name that we call her. Not that we're being bitchy. It's as if she's trying to work her way up the tree and can't find anything to haul her skinny butt up with so she's using us. She needs to take a look and understand she's working at Hopstocks Department Store, not some high-flying law firm."

Susie looked at Abigail. "She does wear a lot of green."

Abigail nodded her head. "I know, it wouldn't be so bad but she chooses the wrong green to go with her black hair and fair skin tones." I raised my eyebrows; hark at Abigail the fashion guru. "It's as if she's trying to brighten herself up. But bright pea green just makes her skin look sullen. She's got a lovely figure though. We all have our good points, right." Abigail turned to Tracy. "Hey, maybe you should offer to do her make-up, you know, introduce her to a kinder, warmer colour scheme. Either that or you could tell her that she should stop dying her hair black."

"I don't think so. I don't think it would go down too well." Tracy looked shocked at the thought. I'd be happy to make the Pea look beautiful. A kinder warmer colour; hmm, let me think, oh yes, I've got it, red…

Abigail ignored Tracy's comment. "Out of the three of us, you definitely have more tact and anyway, it would give you something else to think about. Think of it as a project. Or a lost puppy, that would probably work better for you. You know how you don't like to see people on their own, well Pea Green wouldn't be if you helped her sort out her look."

Susie looked at Abigail, a smile on her face as she turned to Tracy. "Maybe that's it. It would give you something else to think about, like Abs said. Maybe give you back a little of your spark. Not that I'm saying you should forget about Richard, but, you know, it wouldn't hurt to have another focus."

"Perhaps, I'll think about it. I don't really know her." Tracy didn't look convinced, and the thought of her pulling herself out of her melancholy was not pleasing at all to me.

"You're lucky you don't have to work with her. You would be doing me a huge favour though, if you did."

"Come on you, we'd best get back to it." Susie gave Abigail a nudge. "And you can stop piling the pressure on. Tracy said she'd think about it, and I'm sure she will." Susie sent Tracy a meaningful look.

At that moment the detective walked in, flagged by a couple of uniforms. I felt a rise of excitement. It had taken them long enough to process the evidence and come to a conclusion. Hopefully, I was going to like the decision that they had come to. At least things were finally moving forward. I had been thinking that the police would never take the bait. I had left enough evidence behind to sink a fleet of battleships and still it had taken them weeks to take me up on it.

Susie was the first to notice them. Her back stiffened and she walked over to Tracy, pulling Abigail with her, so that they flanked Tracy's sides. Mr Orange had stopped talking to Helen, and Helen was now staring openly at the detective. I watched her eyes travel up and down the length of him, taking in his broad shoulders and starched white shirt, nipped together with a royal blue striped tie. His black trousers were tailored, slimming down his legs and defining the muscle along his thighs. The detective's hair was loaded with gel and had been styled to give it a dishevelled look. No whiskers lined his jaw. He'd taken time with his appearance. I was a high-profile case and could make his career; he was seeking the glory of it. His swagger oozed confidence. I smiled; I would take great pleasure in taking that away from him – when I took his life.

"Tracy Bennett." The detective came to a stop in front of Tracy. "We'd like you to come to the station for further questioning."

Susie puffed out her chest in outrage. Oh, I would enjoy killing her too. "What kind of questioning?" Susie turned to Tracy. "You don't say anything! We'll find you a lawyer."

Abigail paled. "They can't possibly think that Tracy had anything to do with Richard's death. That's insane. It was Slasher, we all know it was Slasher...Oh, God, Susie you don't think that they think Tracy is, Slasher, do you? That would be absurd."

"Abs, this isn't the time. The police might think that they can bully our Tracy into confessing something that she didn't do, but they won't. You don't talk to them do you hear me Tracy." Tracy had shut down, the expression on her face said, *'no one was home'*.

The detective looked annoyed. "We're following up on some loose ends."

Susie opened her mouth to speak. Abigail put a restraining hand on her arm. "He's only doing his job Susie."

Susie gripped at Tracy's arm like she could chain her to the spot and stop the police from taking her. I smiled to myself, such a silly girl, could she not see that very soon Tracy would be no more. "Would you like me to charge you with obstructing justice?"

Susie paled, but her hand still gripped Tracy's. I looked at the anger painted across her face and the hand that held Tracy's arm, like they had been soldered together. I liked the fact that she was willing to fight for her friend. It gave me all sorts of ideas. Abigail tied to a chair facing Susie. I'd make Susie watch as I cut at her friend. The blood would drip from Abigail's body as Susie screamed out her rage at me. She would look at me with such glorious hate. Abigail would die and Susie would have to live with the knowledge that all she had been able to do was sit and watch. She didn't have to worry; her pain at the loss of her friend would be over very soon. I closed my eyes and smiled; such a beautiful thought.

Tracy turned to Susie. "It's OK, Susie, don't worry, they just want to ask me some questions. If it will help to find out who this Slasher person is and get him locked up, then I'm all for it." Tracy gently removed her arm from Susie's. "Don't worry, Susie, it'll all be alright, you'll see."

I looked round; Hopscotch's had come to a very quiet standstill. The music still softly filled the shop; however, everyone had stopped what they were doing, and openly watched the little scene in front of them. It was as if the clocks had stopped ticking, that planet earth had ceased to rotate and time had frozen.

And still it was all about Tracy.

The detective here might think that he was about to make another step on his career ladder. He wasn't.

Because all anyone cared about, all anyone ever saw was Tracy. Rage filled me, this should be my moment! York had been gripped in terror because of me! I Lauren Michaels, was the Yorkshire Slasher, not bloody Tracy Bennett.

I would kill the lot of them.

I took another look around, taking in their faces, some I knew and some were new to me. I would still find them. And then I would kill them. Death had marked them and you can't cheat death.

The detective stood back and Tracy walked out of Hopscotch's flanked by the two policemen.

Abigail had put her arms around Susie, and together they watched Tracy leave them behind.

Hopscotch's bust into life, everyone spoke at once, their voices carrying their surprise, their excitement. The volume increased as everyone fought to be heard. Mobiles glowed as people began dialling friends or family, eager to share their news. Suddenly a man surged forward and started snapping pictures of Tracy as she walked with the detective. Someone else pushed forward phone in hand, snap, snap, snapping. They were like rats caught in the midday sun, scurrying for a patch of darkness. Well they had found their darkness; they had found me.

Tracy saw none of this, heard nothing, as she ducked her head and sat in the back of the police car. A lone tear ran down her cheek as she stared through the car window without seeing, without feeling, lost in thought.

Planet earth began to rotate again and the clocks started ticking.

And Tracy began to slip away.

My strength grew within her, her mind became a soft whisper.

Soon very soon, and this body would be mine....

Chapter Nineteen

The room in which Tracy sat was dull. I suppose these interview rooms in the police station weren't meant to be warm and fuzzy. It was clean and clinical. I appreciated it.

The walls were an off white and I entertained myself with imagining them covered in the detective's blood. I'd never bothered to learn the detective's name; it wasn't important to me. He'd be dead soon. Susie referred to him like Abigail did, as 'The detective'. Tracy didn't make reference to him at all, unless absolutely necessary.

I could feel the cold blade of my knife that was hidden in the secret compartment of my shoe. This knife was special; it was made from bone. Carved to a thin point, and sharpened ready to slice at the flesh of anyone I chose to use it on. I'd had the knife specially made. I never travelled without it and given metal detectors and so forth, bone just made travelling so much easier.

I couldn't wait to use it. To show them just what I was capable of. They wanted The Yorkshire Slasher and today they were lucky, because I was in an accommodating mood. Tracy was weakening, her grip loosening. All I had to do was wait a little longer for the detective here to break her down further. Then they would see me and it would be too late. They'd be dead and I would be free.

I was feeling rather smug.

Tracy was beginning to get twitchy. Her fingers entwined round the dress of her uniform, crumpling up the fabric, twisting it, letting it go, to the do same thing all over again. I enjoyed her unease. Despite what Susie had told her, she was talking to the police without any representation. I looked at the brown file that the detective had slapped on the table when he'd entered the room. I was looking forward to seeing the contents of that file. Tracy on the other hand, probably wouldn't enjoy the contents of that file at all. I shrugged, like I cared.

The detective's buddy was slumped in the opposite chair to Tracy, feigning disinterest. He wouldn't be winning an Oscar for his performance, it lacked conviction. His beady dark brown eyes never left Tracy's face, watching, waiting for a reaction. Tracy looked vulnerable, scared, uncertain and more than a little lost. She sat there silently watching the detective, her eyes never leaving his face. If she noticed the brown folder, she didn't show it.

If Buddy was waiting for a confession from her, he'd be waiting a long time. Tracy wasn't capable of the murders. That was all me. The rhyme 'he's large, he's round and he bounces on the ground', came into my head when I looked at Buddy. Like the detective, his name had been mentioned and again, I hadn't bothered to take the time to listen to it. He'd be dead soon too.

I tilted my head slightly; did fat people contain more blood than skinny people? Could it be possible that when I cut into Buddy here, that his blood would poor quicker from his body and fill the tiled floor more than The Detective's would. Well there was one way to find out. I smiled a rather superior and satisfied smile at the thought.

233

There was to be no recon work to do. No spending time getting to know their routines, getting to know their neighbours' routines – ready for the kill. No, today it was all about the moment. About killing them instantaneously, without thought or planning.

I wondered if Buddy minded dying in a crumpled brown suit that was a size too small for him. His white shirted belly hung over the top of his brown shabby leather belt. He'd let himself go. Maybe he'd always been a slob? Who knew? Who cared? Not me.

"There's a problem with your story Tracy." The Detective was trying to appear familiar, to be on Tracy's level, to understand her. Good luck with that. "The evidence isn't adding up. The foot prints…" A pause as the Detective opened up the file and sieved through the photos.

I was betting he'd deliberately placed the one of Richard's bloody body on top. I took a swift look at my handiwork. The photos didn't really show off the smoothness of the cuts or how I had used different strokes and depths to the cuts, or how the blade had skimmed the surface of the skin in areas, not pressing too hard, to prolong life.

"See here, these are your footprints, Tracy. The question I'm asking myself is, why they are the only ones in the room. See." The Detective pointed a slim finger at the footprints. "Surely if someone else had done this, there would be two sets of footprints. Wouldn't you agree, Tracy?" Tears fell from Tracy's eyes; she didn't say anything.

Taking the photo of Richard from the file, The Detective placed it in front of Tracy. "You did this Tracy."

Tracy shrank back. "No, n-n-no, I-I-I didn't. I c-c- couldn't h-h-have. I l-l-love Richard, we were g-g-g- going to get m-m-married." The ring on her finger caught the light and she watched the tiny sparkles dance along the table. Tears poured from her eyes unchecked. Snot was starting to run from her nose. She pulled out a tissue and wiped it away.

"Come on, Tracy, what's the point in pretending. You dropped Richard a sleeping pill and while he slept, you dragged him onto that chair and tied him to it. He trusted you Tracy. I bet he even loved you; loved you enough to ask you to marry him." The Detective pointed to the ring on her left hand. She moved her hand under the table and began playing with the ring.

"What was wrong? Was the diamond not big enough for you? He never stood a chance did he Tracy? Did you plan this all along? Why the others Tracy, why did you kill them? Were they spoiling your plans, getting in your way?" The Detective took out the photos of everyone I had killed. I noticed that there was a fair few missing.

"Who's helping you? You'd be better off giving them up now. You didn't do all this on your own. Maybe you were pushed, felt you had no choice." The photo of Patrick Barnes was placed on the table over Richard's. "See this void, it means someone was stood there watching while you killed Patrick Barnes. Give us their name. When we catch them, they'll be telling us that it was all you, that you made them do it.

"Give me their name and I'll see what we can do for you." I wanted to laugh at that. I'd like to see them get Fred to talk. "We're searching your house right now, tearing it apart. What do you think we're going to find, Tracy?" The Detective scattered the photos across the table.

I could tell the detective here what he'd find. Nothing, that's what! Did he think I was stupid? That I would leave some stupid bit of incriminating evidence at the house for them to find? I was better than that. Better than the lot of them. It made my blood boil at the thought that the detective here thought I was that sloppy. ME!

235

If the detective wanted to know what sloppy was, he needed to look at himself. The Yorkshire Slasher was here, in the very same room as him and he didn't see me. No, he was still looking for someone else. Stupid, stupid detective.

Tracy started to sob uncontrollably, her hands were shaking. She was starting to lose her grip. She couldn't stop looking at the photos spread across the table, where body after bloody body stared back at her. "It w-w-w- wasn't me; I-I-I didn't d-d-do this. P-p-please, y-you c- can't think t-t-that I d-did."

The Detective leaned closer, his face was so close to Tracy's that I could almost smell the sweet scent of victory that rolled off him. I was looking forward to taking care of that. Did he think for one second that he was really that good a detective to be able to catch me? No, I had led him to this point. I'd had no choice; to destroy Tracy I needed her to see the body count. To see Richard's dead body once more.

It wouldn't be long now. Tracy was starting to fade.

The detective was doing a good job at destroying Tracy's grip on reality. I must remember to thank him as I slit his throat.

"Yes, you did Tracy. The evidence doesn't lie. See the knife marks, they were made by a woman, the same woman that killed Patrick Barnes, that killed Richard Burnhill." More shuffling of photos as the detective selected another photo. "And killed Karen Stillman and everyone else you see here, Tracy. That person was you. Forensic science can determine all this, and one thing it doesn't do is lie."

I gave the detective a considered look. I agreed with him, the forensic crew could ascertain that in all likelihood, given the depth of the knife cuts, the same person had killed all of the people scattered over the table. They would also be able to determine the approximate weight and height as well as probable gender of the killer. However, what the detective and his forensic crew couldn't confirm was that Tracy Bennett had killed any of them.

I'd been careful, very careful. There was no way that he could pin the killings on Tracy with the evidence that he had. He was making a giant leap here. Looking at Tracy, she was fighting what she knew to be the truth and what the detective was telling her, trying to convince her of, that indeed she had killed these people. That she had killed all the people laid out on the table before her.

I thought back to Richard's death. It would be difficult for them to prove, without doubt, that Tracy had killed Richard.

The Detective slapped his hands down on the table. "Come on Tracy, stop the act. I know you killed these people. Look at them Tracy, all dead because of you."

"No!" The word was soft, filled with anguish.

I shook my head at the detective, just keep pushing and see what happens matey.

The detective must have skipped Dr David Canter's teachings on how to catch a murderer. According to Canter, criminals were just 'normal' people and that the police should stop looking for monsters, and start looking for the hidden monster within the 'normal' façade. And still the detective never saw me, never noticed Tracy losing her fight. He never suspected that in just a few short minutes he and Buddy would be dead. Dead because the detective never stopped to see the monster hidden in the pretty normal woman sat in front of him. Never saw the killer ready to make her way to the surface.

"Look at their faces, Tracy, why did they deserve to die?" The detective started moving the photos around pointing to their faces. Richard's was the last photo to join the pile in front of Tracy.

Tracy's hands flew to cover her face, to stop the lifeless stares from accusing her of their death. One of the photographs slid across the desk and fell onto the floor by Tracy's feet.

Tracy screamed. It echoed round the room, bouncing off the walls, her scream was feral, completely wild and full of lost hope. And in that moment, her brain fractured and cracked, just as it had done when Uncle Kevin had raped her, the day that I had been born.

I could see my opportunity opening up.

Her body shook, and reality finally fell away.

Tracy was no more.

I took my hands from my face and looked at the detective. He stepped back when he saw me. He appeared confused, scared. Death can feel like that.

He knew something had changed; there was a coldness in my eyes, a coldness that had never been there in Tracy's. My posture was different too, more confident.

"Tracy?" He didn't sound so sure.

I smiled. "Tracy, who?"

I reached down as if to pick up the photos that had fallen onto the floor. Buddy looked nervous. He should be. Instead of picking up the photo, I pulled the knife out of the hidden compartment of my shoe.

"Say hello to Death boys." I smiled.

Without hesitation, I leapt forward. The Detective wasn't fast enough. They never were. He stumbled backwards. His back hit the wall. The blade of my knife cut a deep line across his throat. Blood flew across the room. The Detective's hands flew up and he started to gag. Blood, Blood, Blood everywhere and not a drop to spare!

Ha, ha, ha, ha...

I was free and I was going to give this room a lot of colour.

Buddy stood up so quick that his chair toppled over. As he stepped back, he tripped over the fallen chair. I advanced on him. I didn't give him the opportunity to fight back before my knife plunged into his heart. I gave the knife an extra twist before I removed it. His hands were sticky with his own blood as he tried to grab my knife. I plunged the knife back into his flesh. His hands fell to his sides, all the while his heart beat out his blood from the holes I had put in his body.

The surprise that clouded his face told me he hadn't expected to die today.

No one ever did.

I looked round the room.

The walls were no longer plain. I had painted them red. I smiled.

I was free.

I could no longer feel Tracy in the body that we shared and I laughed. I had won, Tracy was gone, and now everyone would see me. No longer would I stay in the shadows. I was free to act as I chose.

The Driver was dead. Gone.

I looked at the door to the room, outside I could hear people running, an alarm going off.

"My name is Lauren Michaels and I do not slash, I make artwork." My laugh sounded insane even to me.

Somewhere inside me I felt something stir. Emma Townend. The name drifted through my head, quickly replaced by another, and another, and another. Personality after personality crowded my head, I could hear them chattering.

"Noooooo!" I screamed as the other personalities inside me became known to me.

I would not share. This was my body.

The door opened and a group of policemen entered, guns trained on me.

I faced them.

I saw Death waiting for me.

I nodded my head in acceptance. I would not share.

I had worked too hard to lose now. There was only one solution.

I took the knife raised it above my head and before the officers could react, I plunged it into my flesh.

Blood poured from my body, coated my clothes and hands.

I smiled, now I would be rid of them all and in death there would be only me.

Me; Lauren Michaels! a.k.a The Yorkshire Slasher.

Epilogue

The strong smell of disinfectant hung in the air.

Tracy's eyes fluttered open. Staring at the white washed walls, she sighed. Her stomach hurt. She gently placed a hand over the scar where the knife had been plunged into her stomach. It all felt like a dream, a really bad nightmare. The police. Richard. Tears filled her eyes. Unconsciously her hand rubbed at the scar hidden under the fabric of her clothing. She still had trouble relating to the fact that she had plunged a knife into her own flesh.

No, she corrected, she hadn't done it. Lauren had.

It had been nearly seven years since she had been rushed into hospital, and later diagnosed with Dissociative Identity Disorder (DID). The tests had been lengthy and many, before the diagnoses had been confirmed. Tracy knew that there were many in the medical world that disagreed with her diagnoses. People that did not believe that her condition was real, that Dissociative Identity Disorder actually existed. Given that it appeared that most suffers had a high IQ, it was understandable that they would question the disorder itself.

None of it made any sense to her.

Lauren had been an 'alter,' a real personality that had taken over her body. In fact, they had, to date, identified fifty different personalities within her. Tracy had been told that the initial splitting, which was the act of dissociation, had probably taken place at the moment in which Uncle Kevin had kidnapped her, abused and raped her. It wasn't something that Tracy wanted to dwell on. She found it difficult to think about when Uncle Kevin had taken her.

Tracy had grown up believing and trusting that Uncle Kevin was a good man. When he had taken her, she had first thought that he was taking her to the park for an ice-cream, why would she think any different? Her hands began to tremble and, with a skill she had come to rely on over the last few years, Tracy shut out those dark horrible memories.

From all the tests, and therapy sessions that Tracy had endured, she knew that her condition was rare. In fact, she had learnt that only .01% to 1% of the general population were diagnosed with her condition. Worst of all, there was no medication to take. The most effective treatment was talk therapy or psychotherapy, hypnotherapy and adjunctive therapies, such as movement therapy. It all sounded way too complicated, and a heck of a lot of therapies. Still, if it meant that she could learn to somehow control the other personalities, to keep Lauren from taking her over, she'd give it a shot.

Tracy had long since accepted that she would never leave the mental institution. It didn't bother her. In some ways, it made her feel safer than she had since Uncle Kevin had taken her.

Her routine was paramount, and there were no decisions to be made, life was the same. There were no demands, other than that she remained committed to her therapy. In that Tracy was determined, more determined than she had ever been about anything in her life. She couldn't let Lauren free. Free to kill.

Today was Tuesday.

Tuesday was her favourite day.

Tuesday's Susie and Abigail came to see her.

They were no longer so close. But they had remained her friends, and for that she was very grateful. It can't have been easy for them when they had found out what she had done. No, she must remember, it hadn't been her, that had done those terrible things. Her mood sank, and she sighed into the emptiness.

She wanted to cry. She was so tired.

But today was Tuesday.

No, she would survive this, because that's what Susie kept telling her. Things weren't going to be the same, just different.

"If you walk any slower, you're going to stop." Susie's voice carried down the hall.

"I'm coming, I'm coming."

"No, you're not; you're ogling that man over there."

"No, I'm not."

"Yes, you are, I can see you. I'm not blind."

"Do you think he works here, or just visiting?"

"How the hell should I know? Why don't you ask him?" There was a pause. "Not now Abs, Tracy's first."

"OK, OK, OK, I'm coming."

"Then come a little faster."

Tracy smiled; she had the best friends in the world.

Lauren blinked; she liked it when Susie and Abigail visited. She liked to imagine their blood dripping onto the sterile surfaces, coating the floor.

Who knew, she might get the opportunity someday, soon…